SELÇUK ALTUN was bor
He is a retired banking ⌐⌐⌐⌐⌐⌐, ⌐ ⌐⌐⌐⌐⌐⌐⌐⌐ ⌐⌐⌐
philanthropist. His novels, *Songs My Mother Never Taught
Me* and *Many and Many a Year Ago*, were listed amongst the
top one hundred foreign crime fiction by the International
Association of Crime Writers. He lives in Istanbul.

Also by Selçuk Altun

Songs My Mother Never Taught Me
Many and Many a Year Ago

Selçuk Altun

THE SULTAN OF BYZANTIUM

Translated from Turkish
by Clifford Endres and Selhan Endres

TELEGRAM

First English edition published 2012 by Telegram

1

ISBN 978 1 84659 148 8
EISBN 978 1 84659 150 1

Published in Turkey as *Bizans Sultani* by Sel Yayıncılık, 2011

A full CIP record for this book is available from the British Library.

Printed and bound by CPI Group (UK) Ltd, Croydon, CR0 4YY

TELEGRAM
26 Westbourne Grove, London W2 5RH
www.telegrambooks.com

If I kiss, they'll kill me
And if I don't, I'll die.
K.

ALPHA

I always mentioned the Arabic origins of my name whenever I told it to someone and was embarrassed if anybody mispronounced the last syllable. Once when I asked my grandmother how I'd got my name she replied, 'It was your great-grandfather's name.' My business-minded forefathers had started out as exporters in Trabzon and eventually became the wealthiest family on the Black Sea. I grew tired of hearing how these blockheaded relatives had wasted it all after the Crimean War.

The excuse for my grandfather's going off to Istanbul was my mother's admission to law school when she graduated from the Trabzon high school. But her law practice was limited to matters connected with the family's apartment block in Galata, where they lived, and the commercial building they owned in Şişli. My grandparent's last bone of contention was about their one and only daughter falling in love with their American tenant. In the end my mother married Paul Hackett with her father's consent. Paul was the regional representative of a worldwide business journal. The next year, at a private hospital seventy steps from our home, I came into the world. When I was two my grandfather died, and four months later my parents divorced. Paul Hackett returned to his country without a trace, and we moved into my grandmother's apartment, which adjoined ours.

Our home had broken up because of Paul Hackett's affair with an enticing Canadian woman. I was eight years old when I found this out from our doorman who probably gave me the information with my grandmother's consent. My mother was always irritated to see me in the mornings. This ill temper of hers continued right up to the moment the news reached us of Paul Hackett's death. The old Jewish psychologist I was dragged off to claimed that the situation was due to my mother's 'conditioned default reflex' toward her ex-husband.

My grandmother ruled the roost and my mother and I behaved like two unruly siblings in constant conflict. My grandmother had gone on the Haj. She had made the pilgrimage to Mecca, after my grandfather's death. Whenever people referred to her as 'Haji Ulviye', she would thumb her prayer beads more rapidly. She radiated benevolence and rarely missed an old Turkish movie on TV. I put up with those grossly incompetent films just for the pleasure of hearing her curse the evil characters, using the actors' real names. To please her I went to the mosque early in the morning, prayed on the big religious days and fasted at the beginning and end of Ramadan. You could see Topkapı Palace from the window of the bathroom, which she'd done up with a Middle Eastern flair. She gave me strict warning: 'Don't look at the Palace while you do a Number Two.' I didn't allow myself an audible fart in that bathroom for years.

To my question, 'Don't we even have a picture of my father?' came my grandmother's prickly answer, 'If you want to see what that good-for-nothing looks like, try the mirror!' Thanks to my 'good-for-nothing' father, I didn't look like my mother. She was a horse-faced, curly-haired woman with bug eyes and an ugliness only enhanced by the chic get-ups she was renowned for wearing. It was natural for her to spend many hours at the beauty parlor. Ambitious and efficient, she was a finely honed mixture of mystery and perfidy. As if her thirty-four commercial and twelve residential tenants weren't enough, she'd bought three more buildings on the street below us at a bargain price.

My mother never bought toys for me or threw any birthday parties nor did she ever even help me with my homework. For a long time I lived with the belief that in her mistreatment of me she was exacting a form of revenge on her ex-husband. Disregarding my mother's neglect, I would seek help with my schoolwork from Eugenio Geniale or as we playfully referred to him, the 'Lord of Galata'. He was a Levantine whom the Anatolian immigrants called Engin Baba and a retired professor of art history. From that wise, ageless man, (he always looked like a sixty-year-old), I learned how to read encyclopedias item by item, how to memorize dictionaries, how to tell architectural styles by observing the façades of the desolate stone buildings, how to give orders to the sea and tell riddles to the sky.

The year I started elementary school, it was Eugenio who bought me a stuffed kingfisher in honor of the event. After that I had no eyes for any other toy and I named it 'Tristan' under God knows whose influence. It was a foot long and had a sharp beak. Its back and tail were a dazzling blue, its neck was white, and its wings dark green.

The handsomest building on Hoca Ali Street was the Ispilandit Apartments. The weary structures on either side of it seemed to lean inward while those facing it appeared to bow slightly as if in sacred ceremony. We lived on the top floor of the cut-stone building in two spacious apartments. Every time I stepped into the antique elevator and reached for the seventh-floor button up to our apartment a familiar breath of coolness met me. Stepping into the living room from the elevator was to be practically embraced by the Byzantine and Ottoman silhouette of the historical peninsula. Framed by the windows, in the foreground, a sea extended from the Bosphorus to the Golden Horn and that hazy panorama formed the backdrop of my childhood games. After doing my homework I would press up against the windows and direct the sea traffic with my imaginary control baton. I shrank the Marmara Sea to a pond and made up love stories about the captains, crew and passengers of passing cargo ships, fishing boats and ocean liners. When the sun rose and beamed like a movie projector over the sea, I would start a war between two hostile sets of wave armies. The Marmara army flowed from the Black Sea down the Bosphorus while the Aramram rebels poured in from the other direction. I conducted the war with all possible dramatic effects while poor Tristan's wings trembled on my lap.

The neighborhood buildings, the youngest of which was 150 years old, enjoyed a rooftop life provided by seagulls. I imagined a disconcerted Tristan as I befriended a dwarf seagull who grew fond of our balcony. I named my seagull friend Ali, and tried to feed him regularly. When I caught it eating its own droppings one day I converted immediately to vegetarianism. Whenever I felt the urge to view the Galata Tower – my lucky charm – I would hurry to the kitchen. Pushing the lace curtain aside, that cylindrical monument seventy meters high would seem to take a step toward me. It was initially built of wood in the year 528 by the Byzantine Emperor Justinian, then rebuilt in stone by the Genoese in 1348, and restored by the Ottomans in 1510. Surveying the tower stone by stone, was like embarking on a three-dimensional safari through time. And when I reached its conical hat, I would be seized with a craving for an ice cream. I lost all hope for Turkish art and poetry because none of our painters or poets had ever jumped from its parapets. I would look through my binoculars for interesting and mysterious faces among the weary tourists clustered around the tower while an automaton-like guide recited clichés.

'Galata Tower was always a mediator between Byzantine and Ottoman,' Eugenio told me.

I met the chronic bachelor Eugenio Geniale, whom I took as my adopted father, through Alberto. Alberto and I went to the same schools up to our university years. He lived with his mother and older sister Elsa in the monumental Doğan Apartments not far from the tower. Eugenio was their neighbor. Alberto's Italian father had deserted his Greek mother in order to move to Melbourne. But at least Alberto could be with his father, a yacht captain, during the summers. His workaholic mother was bookkeeper for a hotel and always giggled when she pronounced my name in reverse. Green-eyed Elsa, two years older than I, was my first sweetheart. I thought she loved me too because she would take my arm or pinch me on the cheeks on the way to the movies. But the year she was supposed to start high school she went to visit her aunt in Genoa, where she discovered the world of lesbianism. Eventually she moved to Venice to start a new life.

I enjoyed Okçumusa elementary school, which was 222 steps from home and stood with a theatricality in reaction to the sloping decline of our street. It was there that I exerted all my efforts to win countless honor certificates, first to impress my grandmother and then a few girls who remained standoffish. It was all in vain. After Elsa I never fell in love again, never had any flirtations of the mesmerizing kind. I had my own primal fear of being rejected and those guys who acted like clowns to impress the girls disgusted me. My grandmother, thinking of me as haughty, said that I was the spitting image of my grandfather.

I moved on to the Austrian high school, 155 steps from home. Eugenio said, 'Well, you'll learn good German and English,' and fell silent. In those days it was the thing to liken schools to prisons; to me the place looked like one of those portable hospitals we saw in epic movies. I was surprised at students who were afraid of the language courses, because every word that I learned fed my appetite for more. It was as if I'd solved one more square in a mosaic puzzle. My favorite teacher was Herr T.B., who every now and then passed on to us an aphorism from his favorite author Elias Canetti. He taught me how to play chess and said, 'I won't be responsible if you turn into an addict.' He diagnosed me as a natural polyglot and I didn't disgrace him. By the time I graduated, in my eleventh year, I'd learned Italian, French and some Ottoman Turkish, enough at least to decipher the inscription on the dry fountain next to the Galata Tower.

I made my grandmother buy the Turkish *Britannica*, telling her it was a required school book. Reading five pages a day, I finished the twenty-two volumes line by line in eight years. I was in the eighth grade and busy with 'Entomology' when the door of my room opened ceremoniously. The touch of irony in Akile's modest smile aroused a faint suspicion.

'Your father died,' she said in an easy, ho-hum tone of voice. I was reading with some skepticism the sentence, 'There are more than 700,000 known species of insects and at least that many unknown …,' and wondering where she'd got the news. But all I said was, 'How?'

She just said, 'Eat your grapes and don't ask what vineyard they come from,' making my blood run cold.

The news of my father's death brought peace between us. Akile was relieved. She dropped the role of mother entirely while fully adopting that of a big sister, which was helpful when I needed it. I forgave her.

*

Alberto and I were always glad to stop off in the next-door neighborhood on the way down the hill from Galata to Tophane. In our high school days all the major craziness happened at the Nezih Café, which sat on the border of the two districts. We had to pay a bribe to get into this place reeking of stale tea and cigarette smoke. The excitement started the moment we slipped the first pack of cigarettes into the hand of the garrulous waiter. Nezih's regulars consisted of taxi drivers, bureaucrats, the retired and the neurotic unemployed, and gambling addicts. Alberto and I played cards and secretly hoped a dramatic fight would break out. Once a young drunk came up to our table on some trivial excuse and began hurling insults at us on the lines of 'You infidel Galata chicken-shits, go back where you came from!' when a fine-looking man in his thirties suddenly appeared. Taking the perpetrator by the ear, he dragged him to the door and threw him out. That's how we met 'the Albanian', the blond-haired Iskender Elbasan. Iskender Abi – we called him 'Abi' for 'big brother' – had, after losing his wife in childbirth, moved out of his father-in-law's suburban house and come to Galata. I never visited the jewellery shop at the Covered Bazaar that he partially owned. I smiled and paid little attention to the Nezih café regulars who assumed he was an antiquities smuggler. He was a patient listener who enunciated his words distinctly and lucidly with an immigrant's accent. It was he who first took me through the swinging doors of a *meyhane*, and he who found the Slavic nurse who first took me to bed. One day Iskender Abi moved to the ground floor of the sleepy apartments diagonally across the street from us. As time went by he became my confidant and protector. Akile used to call him the proletarian 'Knight of Galata'.

Eugenio said the Byzantines put the Genoese in Galata for logistical reasons. 'We're a floe that separated from the Genoa iceberg 800 years ago and got stuck to Constantinople.' Maybe that's why when visiting Genoa I wasn't surprised to see reflections of Galata there. Galata in its heyday had been a district inhabited by an upright middle-class minority, my grandmother said, 'But when we first got here it was like a camp of ghosts.' The first to revive Galata were migrants from Eastern Anatolia. Then in the 1990s its aesthetic and practical virtues were rediscovered by foreigners teaching at the new private schools. After that writers, painters, more artists, and some professionals who thought they possessed a bohemian spirit invaded those stone buildings still holding out against time.

The owner of the Tigris Buffet on Galata Tower Street was Devran from Diyarbakır. Rumor had it he'd been tortured during his five years in jail as a political prisoner. This, he well knew, was what drew young folk to his café despite the bland food he dished up. To the left of the entrance was the 'Spark' bulletin board. There Devran posted clichés from left-wing pundits and excerpts from acceptable poems and nonfiction. One of his recommendations helped me make peace with poetry, which high school had turned into an unlovely thing. The title of that masterpiece was a remarkable poem in itself. Thanks to Ahmet Arif's *Fetters Worn Out by Longing*, I began each of my days by reading poetry and began my own poetry collection. Whenever I dove into a poem, I felt a pleasure like that of solving mathematical equations, or maybe skating on a chessboard with countless squares hanging from the heavens. I found silence in poetry and scolded whoever came into my room, my grandmother included. I found the distilled eroticism of the seventeenth-century folk poet Karacaoğlan extremely seductive. I concealed even from Iskender Abi the fact that I sometimes masturbated over his lines. The poems I wrote in my lycée years I showed only to Selçuk Altun. He was a close friend of Eugenio's who favored his bibliophilic side over his writer's side. When he declared my poetry 'Not hopeless,' I tried my hand at translation. My versions of Montale and Cavafy looked to me like the back of a silk

15

carpet. Eugenio said, 'Well, what can you do if a poet's soul refuses to collaborate with you?'

In the old days the real-estate office just below the Tigris Buffet was the watch repairman Panayot Stilyanidis's shop. When I was in middle school Panayot was in his seventies and worked alone. Since hardly anyone was left to have their watches and clocks repaired, he worked mainly on the stubborn old pieces sent him by antique dealers. I was happy when he let me watch him work. It tickled me to hear the duelling salvos between the shop's antique wall and table clocks. I'd stop breathing when he put the loupe in his eye and took his special tweezers in hand. A watch's internal body was as complicated as an aeroplane's control panel for me and, when the tweezers prodded it into ticking, as fantastic as an Egyptian mummy waking up. Panayot the master craftsman would just chuckle when I became flustered over the number of errands he'd asked me to do. In the middle of his desk stood an antique French clock. I watched open-mouthed as the rainbow-colored mechanical bird in its gilded cage oscillated right to left with every second ticked off. Master Panayot's heart stopped ticking five days after he gave me the watch left him by his father. He had no children; he was the last link in the chain of the Stilyanidis family, who had been watchmakers for four generations. After he died his widow sold their building to my mother and went home to Chios with the rest of her husband's ancient clocks and watches.

*

When people asked what I wanted to be when I grew up, I answered impatiently, 'A watchmaker.' When my grandmother inquired what subject I wanted to study I said, 'Semiology,' and paused. My ideal was to be Umberto Eco's student at the University of Bologna. Haji Ulviye, discovering that semiology meant sign language, asked whether I was an idiot. Then, with my mother's connivance, she made an offer: if I chose engineering or business she would underwrite my education in America. With Eugenio's guidance – he'd taken a PhD from Berkeley – I applied to a dozen schools. At the insistence of Selçuk Altun I added Columbia to the list at the last minute. When the letter of acceptance from Columbia University Department of Economics arrived, I read it three times, at different hours of the day.

It was only later when I was filling in the registration forms that I learned Columbia was in New York City. For my four undergraduate years I lived in an encyclopaedic city. I saw that actually it was only the rich and the daring poor who enjoyed New York; the rest of us had to be satisfied with philosophizing the ordinary.

The years went by quickly, with no love stories and adventures and before I knew it I was flying home to Turkey with a bachelor's degree from Columbia University. Was it me or my country that something had happened to? On boarding the plane to Istanbul from New York, I wondered what irritating headlines full of trivialities I would encounter on landing. A great many of my fellow citizens seemed to feel no worse about the constantly updated corruption than about a missed goal by their favorite football team. In truth, they didn't even read the newspapers, just glued themselves passionately to the TV soap operas. I was prejudiced about the Parliament they'd elected, too.

I took a job in the investment department of a big bank to appease my family. But I couldn't endure my blockheaded colleagues or the clumsy management. Besides, I have to admit, I hated taking orders. At the end of my first month I resigned, certain my grandmother's would declare: 'Just like his grandfather.'

I thought I might try an academic career in economics. Haji Ulvıye liked serious titles like Governor/General/Professor. She agreed to finance my sojourns outside the country so long as the process ended in a professorship. My favorite Columbia professor was Assael Farhi, the son of an Istanbul Balat family, who used to teach on a doctoral program at the London School of Economics. I applied and was accepted for the winter term, which meant my current 'holiday' was extended for three months. I went to Italy for two weeks. There I dropped in on Elsa, who was running an art gallery in Venice. She shared her spooky mansion with a woman artist who smelled of paint thinner.

'You look like one of those antique Mediterranean gentlemen,' the artist said, 'the type that women would just love to exterminate.'

Over dinner at the mansion Elsa filled me in on Alberto. He had emigrated to Australia and was now teaching chemistry at a Sydney high school. His wife worked in the human resources department of a hospital and was six years older than he. I booked a ticket to Australia, excited to see Alberto again, but things did not go well. His wife did not miss a chance to scold him. I endured their soulless house for a week, then took a train up to Adelaide. Just because its name was Ararat, I stopped off at a remote station in the outback for two days. From Sydney I flew to Alexandria, my last stop. There I wandered among the places where Cavafy had once sequestered himself reciting his last poems like a long prayer.

It was mid-autumn when I returned to Istanbul, where I was thoroughly bored by an old high school friend's wedding. The cheap wine they served gave me a headache in the bargain. On the way home I sank down on a bench in front of the Tower and chatted with the kids hanging out there, whose families were migrants from eastern Anatolia. They weren't impressed when I ticked off the names of the small towns and smaller villages they'd all come from. I rose, hoping to sober up by strolling the silent and deserted streets in the pleasant evening. I began walking in the direction of the thin wind that was blowing towards me. The street, so narrow a bicycle could barely get down it, was a source of annoyance. A little way into it I saw a girl of seven or eight crying in front of a half-abandoned building with a single light burning on the third floor. She wore a one-size-too-small sweatshirt and sweatpants and no shoes. She was shivering. I couldn't keep from thinking that her teardrops were prettier than pearls. Moved, I took off my jacket and wrapped it around her. The dark olive-eyed girl was Devran Abi's daughter Hayal. Her father had often brought her to his café when she was a baby. She was a sweet girl. I remembered how she would run to me and wrap her arms around my leg whenever she saw me. Devran had died of cancer, may he rest in peace, when I was in New York. His widow then married an old friend of his whom Devran had considered of dubious character. Now Hayal told me that her mother had died in hospital two days earlier, and her stepfather had put her out of the house.

I knew there would be no answer, but I rang the worthless bastard's doorbell all the same. I turned to the shivering girl and said, 'Come and stay with us tonight. You'll be rid of that drunk, God willing, by tomorrow.' With that I picked her up and hoisted her on my back. She cried until she fell asleep with her head on my shoulder. The tick-tock of her little heart and the warmth of her body were too much for me; tears came to my eyes. I was a well-regarded idle man who hadn't yet done any good deeds for anyone. My mother received the surprise as she was watching TV.

'Akile,' I said, 'this princess is my new sister.'

The next day Iskender Abi and I buried Hayal's mother. In exchange for a bit of money the stepfather turned the child over to me and left Galata for good.

Hayal was as sturdy as her father. She overcame her trauma with a little help from a psychologist and grew into a smart and charming young girl. She's a student now at the Austrian High School; she wants to be a doctor. She parts her hair in the middle because I like it like that. She calls my grandmother 'Haji Grandma', and my mother, 'Mama Akile', She goes with Haji Grandma to my grandfather's grave, to the spa in Gönen, and to visit her sister in Artvin. Is it a rule that an old annoying custom should haunt you from the cradle? Since older brothers are supposed to marry first, Hayal is convinced, in view of my confirmed bachelorhood, that her turn will never come. 'Mama Akile,' she likes to complain, 'I'll never have a chance to get married.'

*

I spent my four years in London as a postgraduate living in an apartment near to the British Museum. I could walk from there to the university in fifteen minutes. From the front the brick building looked like it was built by Lego. Only after I moved in did I notice a plaque in the lobby commemorating the fact that the Nobelist Bertrand Russell had lived there. During one of her religious holidays my mother came with Hayal to visit. I took Hayal to the London Zoo, since she wanted to go – before that I hadn't even gone to circuses, believing they were a symbol of enslavement. But at the lions' cage – was I awake or dreaming? – my eyes locked with those of a young lioness. We gazed at each other a long time, then she came to the edge of the cage and bowed her head as if she wanted me to pat it. The rest of her family stood gazing sympathetically at me, like they were waiting for my signal to attack. The other big cats, the tigers and panthers, said hello to me from a distance by wagging their tails. The next month I went again to the zoo and again enjoyed the same rites of hospitality. It occurred to me that these noble cats perhaps recognized a real friend at first sight. I thought of Tristan with great longing. Thanks to Tristan I'd learned the Latin names of hundreds of bird species. When my grandmother refused to buy me an aquarium, I bombarded her with the names of the twenty-seven kinds of shark that lived in our seas. The better I got to know people, the more I respected animals. I always loved children, especially mischievous little girls with runny noses. I used to go to Tünel Square just to hand out change to the child beggars there. My grandmother said, 'If I don't will my fortune to the Children's Charity Foundation I'm afraid you'll do it for me.'

For the last six years I've been teaching two days a week at Bosphorus University. Last year, when I was promoted to associate professor, my grandmother asked, 'What does it mean?'

'Well, if professors are generals, then I'm a colonel,' I said.

'All right,' she said. 'In that case, congratulations.'

I started teaching one day a week at Kadir Has University too, simply because I never felt bored on my walks to that nostalgic building on the Golden Horn. The students, who lose their innocence as soon as they start making money, all call me 'Hocam', which means 'my professor' and it warms my heart. In my free time I read poetry, study semiology or play chess, and compose Sudoku puzzles. If I happen to go out into the city, I'm appalled at the colossal new skyscrapers. And I feel truly sorry for all those people running around like robots in blue jeans. As I confessed to Tristan, I'm more than ready to work for any honest political leader who could save the country from turning into Boorishstan. Other than that I find no reason to be acquitted of Galata.

During my first summer vacation while I was at Columbia, I became my grandmother's neighbor by moving into my mother's perpetually empty apartment. I furnished it with antiques from old Galata mansions: my desk, my weary armchair, my end tables and the busts on them of my family members. Eugenio, hearing that I'd already introduced the busts to Tristan, said, 'You're a one-of-a-kind animist.' I hung some old maps on the living-room wall in the places vacated by my mother's library shelves. One of the maps was a 1559 engraving by Sebastian Münster. It was the most exciting object among a treasure trove that one of my grandfathers – not even my grandmother could remember which one – had left behind. The map, which Hayal described as a graphic novel squeezed onto a single sheet of paper, pictured Galata before the Conquest. Everything was in a jumble behind the ancient citadel walls, with our Tower standing erect and powerful beside an aqueduct.

I collected quite a few old map books with money I squeezed out of my grandmother for school expenses. I took courses in Latin to examine them more thoroughly. All the city names on those maps never failed to be poetic. The ones I focused on, letter by letter, drew me inside their walls. I was taken on exemplary tours; I supposed I was expected to experience what had happened to humanity because of individual mistakes.

Alberto, whose mother forced him to listen to classical music for half an hour every night because she thought it sharpened the mind, used to cheat off me in school every chance he got. To me, classical music was like an insistent lullaby, and pop music assorted canned vegetables. In Istanbul a great many musical-instrument shops were to be found on Galip Dede Street, which connects the Galata district to Istiklal Avenue. Hayal once asked, 'Abi, are you trying to make people think and laugh at the same time?' I told her I hurried down that street to keep the instruments hanging in the shop windows from squirting anti-musical notes at me. My own musical notes were, and are, the sound of the wind rustling through the labyrinths of our neighborhood, the screams of seagulls, the foghorns, the train whistles, the prayer calls and church bells and giggles of little girls – natural and free of expectation. If I'm in the mood for a symphony, I take a very long journey.

Our rental income is deposited into my grandmother's bank account. After expenses, what's left is divided half into dollars, half into Turkish lira and put into three interest-bearing accounts, one for each of us. But my mother and I aren't allowed to touch our accounts. My grandmother puts $7500 into mine every month; this amount is adjusted periodically on the basis of parity with the prime minister's salary. I'm sure, incidentally, that my mother's is indexed to that of the president. Hayal has to kiss her grandmother's hand to get her allowance.

I collected watches and took theme trips. Having no reason to save money was the source of my freedom. In my student years I wandered across Anatolia to see its castles, ancient bridges and lighthouses. I went to Geneva to admire the watches in the shop windows, to Tarifa for the killer whales, to Druridge Bay for the bird sanctuary, to Umman for the stingrays, to Odessa to play chess with a master who was a transvestite. People were surprised at my not knowing the silent woman in the group on a picnic with Marieta and Schalk in Namibia's Harnas Nature Park. Marieta and Schalk were two tame lions; the woman with violet eyes was a Hollywood star named Angelina Jolie.

Hayal loves watching the fishermen on the Galata Bridge. I go there with her if she's not on good terms with her boyfriend. According to some banners hung on the bridge on orders of the mayor, today, May 29, 2008 is the 555th anniversary of the Conquest of Istanbul from the Byzantines.

That means I'll be thirty-three tomorrow. Those banners remind me of all my uncelebrated birthdays. But then, as Oscar Wilde said, 'After twenty-five everybody is the same age.' On my birthdays I grow tired of never getting tired.

I ought to call Madam Olga, who knows me as Engin Galatali, from a phone booth. Not because I make love to two girls at the same time but because I started reading the poems of her countryman Joseph Brodsky, Olga the retired teacher calls me, 'My Sultan'.

BETA

At the beginning of my teaching career Eugenio told me, 'Each of your students is like a candle given to you for safekeeping. Don't forget.'

I did more than my share; I warmed my heart with their flickering light. Creating a stress-free atmosphere in my classes, I succeeded in becoming their confidant. Once a year I took them to Galata and guided them through the labyrinthine neighborhood. Female students wrote me love letters. Male students, owing to my love of poetry, tried lining me up with women in the department of literature. I was well aware that they respected me for my unusual journeys.

I proposed to fly to the capital of Eritrea on June 15, 2008. I wanted to acquaint myself with the minimalist architecture of Asmara and at the same time meet up with Leo Punto, who had settled in the city for its beautiful name, for a game of chess or two. After that I planned to meet my old grad-school friend James Hill in Dar es Salaam. We intended to conquer Kilimanjaro, above the Serengeti Plain.

On the morning of June 5, I opened a courier-delivered envelope and it became clear that I would have to cancel my plans for Asmara. On the purple sheet of paper that fell out of it was a mysterious invitation:

Distinguished Sir:

    I was a friend of your grandfather, may he rest in peace. I would be pleased to see you at the Four Seasons Hotel in Sultanahmet tomorrow at 14:00. Please bring with you that Christophoro de Bondelmontibus map you have at home, but don't take it from its frame. I have no interest in the Constantinople map. The other item is much more important, and I have excellent news for you.

    One of my assistants will meet you in the lobby.

    With the hope that our meeting will remain confidential between us, and

    My deepest respect,

    Nikos Askaris

It was handwritten in black ink; I read it twice. The first irritating point was the exaggeratedly respectful final sentence of this friend of my grandfather. It seemed forced to me and perhaps an early warning of an oncoming burden. As I dusted off the framed map drawn in 1422 by the Florentine priest Bondelmontibus and laid it on my desk, I wondered about this Askaris, who had not omitted the diacritical mark in my name. On the engraving under the glass my eye took in Galata. The walls that besieged the city from the north and the west seemed to be dancing the *halay* in a circle around the Tower. The Byzantine remnants inside the city walls appeared as timid as pawns on a chessboard. I phoned the hotel and asked for Nikos Askaris. To the man who answered in a high-pitched voice I said, 'I'm calling to hear you say that you're not making an illegal proposal.' When Askaris replied in accent-free Turkish and pronounced the second syllable of my name correctly as well I felt somewhat relieved.

I wrapped up the little map with care and prepared for the meeting. Suddenly, I was wondering about the nature of a potential burden. I changed my mind and decided not to call Madame Olga. All of a sudden I had a craving for George Seferis. I took *The Complete Works* from the shelf and opened it at random:

> What are you hunting, old friend?
> After so many years
> Under foreign skies
> Far from your own land
> You've come home from exile
> Hanging on to all those memories.

*

Whenever I go to Sultanahmet Square I seem to step back into different eras from the past. This time I found myself in the festive atmosphere of the Byzantine hippodrome. The shouts of the fanatical spectators followed me all the way to Sultanahmet Mosque …

At the other end of the square the Four Seasons Hotel stood like a sentinel. Constructed originally as a government building to house public services, the building had a dark history as a prison for so-called thought criminals. As I entered the calm lobby, a large man with a beard materialized before me.

In almost perfect Turkish he said, 'Welcome, sir, I'm Theo Pappas and I'm here to take you to Mr Askaris, if you will allow.' As I fell in behind this apple-cheeked man who appeared no older than forty, I was thinking how he looked simultaneously like a priest and the head of security. The prim and proper courtyard we were crossing must once have been the prison's exercise area.

'Mr Askaris's suite was once the prison warden's office,' said Theo with a smile.

Nikos Askaris was a small ugly man in his sixties, with a thin beard; he wore his face like a mask. I wondered what sort of plusses he owned to offset this outlook. Another man in the spacious room with a red beard and glasses was Askaris's other assistant, Kalligas. The three had two features in common: they were all bearded and wore suits. I would have bet they worked for a church or a charity organization. On the table lay two packages. I laid the bag with the map requested in the letter next to them and asked for white wine from the minibar. Askaris took mineral water for himself and beckoned me to the table. Papas and Kalligas seated themselves on chairs immediately behind him. Kalligas, who looked about thirty-five, also spoke very fluent Turkish. I was almost getting used to their determination not to fail to show absolute respect toward me.

'Before we broach the main subject, sir, I'd like to ask a question, if I may. In two sentences, how would you define Byzantium?' said Askaris.

'Once upon a time Byzantium was synonymous with intrigue, but this image has gradually changed. For me Byzantium mingled East and West and became the most prominent civilization of its own time, and then it triggered the Renaissance.'

'What a wonderful summary! It might be added that

no other empire ever stayed alive and active for over eleven hundred years. In Byzantium sovereignty did not always pass from father to the eldest son. In order to allow the most deserving person to ascend the throne, there was a flexible selection process, and because of that there were occasional periods of bloody conflict. But didn't Rome and Hellenistic Greece have similar problems? Since in those ages communications were not as advanced as in Byzantium, their recorded history is incomplete.

'The greatness of Byzantium begins with her will to continue the legacy of Greece and Rome, to which she was the natural heir. As you said, that heritage was enriched by a touch of the East.

'Byzantium laid the foundations of modernism. She initiated state social institutions. She disciplined the military, educational, financial, legal and technological sectors. She made sports and entertainment an integral part of life. To raise the quality of life she formed organizations for the improvement of health care, city planning, the crafts, fashion, jewellery-making, and social manners. As a role model she influenced her neighbors in science, culture, and the arts. You also noted that the Byzantine scholars who fanned out into Europe after the fall of Constantinople paved the way for the Renaissance.

'During the Middle Ages the East was generally superior to the West, military-wise. The Byzantines saved the future of Europe by blocking the path of the Eastern armies to the unprepared continent. In short, Byzantium was the most significant civilization in history, and if humans ever offer prayers of gratitude for the gifts they've received, the name of

Byzantium ought to come after God and before Jesus.'

I was not impressed that Askaris turned out to be a cheerleader for Byzantium. I slowed him down by asking for another glass of wine, then got set to listen to the second part of his spiel, which was intended to connect his monologue to the agenda. I was curious about his proposal, but I knew I was not going to say yes. Maybe this explained my calm demeanor, which appeared to surprise the team. What I was actually curious about was how these three boring Greeks had learned to speak Turkish so fluently.

Askaris and the two behind him took their seats again, and the horse-faced Askaris continued in an even higher pitch.

'For eleven centuries eleven dynasties ruled Byzantium. During the last, the Palaeologus dynasty, eleven emperors held the throne for a total of 192 years. The Palaeologi ruled the Empire for the longest stretch and during her most trying times. It was founded by Michael, who came from a noble family. In fact his last name, meaning 'old word', is a sign of deep roots. The Palaeologus dynasty's performance during their rule has to be considered a success, given the conditions of the times. The last emperor, Constantine XI Palaeologus, was forty-five when he ascended the throne in 1449. He was a model leader. Both the army and the people claimed him as their own. When he rejected Sultan Mehmet II's terms of surrender, the Ottoman army of 80,000 men began the siege of Constantinople on April 2, 1453. The Byzantine army had about 7,000 soldiers, whose task was to defend a city whose population had been reduced to 60,000. The emperor put his trust in the city's walls – which invaders had failed to breach for 800 years – and the support of allies like Pope Nicholas V and the European monarchs. But help against the fifty-five-day siege was late in coming, and merely symbolic at that. It was like the Pope wanted to stab Orthodox Byzantium in the back because she had never recognized his sovereignty.

'The army had lost its defensive strength, and the people, in dire economic straits, were anxious. Constantine distracted the people with empty promises and paid his soldiers' wages by melting down the precious metal vessels belonging to the churches. But his heroic efforts were not enough; on May 29, 1453, Constantinople succumbed! The corpse of Constantine XI, dressed in his imperial vestments, was paraded through the city. The 53,000 civilians and soldiers who were taken as slaves by the Ottoman forces were dead certain to a person that the body was not that of their emperor. Most of them were of the belief that he had disappeared into the massive walls and would emerge when the day of independence came again.

'George Sphrantzes wrote that Constantine XI died in combat on the city walls. In time this claim gained authority. The same historian also concocted the story that the Ottomans brought an army of 200,000 soldiers to the siege of the city. Sphrantzes, who was born in 1401, was not only the confidant of the emperor but also his match-maker and private secretary. The historian Nicola della Tuccia, the poet Abraham of Angora, and the Byzantine bishop Samile, on the other hand, all wrote that the emperor escaped by ship.

'At the time of the siege the emperor was forty-nine years old. If you consider the average life span in those days, he must have been about as strong as our own seventy-five-year-old grandfathers. Perhaps he couldn't fight sword-to-sword with the Ottomans, but he did even more. As commander-in-chief he coordinated the deployment of the army along five miles' worth of defensive walls. As the Ottoman victory neared, his close circle implored him to retreat to the Morea. He could remain there in exile for some time and return to the throne when circumstances were right, just as the dynasty's founding father Michael had done. Seeing his army dissolving before his eyes and furthermore feeling the pressure of these unheroic suggestions, Constantine fainted. His robes were put on an officer whose head had been crushed. The emperor's hands and feet were bound and he was put on the last Genoese boat to leave the city. The history books missed the fact that the emperor had been hijacked.

'Among the noble names on the boat's passenger list were six Palaeologi, two Cantacuzeni, two Comneni, two Laskaris and two Notaras. Loukas Notaras was the Grand Duke of the palace. Both he and Sphrantzes were Palaeologus sons-in-law, but they never liked each other. Notaras was a mysterious statesman – he was a citizen of Genoa and Venice both, and had great fortunes in both places.

'Notaras and Sphrantzes surrendered to the Ottomans because the Sultan granted the nobles their lives. Notaras, one week after the city fell, was killed for unknown reasons; Sphrantzes, on the other hand, fled to Mistra, the last out-post of the Empire.

'Let's go back to the Genoese boat. According to its skipper, Captain Zorzi Doria, the Byzantine passengers disembarked at Chios and Crete. From there they scattered to the Morea, Corfu and assorted Italian towns. The emperor and his relatives, with Loukas Notaras's daughter and sister, first went to Venice. There they transferred the fortune that had been accumulating in the Notaras family accounts to the emperor's relatives.

'Constantine never set foot after this on the soil of either Venice or Genoa. He lived the rest of his life hiding in Italian towns under his mother's last name, Dragas. He married a noble widow from Ravenna and gave his mother's name, Helena, to his newborn daughter. He concealed his true identity from everybody. Even his wife knew him only as an elderly Byzantine prince. The emperor's previous marriages were short-lived owing to his wives' early deaths from disease. Those two unfortunate empresses were both Italian. Constantine lived for twenty-two more years, suppressing his deep depression, and dying at seventy-one. He always knew that he would never return to Constantinople but he was never resigned to it. In fact, he compiled a 'revenge list'. Europe, by deserting her in her hour of need, had badly betrayed the Byzantium that had always guarded the former's flanks from the Asian barbarians. I'm in no position to pass along detailed information about the list, but I can tell you two interesting tales.

'Nicholas V, the Pope who was the target of so many Byzantine curses, died suddenly at the age of fifty-eight. It was a shock: he had always been quite healthy and free of serious illness. It was said that the cause of death was 'gout' in order to hide the fact that he was poisoned. Second, Sultan Mehmet II died in 1481 when he was only forty-nine. How interesting, isn't it, that history records the same causes of death – gout or poison – for him as for the Pope.

According to the East it was the Christians who poisoned Mehmet; according to the West it was his son Beyazit II. Personally, I think these two names were at the top of the revenge list.

'Constantine never met Sphrantzes again. Maybe he wanted to avoid taking a risk. His confidant died in 1477 at a monastery in Corfu. The three nobles who were the emperor's companions on the boat never left his service. When Constantine died in 1475 he entrusted his secret fortune and his throne-in-exile to their hands. They founded a secret society named Nomophylax (Nomo), which means Guardians of the Law. Over time they doubled the inherited fortune and carried out the assignments on the list one by one.

'Constantine's only grandson, Massimo d'Urbino, was an ambitious merchant. There was hardly a port in the East that he hadn't visited. He married a Greek woman from Smyrna and settled in Istanbul in 1503. When his only daughter, Irene, married a pasha's son and converted to Islam under a new name, Emine, the Byzantine Empire-in-exile was conveyed to the Ottomans. One of Nomo's jobs has always been to select an emperor from the family tree of the lady Emine, for Constantine wanted only his 'elected' grandchildren to deal with the contents of that list. No one is assigned to carry out any of these tasks unless he has been chosen emperor and thus 'elected'.

'Nomo has been at work for the last 533 years; in all this time the Byzantine throne-in-exile has never been empty. The first act of the new emperor is to take an oath of secrecy – he may not share his secret even with his wife. The punishment for treason is … death!'

Askaris paused to gauge my reaction. Perhaps my face wore the expression of an actor bored with his script. He asked my permission to open the package I'd brought. I was a bit skeptical as he took a pair of tweezers from his pocket. But when he touched a certain point on the map's border, the metal frame parted at the bottom. He half-closed his eyes and seemed to be silently praying; it was clear that he would react to nothing I said or did. Then with his tweezers he deftly pulled a piece of paper from between the map and the metal frame. Was there a half-portrait on it? The picture revealed a long-faced, bearded man in a helmet blazoned with the double eagle. It was His Majesty, looking like he was waiting for the perfect motive to dress somebody down. Askaris now dug into the purple pouch that lay on the table and pulled out another map. Using the same method again, he extracted a sheet of paper from it and placed it under the first one. The portrait was now complete down to the ornamented belt. And the way his majesty held out his hands, it looked like he was pleading for help.

Askaris and his two assistants suddenly rose and stood at attention with their eyes cast down. Askaris said, 'Most respected sir, this is an engraving of the last Byzantine emperor, Constantine Dragas Palaeologus XI … and you, sir, are his last descendant, which is to say, you are the current Byzantine emperor-in-exile, Constantine Palaeologus XV …'

I felt nailed to the table by my elbows. I did not let Mr Owl Eyes repeat his sentence, so as not to increase the chill in the air. Every cell in my body was flashing a message to my brain. Was my head going to pound and the sore on my tongue suddenly explode? Surely I was the victim of an elaborate mistake. I told the trio standing in front of me like a squad of bodyguards to sit down.

'I wonder, one, what kind of proof you have for these outlandish statements. And two, if you're not Turkish, how is it you can speak my language so perfectly?' I said.

Askaris leaned enthusiastically forward, then took a purple album from the leather bag. He moved closer. On the pages he ritualistically turned over were engravings or photographs of eleven people, from d'Urbino to me. I forgot the resumés he recited to me as soon as he turned the page; my only reward for this session was to learn that our family had moved to Trabzon in the eighteenth century. The more Mr Owl Eyes spoke, the smaller were my chances of catching his mistakes. I made a quick situation analysis: when the modern law requiring families to have last names was passed, my grandfather made the most suitable choice for us – ASIL, that is to say, NOBLE. My namesake excepted, all the names given to my grandfathers had been the Islamic equivalents of those of the Byzantine emperors: Yahya/John, Mikail/Michael, Ishak/Isaac, Rumi/Romanus. I was about to inject a little humor into the situation by observing that this systematic approach hadn't left out my mother – Akile/Sophia – when something at the back of my mind caught my attention. It was that when my turn came to be named after my grandfather, Yahya Asil, I was still a baby, but the announcement was postponed for thirty years. The most dramatic possibilities began to revolve in my brain like multiple-choice questions on a test.

Mentally changing the subject I asked for information on Nomo, and Nikos Askaris's forehead wrinkled.

'The grandchildren of the three nobles who founded the organization continued the mission. Nomo's administration was generally passed on from father to son; those without sons adopted them. Their wives believed that their husbands were simply rich investors. Always there were three people in the administration, and they never contradicted one another.

'They never failed to increase the fortune they had inherited, never cut corners and never took risks. Nobody knows how many billion dollars the Nomo balance sheet is worth these days, but it's said that they don't invest in real estate or the stock market. Where organization members live and where they meet are secrets as well. They keep an eye on the emperors they have elected, but only meet personally with those they consider worthy. Somebody wearing a disguise passes along my orders to me. He's probably not in direct contact with Nomo members either. The only shred of information I can offer you is that my adequate Turkish is precisely the reason why I'm here. I can't tell you anything more. Of course you will have surmised that we don't use our real names in the course of our missions.

'We can show you a copy of the will your grandfather signed and left with Nomo. You'll see the same signature on the bottom right corner of the map you brought. The moment you take your oath accepting the honor and obligations of the imperial crown, you will be assigned a special mission.'

'Even if I believed that I was a descendant of Massimo d'Urbino, how would that prove that I'm a descendant of the last emperor?' I said.

'In fact there are proofs in the will, or at least clues that will pass as proofs. But it's true that you're not in a position to analyze all this. If you could manage to get in touch with Nomo, they can furnish you with all the proof you want, even DNA testing. For this reason I imagine there's a royal test somewhere waiting for you. We are at your service, if you allow it. This is a turning point in our history, since the time has come to deal with the last item on Constantine XI's list. When this mission is accomplished, it will mean that a very significant trial has been passed. It is then that you, together with the members of Nomo, will decide the future of the organization. This could even mean shutting it down.'

'First I want to know the reason why I'm the one chosen for this grand finale, and why you've waited till now to make this announcement.'

The trio visibly relaxed; obviously I'd asked the expected question. I compared Kalligas, who asked permission to answer my question, to the conflicted rabbi of art films. Maybe that red beard of his was false; I was tempted to pull it.

'Byzantium was influenced by the East and could not completely give up the polytheistic beliefs of the pagan period. The power of the mysterious has always been recognized. Look. Eleven dynasties ruled the Empire, which survived for eleven centuries. There were eleven emperors in the last dynasty. And you're the candidate for the eleventh emperor-in-exile. The symbol of Byzantium is the double-headed eagle, the numerical expression of which is eleven (11); eleven is the symbol also of leadership and unity … We lost Constantinople on May 29; you were born on the morning of May 30; no other emperor was born on such a meaningful day … Five is the number of destiny; it is the 555th anniversary of our loss of Constantinople … Three is the blessed signifier of relief, and you have just turned thirty-three …

'I'll give you a few examples drawn from your own CV. Despite family difficulties, you did not turn into a problem child. You were a hard-working, honest and popular student. You continued your success in some of the most prominent universities in the world. You're an intellectual and art-lover who can speak five languages. You didn't try to sneak out of your compulsory military service. You could enter the political life, if conditions were favorable, of any country whose passport you carried. You've got too much honor to take orders from other people, and too much pride to flirt with the girls. You go to bed with two women at a time; if you happen to come eye-to-eye with a lion it turns into a housecat. Your air of mystery is respectable. Sir, you are the emperor that Byzantium-in-exile has been awaiting for the last 555 years! Thanks to you, the soul of Constantine XI, who died unfulfilled, will find peace. We proudly address you as Your Majesty.'

These compliments, arriving in larger and larger doses, were beginning to bore me. Still, I believed what these Nomo workers told me, and I was almost sympathetic to the organization that had trailed me even to love hotels. As a puzzle-lover myself, I was curious about the test awaiting me, and even more so about the last item in Constantine XI's last will and testament. Maybe I'd found the project that was to pull me out of Galata again.

'My grandmother always said you should think twice even if you're just buying underwear,' was the aphorism with which I concluded the meeting. Theo, the least ambitious and most lovable of the three, was getting my bag together. In his eyes I saw the innocence of a child confiding in his doctor.

41

They walked me to the exit. As we traversed the courtyard Askaris, bursting with historical titbits said, 'This hotel rose up on the foundations of the Palatium Magnum – the Great Palace – which Constantine I, the Great, began building in the fourth century. In 1204 the so-called Crusaders but really the Latin Looters, first plundered, then demolished it.'

We said our good-byes agreeing to meet again the next day at the same time. I knew that nobody was going to tell me to keep this meeting a secret.

*

As a child I used to think that my body might split in two because its right side was Turkish and its left was American. The archaeological excavations next door to the Four Seasons reminded me of that division, causing me to wonder if I were Byzantine above the waist and Ottoman below.

Making my way through Sultanahmet, the weary heart of Byzantium, was I walking through a now-dead minefield planted by my forefathers? The call to prayer suddenly started up from the Ottoman mosques and I realized that I was gripping the ground more firmly with my toes and holding my shoulders high. I passed through Sirkeci on my way to the Galata Bridge.

A disturbing stanza from Karacaoğlan came to mind:

In the world not left to Sultan Süleyman
These mountains one day will be uprooted
And souls rotting for a thousand years
By God's will one day will be revived.

GAMMA

Before Istanbul was even Constantinople, the district was known as Sikodis which in Greek means 'fig orchard'. The last three fig trees of Galata belonged to my family. They stood in the garden to the right of our apartment building. There was also an ornamental pool in the garden; my grandmother thought it looked like a tomb and for that reason we weren't allowed to enter the garden. In summertime, when the fragrant scent of figs enveloped the whole street, she'd say, 'The tree is crying because it can't bear fruit.' I would close my eyes and inhale that perfume. When I was still at high school, the meaning of mystery to me was taking in the fragrance of that fig tree and storing it up inside myself.

I was happy to learn that the name of our district derived from the 'barbarian' Galatians. It was the first time I'd heard the rhythmical word 'barbar', and I thought the Galatians must have been heroic horsemen with roots in Gaul. According to Apostol the barber, the most saintly citizens after the prophets were the Byzantine rulers who accepted Christianity as their official religion and standardized the Bible. Whenever I took my seat in his antique chair he would squeeze one of my ears with his scissors and say, 'Wow! I almost cut it off.' His son could not manage to take him away from us to Thessalonica, at least until his legs froze up and he couldn't walk. Apostol claimed that when the Byzantines gave Galata to the Genoese, a wind with a tail appeared over the roofs of the neighborhood.

The Galata streets are like cards in a mismatched deck. The goal of anyone who dives into that maze is definitely to not rush to get out on the other side safe and sound. Each street is a line from a poem that I would not dare to memorize. In Tristan's view, Galata and I were the missing chapter in *Gulliver's Travels*. I knew the monumental buildings by the way they sighed. The streets, paved with stones from the old city walls, kissed my feet with each step I took. I always began my time travel by rubbing the blackening walls that remained from the fourteenth-century Palazzo Communale. I would watch the army of ants ceremoniously descending from beneath the cracked facade. People say that 'the most aesthetic stairs in the world' are the Camondo Stairs curving up from the old banking street, Bank Avenue. The Camondo family, generous benefactor of the Louvre Museum, were also the former owners of our apartment building. Because of the way our neighborhood streets zigzagged it was difficult for the city to tear down our deserted but magnificent old buildings. Their rank decreased in proportion as their distance from the Tower increased. In my opinion they gave the impression of aristocratic men in tuxedos and elegant women in tulle evening gowns. Do weary buildings draw closer together at night to share their troubles?

The sounds of the call to prayer, church bells, and the screams of gulls all somehow accentuated our quota of silence. Whenever I see those neat symmetrical cities in graphic novels, I'm driven to go out into a Galata street on a late afternoon. Galatians enjoy life on a different timeline.

Their stance is dramatic, and I like it. If you want to see how small a tribe we really are, then you should count those few lit-up apartments. You can find more buildings than people in Galata, and it is a reality of the night, that the streets in which children's voices echo during the day are deserted, even by the cats. But those lanes of loneliness are my music teachers.

Am I going to part company with the streets I strolled in meditation? I was passing by the hospital where I was born when I saw a puff of smoke fluttering up to the sky as if on wings. The sight gave me goosebumps because I realized that after Eugenio I was planning to be the next 'Lord of Galata'.

Whenever I climb the Galata Tower I feel like singing a l-o-n-g *ezan*, the call to prayer. This time I was touring its balcony as the 'Candidate for Byzantine-Emperor-in-Exile', but I couldn't find an adjective to define my condition in any of my five languages. If Eugenio had been in my shoes he would have launched a tirade, right fist raised: 'Ah, you were once the property of my forefathers, you ungrateful city.' I fixed my gaze on the Ottoman mosques hiding behind a fragile screen of fog. My grandmother gave me fifty dollars when I first learned to count them all from our living room without faltering. She was sixty before she discovered that her Georgian forebears had converted from Christianity and was grateful that she'd been brought as a bride into a purebred Muslim family.

The secret that had been handed to me was of course a hoax, but I was tempted all the same. I wondered about that last item on Constantine XI's list, and wanted to confront Nomo before buckling down to their mysterious test.

Otherwise, whenever I sat down to a chess game I would be conflicted. My grandmother believed there was an angel who could be heard but not seen, named 'Hatîf'. I especially liked him because of the first two letters of his name. On my therapeutic tour of the cylindrical balcony of the Galata Tower I made myself believe that I could hear a half-human, half-bird sound, something like 'Be'. Relieved to have heard Saint Hatîf's murmur of approval, I descended to earth.

Making my way home I passed Apostol's barber shop, now a posh dress shop. I would always pause and stroke the cast-iron door handle whenever I passed by. When Apostol washed my hair after a haircut, I could always expect him to say, 'Young rascal, you're not handsome, but you're lucky – your face is like an old bust of a prince.' He always gave back half the price of the haircut, saying, 'Go buy yourself a chocolate bar.' Just before he migrated to Thessaloniki they gave him a going-away dinner. I was the only student there and I caused him to cry when I read a poem by Oktay Rifat.

*

I woke to the call to prayer, the morning *ezan*, rising up from the Bereketzade mosque, which happened to be the first place of worship built after the Conquest. I was so busy brushing up on Byzantium on the Internet that I forgot to eat breakfast.

The entire team was waiting for me in the hotel lobby. All three were dressed fashionably in sharp black suits with purple ties which made me a little uncomfortable. (Purple was the official color of the Royal Palace.) Did they know how I would answer, were they mocking me already in the first round? As I went down to the meeting room just below the lobby a thought about 'prison poetry' crossed my mind. I don't know why but I wondered what it would taste like being locked up in jail.

They offered me a seat in a handsome armchair and a sheaf of papers. I felt gratified to be handed documents in Turkish, Greek and Latin concerning my election as Byzantine-Emperor-in-Exile. At the bottom of the Turkish text were signatures belonging to the Paleaologus, Cantacuzenus, and Comnenus families. (The Comneni ruled from 1081 to 1185.) While donning my formal robes for the investment ceremony I asked, 'Why isn't Nomo here to honor this historic occasion – or are you the Nomo members in question?' Pappas, who was giving me a hand with the vestments, couldn't keep from smiling. Askaris glared at him and said, 'If they're not watching us right now, they're certainly listening, my dear sir. Everything is for Byzantium and your safety.'

A little later I placed my right hand on a dark silver box engraved with the Byzantine coat of arms and took the oath: 'I swear that I will not reveal my secret to anyone … that I will work for the greater good of Byzantium … this I swear.' And with my affixing the freshly created signature of Constantine XV to the decree placed before me, the ceremony came to an end. Askaris, Kalligas and Pappas genuflected on their right knees and with their rusty voices recited a passage that sounded like a hymn.

I was briefed on my duties and responsibilities: after two months of education in 'Byzantine reality', the testing process would begin. To pass the test I would have to quickly solve the riddle of the last task on the list in Constantine

XI's will. Then I would meet with Nomo to discuss how to actually carry out the assignment. If I met these challenges successfully, I would also have met the criteria for 'the Elect'. My deadline was the evening of September 30, 2009.

During this period I would be known as an employee of the London investment firm, RSIB Finance. I would be a researcher in economics, and every month £30,000 would be deposited into my bank account (Nomo must have been a privileged client of the same investment firm.) My education would take place at the Center for Research in Byzantine History in the same city (they were probably its anonymous sponsors as well).

As in the case of every majesty, of course, there were restrictions. I would ask no questions about my grandfather's activities or those of Nomo, and I would never attempt to pry into the CVs of the team.

*

First I broke the news to my family that I was going to London to work as an economist at a brokerage firm. I would take unpaid leave from my teaching posts. My mother wondered how I'd found this new job (with the help of a friend from the London School of Economics). And I knew my grandmother would say, 'Allah be praised!' the moment she heard that my salary would quadruple that of the president of our Republic.

While I was applying for leave a thought flashed through my mind: had Kalligas forgotten to mention my passion for chess when he was ticking off the positives in my career path? Or did they just have a low opinion of my talent?

DELTA

As a metropolis London was neither as old as Istanbul nor as young as New York. When I went there for my doctoral studies, I was already a little late in appreciating it. I considered Piccadilly a melodic name for a neighborhood, the Royal Academy of Arts reminded me of a Seljuk caravanserai, and I was sure that the customers of the Le Meridien Piccadilly hotel had all come to town on very important business.

The Le Meridien receptionist, hearing that I would be their guest for approximately three weeks, bestowed on me Suite number 905 on the top floor. I liked the room, which was spacious enough to host two prostitutes simultaneously. Outside the cage-like windows the city's historical panorama twinkled like an oasis. I shifted my focus to the Big Ben clock tower. It seemed fragile, like those famous people who've grown tired of posing for photographs and brought to mind Galata Tower. (In my childhood fantasy all the towers of the world were cousins.) I lowered my gaze to the other side of the street, where my eye was caught by Waterstone's. There, in Europe's greatest bookstore, quite possibly the last book of some marginal poet was waiting for me to find it. It was a tempting prospect.

New Chatham House was the most depressing building on the street. It was behind the Royal Academy, an exhibition space. So as not to shorten my route, I passed regularly through the Burlington Arcade. The arcade, where each shop sold a different kind of luxury item, sported security guards who looked like circus ringmasters. It was comical, the way they arrogantly clasped their hands behind their backs as they passed out warnings to passersby. I always watched the talentless but uniformed shoeshine man for a while. Evidently it was to spare his ornamented brush that he wagged his big head from right to left. These claustrophobic shops, run probably by the same families since 1819, had two levels. At one time I believed that when the arcade closed for the evening the shopkeepers went upstairs to live.

New Chatham House from a distance looked like a rectangular chunk of coal, and its undesirability increased as you drew closer. The goal of the receptionist at the main door was to provide a miserable start to your day. I didn't want to know who the tenants were on the other five floors, but the whole top floor belonged to the Center for Research in Byzantine History. According to the Internet the Center's library held 40,000 books in seventeen languages. The rest of the twenty-thousand-square-foot space was given over to seminar rooms, exhibition halls, and archives. The furniture in the library section, except for the bookshelves, was modern. I liked the harmony between the purple rugs and the gray granite floor.

I finished my brief exploratory tour and went up to the information desk. It was presided over by a white-haired woman with a doll-like manner who sat me down in a chair opposite her desk. She held still long enough for me to read her name (Mrs Jocelyn L. Hartley-Singros) on the card hanging from a chain around her neck. I digested the long name and briefly whispered mine to her and was done.

'I'm an academic from Istanbul. My field is econometrics. I want to learn Byzantine history through and through. If you can help me I'll be very grateful, Mrs Hartley-Singros.'

'My husband was a Cypriot,' she said, 'and you pronounced his last name as perfectly as a Cypriot. How nice, at last, to see a Turk here! May I ask how much time you've set aside to reach your goal?'

Reacting to the irony in her tone, I frowned and said, 'Under the right conditions, maybe a month.'

I don't know what kind of look I gave her, but Mrs Hartley-Singros leaned forward on her desk.

'I'm glad to see a young scholar like you have an interest in Byzantium,' she said. 'I recommend a program on two levels. First, a chronological history; then, Byzantine civilization and the books that underline the way it was institutionalized. If you wish, I can prepare an essential list for you.'

In something like panic she began compiling a reading list while I perused the CRBH's brochure. Founded ostensibly by a ship-owner of Greek extraction, the Center opened in 1853, most likely with my ancestor's money. Thanks to the benevolent legacy of the 'founder', the Center had no need to go to the outside world to meet expenses. It accepted neither donations nor members, a fact that was enough to confirm my suspicions.

As aids to my education in Byzantium from its birth to death (330-1453), the names of three authors were proposed, the first two of whom were academics. I was to choose one of them, but I preferred to read all three, which meant covering 2222 pages in ten days. Actually, I was curious about how it would feel to be a spectator of the same epic drama as staged by three different directors.

I absorbed the books, their appendices included, with great patience. I felt as if I was tracking down a secret code that I would recognize the instant I saw it. I doubted myself only on occasions of feeling exceptionally calm despite the long trips time travelling between the fourth and the fifteenth centuries.

*

Byzantium. From the Caucasus to Spain, from South Europe to North Africa. Only two centuries after it was founded it would be the greatest and most civilized empire on earth. Because of contradictions inside and developments outside, it sifted away like sand in an hourglass. When Mehmet the Conqueror took Constantinople in 1453, it was an empire on its deathbed. The truly fatal blow had come from the army that set out on the Fourth Crusade by order of the Pope. In 1204 this crazed group of criminals plundered the city during a so-called detour and founded the Latin Kingdom. When they were driven out in 1261, the city lay poverty-stricken and in ruins. It never pulled itself together after that.

The main internal cause of this melancholy ending was the flexibility of rules for the transmission of power. An emperor might choose his successor but the army, the church, and even civil leaders could intervene. The aim of the process was to let 'the best man' emerge. If an unexpected person seized the throne through intrigue and treachery, that was okay too, for it was God's will. Basil I (867-886), a villager from Adrianople, came to the throne in this way and eventually qualified as 'Basil the Magnificent'. It was an unfortunate example of God-granted power. In fact it was unavoidable that the system would create perpetual administrative chaos. The Byzantium that survived for eleven centuries was ruled by eighty-eight emperors; sixty-five of these were subjected to palace coups; twenty-nine were murdered; and thirteen took refuge in monasteries.

If I had to squeeze history into three words, my formula would be: History = Ambition + Chance - Simple Mistakes.

By the end of my third day the Library Information Specialist and I had drawn closer. We took coffee breaks together and traded Byzantine riddles.

'Which emperor was crowned after his son was crowned?'

'Zeno (474-491).'

'Which emperor are you least sorry about his throat being cut?'

'Phocas (602-610). He was Byzantium's ugliest, least talented, and most violence-prone emperor. He fomented an uprising and had all the sons of the emperor Maurice killed before his eyes, including an infant in the cradle, before having the emperor himself torn to pieces. He was so ugly that he had to grow a beard to hide his face.'

'How did Heraclius (610-641) cross from Europe to Asia as he was going to war with the Persians?'

'The sight of water frightened him. So they put a line of boats one after the other across the Bosphorus for him to walk on. Walls of potted plants were erected on both sides of the walkway to hide the water. The journey ended in victory.'

'Who was the most famous astrological Gemini of Byzantium?'

'The empress Irene (797-802)! So that she could dominate Byzantium she had the eyes of her son Constantine VI plucked out and imprisoned him in the room where he was born. She crowned herself empress. Charlemagne, the founding father of Europe, proposed to marry her in order to create the greatest kingdom of all time. As plans were being made to move the capital from Aachen to Constantinople Irene was dethroned.'

'Which emperor's mother was a Caspian Turk?'

'Leo IV (778-780).'

'What was the most effective message Byzantium sent to its aggressive neighbors?'

'It was sent by Basil II (976-1025). He defeated the Bulgarian army in 1014 and sent his prisoners back to their own country. Before sending them off he blinded all but one out of every hundred. Those he left with one eye so that they could guide the others. The Bulgarian king, Samuel, on seeing his 14,000 soldiers in this condition, died of a broken heart within two days.'

Steven Runciman and Cyril Mango were the authors of two of the books I chose for cultural and socio-economic perspectives on Byzantium. What these two scholars had in common was that they had both lived in Istanbul for a long time. As I turned the pages of their books I came to agree with Askaris more and more that Byzantium had brought civilization to her contemporaries and modernism to all humanity. With every paragraph I seemed to rise another step toward the clouds. Meanwhile I continued to pray that

I wasn't the victim of a big bad joke.

Byzantium was a divinely chosen nation, the inheritor of both the Roman and Greek cultures. The Byzantines were not totally wrong to sneer at the Catholics, since it was they who formed the first Christian state and built that most magnificent church, Haghia Sophia. For a Byzantine to be uneducated was almost as great a crime as being unlucky. They survived for eleven centuries because of their legal system, which was founded on written laws, yet lived in chaos because of their governing system, which was without written laws.

I ploughed through books containing pictures of icons, mosaics and frescoes. The everyday clothes of Byzantium citizens, the uniforms of foot soldiers, even the saddles and stirrups of their warhorses flaunted charming designs.

I came across it in the architecture books section, as if it had been waiting just for me on its special stand. In gilded letters on the purple leather binding of the giant book was stamped *Promenade in Byzantium*. This monumental example of the art of the book was number 003 in an edition of 999. It was the work that would be the turning point of my life. But my first job of the morning was to inhale the scent of the copyright page and then wrap the book in a great hug. No matter how often I turned the 333 pages as slowly as I could, I remained as unsatisfied as a child called in early from the playground. The book was a compilation of computerized reconstructions of all of the existing great but run-down Byzantine monuments.

Here were III architectural masterpieces, all functional and respectful of space and of an aesthetic reinforced by plain and symmetrical elements! Palaces, churches, city walls, hippodromes, aqueducts, triumphal arches, towers, barracks, schools, hospitals, libraries, cisterns, pools, parks, bridges, stadiums, hotels, bath houses, municipal buildings, fountains, stables … every one of them had an authentic and proud face, and it grieved me to think what a symbolic metropolis Istanbul could have been if only these buildings had survived. Below the image of each building, portrayed from different perspectives, was a description of it in four languages. It was natural for the Great Palace to receive the lion's share of attention. It was a monumental city in itself, begun by the father of Byzantium, Constantine himself, in the fourth century and continued for another six centuries with one beautiful addition after another. The palace complex began where the Sultanahmet Mosque stands now and continued without interruption to the Marmara shore. This masterpiece for the centuries was turned into a ruin by the crusaders who stopped off at Constantinople, ostensibly to break their journey, on their way to Jerusalem. I used to trace the Arabian Nights-like Great Palace stone by stone and curse that benighted mob the Byzantines put down as 'Latins', along with the Pope who manipulated them and the Venetian duke who collaborated with him. I remembered how the Conqueror extended protection to all the Byzantine monuments beginning with the church of Haghia Sophia, which he took over for a mosque. And has Europe, I wonder, shown the crusaders who plundered Constantinople – not excepting its matchless library – one-tenth of its reaction to the Arabs' destruction of the Alexandrian library?

Emperor Constantine I had no hope for a Rome riddled by polytheism. Converting to Christianity, he founded a new capital for himself. His goal in 330, as he laid the foundations of the new city – first called East Rome and then Constantinople after him – was to make it more magnificent than the original Rome. Most of the emperors who followed him embraced this goal as well. In the end, Constantine's city lasted nine centuries as the capital city of earth.

I was fascinated by the four-page engraved map in the middle of *Promenade in Byzantium*. I saw the refinement of miniatures reflected in the drawings of the 111 architectural sites. For turning the pages there was a pair of white gloves, and a magnifying glass to examine the engravings. I took the glass in hand, murmured a short prayer for an auspicious beginning, and set off on a journey between the fourth and fifteenth centuries. I heard the curses of the fishermen sailing out to open sea from Eleutherios Harbor; the grumbling of the night watch patrolling the Nike Way; the weary murmur of water flowing through the Valens Aqueduct; the buzz of the crowd ready to explode at the Hippodrome; the quavering prayers rising from the Church of the Pantocrator; the giggling of young women strolling the Mese Boulevard; the aroma of spices diffused by a ship putting into Phosphorion Harbor; the loud voices emanating from a tavern at the Platea Gate; the breeze off the Golden Horn timidly caressing the Fener seawalls; the whisper of mold in the Aegeus cistern; and the sorrowful plaint of an emperor going to bed with a long face. I heard them all.

The residential districts of the city, which boasted 500,000 people by the fifth century, were represented by gray-edged squares. The richer folk had courtyards, but all the other houses at least had bay windows or balconies. I read that the details of urban planning, such as the width of streets and the height of buildings, were all spelled out in written regulations.

I didn't put down the purple-handled magnifying glass until there was not a single cistern or street left unexplored. The element of mystery in my journeys constantly grew. And the common feature of the emperors I met in the palaces, when it wasn't desperation, was unreliability.

My education at the Center would be over when I read two more books and watched a six-part documentary on the Palaeologus dynasty and Constantine XI. My tutelary period, which began as instructive, ended as beguiling. If Nomo was watching me they should have been impressed by my opening act.

*

The Imperial Twilight was a striking title for a book about the last dynastic period and that drew me to it. The book by Constance Head seemed to stumble slightly as I helped it out of its corner on the shelf. The second reason I chose it was that it was 169 pages long and I didn't want to read a long and tedious tragedy about my ancestors. First I dove into the black-and-white photographs, most of which were reproduced palace engravings now held by public libraries in Europe. There was a hint of slight innuendo in the expression of the contrarian Michael Palaeologus, the founder of the dynasty. In another engraving all nine emperors looked as if they'd got an order to smile timidly. Or were they sending a message of apology? They all had horse-faces, long noses and goat-beards. I wouldn't have had much difficulty in visualizing my grandparents on a branch just above them on a schematic family tree.

The Palaeologi were Byzantium's last and longest-lasting dynasty (1261-1453). The eleven emperors of the eleventh dynasty were installed from father to son, older brother to younger brother, or grandfather to grandson. John V Palaeologus shared the throne with his father-in-law John VI Cantacuzenus for some time. The Palaeologus dynasty ended the plunder-and-confiscate period of the Latin Empire (1204-1261). With limited resources they made great efforts to reconstruct the ruined capital and tried to live in peace with European kings, the Vatican, the Seljuks and the Ottomans. Besides Constantinople what remained of the Empire consisted of five islands in the Aegean plus Mistra and its surroundings in the Southern Peloponnesus. On the other hand, the throne-wars, in which the women were also involved, looked like a fight for the captain's chair of a rusty and soon-to-be-sunk Titanic. Recorded history catches up with Michael for the first time in Nicaea, now Iznik, at the palace of John III Vatatzes (1222-1254), the emperor-in-exile. The emperor regarded the noble Palaeologus as an adopted son. Michael was charismatic, ambitious and a good soldier. While serving as governor of Thrace he came under suspicion for his anti-imperial rhetoric. But he saved himself from serious punishment with his silver tongue and, what's more, managed to marry Theodora, the daughter of the emperor's nephew. The following year the emperor died from an asthma attack and his son Theodore II Lascaris (1254-1258) succeeded him. Since Michael understood all too well what the new emperor was thinking where he was concerned, he hid out with the Seljuks and fought alongside them against the aggressive Mongols. Theodore II established good relations with the Seljuks and took Michael back, installing him in his previous position after swearing him to fealty. Michael however seized the first opportunity to be thrown into prison again, and talked his way out of it again as well. The emperor ruled for four years before he became ill and died; the son who replaced him, John IV Lascaris, was only seven. Michael had the new emperor's mentor killed and became co-emperor, keeping his young partner in the background.

In the winter of 1261 the most delicate method of blinding was used on the unfortunate eleven-year-old emperor: his eyes were exposed to a strong ray of light until they could no longer see. Patriarch Arsenios excommunicated Michael for this cruel act; Michael in turn denounced Arsenios and appointed a new patriarch who would approve him as emperor. There are conflicting reports about how John IV's story ends: that he was held captive in a castle on the Black Sea or the Marmara coast until his death; that he was imprisoned in a monastery; and that he regained his sight and departed for Sicily.

During the summer of 1261, as Michael VIII Palaeologus was entering Constantinople the Latin army slunk away without a fight. The emperor assigned his army to reconstruct the 'city of cities' that lay in ruins and levied special taxes for the work. Once domestic peace was achieved, he conspired with the Genoese against the Venetians and with the

Mongols against the Seljuks. This is when the settling of the Genoese in Galata took place. The Sicilian king, Charles, was an in-law of the Latin king, Baldwin II, whom Michael had evicted from Constantinople. He had a revenge attack in mind, for which the Pope gave approval. Michael VIII went to the Pope for help in negotiations with Charles. What he got was the reply that unless the Orthodox church joined the Catholics and thus resolved the 'religious dilemma', Byzantium could go to hell.

The emperor promised the desired union, but back home he encountered fierce opposition from the church, the army and the people. Luckily, thanks to certain fortuitous developments, Europe was unable to carry out its planned attack. But when the emperor died of a cold he caught while going to Thrace to suppress a revolt, he was treated like a traitor. Michael VIII Palaeologus, who had worked so hard to save the future of Byzantium, was, with the consent of the church, damned by his widow.

From that time on Byzantium lost much of its attraction for the ambitious kings of Europe, and also much of its power, freeing its emperors to make critical mistakes. Inter-family throne-wars helped speed the sands of time, though they slowed occasionally when an emperor of common sense managed to get hold of the throne. Until Manuel II Palaeologus was crowned, Byzantium was treated like a bankrupt merchant. When his turn as emperor came up, Manuel II – a philosopher diplomat, bibliophile and aesthete – had just turned forty. (I call attention to his habit of keeping a diary.) He had a respectful attitude and enjoyed generally good relationships with both the European powers and the Ottomans. Suffering a stroke at the age of seventy-four, he tried, with the help of Brother Mathias, to become a priest but died in a couple of weeks. He had six sons by the Serbian princess Helena. The eldest of these, John VIII Palaeologus (1425-1448), succeeded him.

John VIII was an aristocrat. A social creature, a music lover and somewhat mysterious, he was also a good soldier and hunter. His heart was on the side of a united Orthodox and Catholic church. He married three times but never had a child. Because of his Catholic sympathies he was refused a proper imperial funeral. Of his three brothers, John trusted only the oldest one, Constantine, and in his will bequeathed the crown to him. Despite this the least talented brother, Demetrius, tried to snatch it; but their alert mother, Helen Dragases, stepped in to prevent it.

The mother of Byzantium's founding father, Constantine the Great, was named Helen. There was an oracle that when a second Constantine with a mother named Helen became emperor, the end of the empire was nigh. Of course, when Helen Dragases' son Constantine XI Palaeologus (1449-1453) became emperor at the age of forty-five and did not change his name, the oracle was happily relegated to a marginal note by all the historians.

*

I read the book carefully and like a diligent student took a lot of notes. It was as if I were patiently writing a talisman for myself by reducing the feckless behavior of my forefathers to dry sentences. I stopped at page 143 and took up a thin biography, hoping to get the Constantine XI story over with in three short chapters. I planned to finish Donald M. Nicol's *The Immortal Emperor* in two sessions. I thought about browsing the shelf of 'Turkish sources', and so I did. Every one of the 150 books, most of them from university presses, had been rebound, probably because of their cardboard covers. My hand reached for Semavi Eyice's *The Architecture of Late Byzantium*, on the monuments of the Palaeologan period.

Under the section written in Ottoman on the Chora church restoration was a note in English, in purple ink: 'These frescoes are what make the Chora even more important than Haghia Sophia!' I was amazed. That graceful Gothic handwriting was not unfamiliar to me. Hadn't I seen a message from that pen in Istanbul? I photocopied the page for later study. If my hunch was right I would follow it up in the US, and do so without informing Nomo. Perhaps my mission had just taken a more sensitive turn. To visit America would require a plausible excuse; I resorted to the Internet. Among Byzantine centers there, Dumbarton Oaks stood out. Located in Washington, DC, it had a research library and a small museum.

'It's number one in its field,' said Jocelyn, with a sneer in her tone.

The Immortal Emperor was available at academic bookstores. I was a little surprised to catch myself admiring the statue of Constantine XI on the cover of the copy I bought at Blackwell's. I decided I would wait until Istanbul to read it; I would head home after two more days of watching documentaries at the Center. I informed Askaris of my desire to complete my education at Dumbarton Oaks after, of course, visiting the Byzantine monuments of Istanbul. He nodded respectfully, I was glad to see, after first greeting the idea with widened eyes.

*

The library closed at 5:30. I usually exited my adventures in ancient time with a buzzing head. It was a pleasure to regain my balance by falling into the charming rhythms of London. Had my grandmother sent the angel Hâtif, whose voice was just loud enough to be heard, to look after me? At a private moment of my day he would whisper two or three words in my ear and slip away.

Every other evening I walked to Heave(geteria) on Bentinck Street for dinner. I discovered this vegetarian restaurant on my way to Daunt's bookshop across from which on a corner of the three-way crossing, was a building that resembled the Galata Tower. If I had no particular agenda for the evening I would stop in after dinner at Waterstone's, across from my hotel. More important than the 2 million books sprawling throughout its five storeys was that it stayed open until ten. There I discovered the poet Pascale Petit and read Aeschylean drama. I tried to guess which of the drooping people around me were Nomo operatives. But I didn't want this game to turn into a habit. If I believed that I was being followed, I preferred to think that it was for my own security rather than for fear of my betraying the mission. I probably shouldn't have stopped in at that café in Golders Green with chess-lovers for regulars. I decided to hide my deeper self from Nomo while allowing my normal habits and desires to show through. (Emperor Basiliscus died of hunger in prison in 477, Emperor Zeno was buried alive in 491 …)

My excursion to see my usual dealer in antiques and rare books and to peer into the windows of the clock and watch emporium coincided with rush hour. I began to think that the Brits all locked themselves in their houses because there were people from seventy different nations murdering their language. Some evenings I went on bus tours of shop windows full of international brands. I saluted the weary mannequins. At twilight I followed the trail signposted by the great stone buildings. I dove into bars with tragicomic names and drank chamomile tea to amuse the dull drunks. In my room the vodka bottle was never far from my hand as I watched DVDs of Coen Brothers films one by one. (Emperor Maurice had his throat cut in 602, Emperor Phocas was torn to pieces in 610, Emperor Heraclius died in 641 under torture …)

On my first weekend in London I asked Askaris to find two prostitutes for me. We were both embarrassed as I specified: 'They should not be bony or quarrelsome.' That night M. from Prague and O. from Brno went with me up to my room; both were lively, and taller than me. To impress them I recited a stanza of their compatriot the poet Jaroslav Seifert – Nobel Prize, 1984 – and they were as startled as a couple of novice nuns who've stumbled on a pornographic graffito. (Emperor Constantine III was poisoned in 641, Constans II beaten to death in 668, Emperors Leontius and Tiberius II beheaded in 705 …)

I went to see the lions incarcerated in the London Zoo. Abi, a playful cub the last time I saw her, was now the princess of the cage. Lying on the wooden platform, she was on the brink of dozing off, while her mate Lucifer was already in deep sleep.

'Abi, hey girl, Abi,' I called.

Suddenly she perked up. Our eyes locked, and she began to nod her head up and down. Slowly she rose onto her front legs as if posing for a sculpture. With a movement of her head she indicated the sleeping Lucifer, suggesting, 'I can't come down to you now because of this guy.'

I went to the London Aquarium. There I was at first annoyed by the endless hordes of children screaming their heads off in the dim cavernous space, but then I remembered that I'd never screamed so happily in my own childhood. I looked at the stingrays and the sharks and the sea monsters that occupied a niche somewhere between seahorses and plants. Did the stingrays seem to be challenging mankind? No? With menacing looks they nosed up to the humans standing at their end of the tank, then retreated with wings flapping like a curse on the crowd. Were I an emperor, I thought, I would definitely have an aquarium full of stingrays and sharks.

I went quickly past my old student lodgings and into the British Museum. It was something of an embarrassment to see the weakness of the Byzantine section amid the treasury of objects pilfered from the four continents. I took up a position on the bottom step of the quiet stairs in the courtyard, closed my eyes and rested my head on my arms and my arms on my knees. Four silent tornadoes rose up from Anatolia, Mesopotamia, Egypt and China and united high in the air. In a discipline of constellations music was improvised while being tossed to and fro … (Emperor Justinian II was beheaded in 711, Emperor Philippicus had his eyes gouged out in 713, Emperor Constantine VI lost his eyes in 797, Emperor Leo V was stabbed and then beheaded in 820, Emperor Michael III was stabbed to death in 867 …)

Another night Askaris sent two Jamaican girls to my room. I didn't know they were going to be identical twins. M.'s left leg was false to her knee. Since she was a reader of the poet Derek Walcott, I invited her to see 'The Mousetrap' with me. The play, inspired by an Agatha Christie story, has been staged 23,000 times since 1952. I shivered when the murderer made his entrance in the first scene. I was thinking about my ordeal, which would come up in six weeks. M. believed I was the heir apparent of an organization involved in some kind of shady business. (Emperor Constantine VII was poisoned in 959, Emperor Romanus II was poisoned in 963, Emperor Nicephorus II Phocas was stabbed and then beheaded in 989, Emperor John I Tzimiskes was poisoned in 976, Emperor Romanus III Argyrus poisoned and strangled in 1034, Emperor Michael V died in 1042 as his eyes were being gouged out …)

I had no idea where my three assistants were staying, so I met them for dinner at my hotel restaurant. Askaris's dialogue with the waiter was impressive; he spoke with an upper-class accent and wielded a rich vocabulary. I was willing to bet that he'd graduated from an elite British university and lived in London. Kalligas's English was good too and he had a general air of self-confidence. Pappas, on the other hand, barely knew English at all. His struggles with the menu were amusing. Maybe he'd been hired as a personal favor to somebody, I thought – then what might the reason be? If he was a bit on the shallow side, at least he had a warm heart.

I gave orders to my team and asked them to account for themselves when necessary but never inquired into their pasts. So, to rescue the evening, I began improvising on this and that, warming to my subject as I saw success in surprising my audience. I summarized my educational history, then delved into passages from private life. Askaris was a wise but pragmatic man who liked to finish what he started. Yet he seemed to want to conceal his virtues. I could tell that he was a bit disturbed that I was sharing a table with Kalligas and Pappas. I met with him twice more before returning to Istanbul; his manners were always efficient and measured and I felt myself warming toward him. I was sure that his mysterious job had prevented him from marrying or developing a hobby. We met the first time at the hotel bar and he was embarrassed to ask my permission to leave, after his second mineral water, to catch the train to Winchester. (Emperor Romanus IV Diogenes had his eyes gouged out and was poisoned in 1071, Emperor Alexius IV Angelus was strangled, then beheaded in 1183, Emperor Andronicus I was torn to pieces after torture in 1185, Emperor Isaac II died as he lost his eyes in 1193, Emperor Alexius IV was strangled in 1204, Alexius V Murtzuphlus had his eyes gouged and his tongue cut out the same year – 1261 – that Emperor John IV Lascaris was blinded …)

I presented Jocelyn a farewell bottle of perfume on my departure from the Center. I wasn't brave enough to disagree when she said in her confident tone, 'Don't try to hide it, you're here to research your Byzantine novel.'

'Or a mysterious play from which I'm not absent.'

'Does it have a title?'

'… Sultan of Byzantium …'

'Well, that's a provocative one for Anglo-Americans who aren't total strangers to sultans and Byzantium. And 'Sultan of Byzantium' was what they called Mehmet II after his capture of Constantinople.'

(The son, Andronicus IV Palaeologus, and the grandson, John VII Palaeologus, of Emperor John V Palaeologus were partially blinded in 1374 in response to the emperor's orders and the meddling of the Ottomans …)

EPSILON

I was hanging up the map with the clues long after my meeting with Askaris when I remembered something beneath my pile of atlases. I'd never picked up this heavy book, assuming that it was just another of my grandfather's tragicomic purchases. The letters on its spine proclaimed 'Manassis'. Anxiously I lifted the cover of what looked to me like a box made up of straw. The book was printed in Venice in 1729. On the left side of the thin muslin-like pages was a text in Latin, and on the right side one in Greek. Together with the words of Constantine Manassis, I found passages from two authors whose names I had not encountered anywhere else. My own research told me that twelfth- and thirteenth-century historians had nothing to do with the Palaeologus family. The book seemed to have done time as a file cabinet: I found fifty-year-old business cards from Genoese restaurants stuck in its pages. One yellowing sheet of paper marked off in squares held directions to nightclubs. They were written in ink in old Turkish. In view of the grammatical mistakes, the author was surely my grandfather.

Another, less worn-out sheet of paper contained a pentagram drawn with a ruler. Its only difference from the stars you see on flags was that the lines were elongated to form five isosceles triangles, with the bases delineated by dots. In two of the triangles were numbers. Another two were full of Latin letters, whereas the fifth one contained a sentence written in Arabic. I thought this document was a list of clues or maybe a cheat sheet for roulette. Or was it perhaps an attempt at using gothic letters to enhance the sophistic plot to siphon more money from my naïve grandfather's pocket?

As soon as I got back to Istanbul from London I pulled out the photocopy I'd made at the Center and compared the handwriting with these documents. It certainly looked like the two pieces of writing had come from the same hand. Now must be the time, I thought, to find out whether that hand belonged to Paul Hackett, for three years the son-in-law in the Ipsilandit Apartments. I'd been conditioned to hate my father as the reason for the dissolution of our family, but I was curious about Paul Hackett simply because of my grandmother's charge that, 'Except for your curmudgeonly manners and the pride you got from your mother, you're the spitting image of your father.'

During my last year at high school, when I was applying to universities around the world, Eugenio once asked, 'Is it because Virginia was your father's school that you don't want to go there?' I remembered how he slowly shook his head when he saw that I had no idea what school my father had attended. The publishing company Paul represented had gone belly-up; now the only chance I had of connecting with his past lay in whatever clues I could pick up at the University of Virginia, if I could go there. I composed a proleptic consolation for myself against the eerie possibility that the handwriting was his. I had no right at this point to promote my life from mystery novel to television soap opera. I don't know why, but a sarcastic graffiti at LSE came to mind: 'Where science ends, prayer begins.'

The night of my return from London, I took the family to dinner at the Müzedechanga. I liked this museum restaurant in Emirgan because the shallow bourgeoisie overlooked it. We took a table with a view of an Ottoman Palace on the Asian side of the Bosphorus. As the second bottle of white wine was being uncorked, I thought I saw a *muezzin* in a turquoise caftan on top of the building's tower. While looking hopefully around at his environment, would he be moved to recite a classical Bosphorus poem? He slowly disappeared behind a curtain of fog. Had I seen this illusion when I was a student, I would have thought, 'If there *are* still people who can see the man in turquoise, I wonder how many?'

At home that night I browsed my pile of poetry magazines. The rhythmic sounds rippling from the pages as I flicked them seemed a challenge to the night, cracking like a whip in the intensifying silence. I rose and went to the balcony to contemplate old Istanbul. I saw a horde of horsemen galloping across the plain bathed in the light of churches and mosques. In the forefront was a prancing white horse that seemed to be saying 'Let's go!' to the commander it was waiting for. I was as thrilled as a child on his first trip to the amusement park.

*

Instinctively, I picked twenty-two Byzantine monuments that I hadn't visited yet. I was a stranger to the names and faces of all but four of them. My excursion might be received by Nomo as an act of deception. But I had no private agenda for this safari, although I thought I might receive a sign of some kind while paying my twenty-two visits. One gift of Persian is the word 'serendipity': in the course of searching for one beauty, to end up with another …

It would have been disrespectful to chronology not to begin my trip through the time tunnel with the city walls: this ring of stone from Sarayburnu to Ayvansaray, from Yedikule to Topkapı, had made Constantinople the best-protected city on earth from the fifth to the fifteenth century. I executed a slalom on and around them both with and without a car. Iskender Abi drove the Lancia that I took out of the garage once a month. I knew he would ask 'How long are those huge walls?' at the first opportunity. I rewarded him with the information that they were a little over twelve miles in length and incorporated ninety-six watchtowers. I waited for the next question – 'What's a watchtower?'

I felt the thrill of entering a foreign country without a passport as I passed outside the walls from Samatya, the only place whose name has remained unchanged since the beginning of Byzantium. There was once a wide moat in front of these walls, and on the other side of the moat another row of walls thirty feet high. Invaders who made it past those two obstacles would come back empty-handed from the ninety-foot inner walls. If you looked closely from the outside, the walls looked like heavyweight wrestlers standing shoulder to shoulder, whereas from the inside they resembled a troop of retirees who could hardly stand straight. This picture was an accurate portrayal of the Byzantium that was handed over to Palaeologus.

I walked along the walls, mentally skipping the 'restored' sections. I scrutinized them as if I were reading my own coffee-grounds, and interpreted the lack of insight as: 'No obstacles on your road.' It was mildly satisfying to see Iskender Abi watching me prostrate to the walls out of the corner of his eye as if he were reluctantly witnessing an outlandish and bizarre ritual.

Traversing the coordinates of the Imrahor Mosque (St John the Baptist Church), Molla Gurani Mosque (St Theodore Church), Fethiye Mosque (Pammakaristos Church), and the Gül Mosque (St Theodosia Church), I zigzagged from the fifth to the tenth, then the thirteenth to the twenty-first centuries. My guide to these mysterious and remote corners of the city was the Byzantine expert Cevat Mert. When he remarked that in the thirty-three years of his professional life this was the first time he had directed a tour like this, I explained that I was doing 'preliminary research for a Selçuk Altun novel'. I'm sure he was convinced.

I thought of the most important playwright in history – Samuel Beckett – as I wandered in and out of the mini-museums and churches-become-mosques. His masterpiece, *Waiting for Godot*, was received with unworthy criticism when it was first staged in 1953. He made a gesture to the theater world by emphasizing that the whole play was a symbiosis. It was tragicomic how the sole clue he gave went unnoticed – in fact it could have been the stuff of a play within a play. Symbiosis is a biological term that means, 'the interaction between two different species as they live together.' If you take this into consideration regarding GODOT, you can see that the words GOD and (idi)OT are intermingled. It may also be easily understood that the leading characters, Vladimir and Estragon, were acting out 'God' and 'Idiot' and exchanged roles according to their zig-zagging moods to create an eccentric harmony. Beckett generously provided secondary clues via the nicknames of Estragon (Gogo) and Vladimir (Didi). Hence GODOT would never come; Estragon and Vladimir were GODOT. They were not waiting for anyone. While they were joking 'absurdly' with each other they were also setting a trap for the sleepy audience.

Suddenly a magpie landed on top of a nearby disused Ottoman fountain and crowed twice towards me, as if it was waiting for an answer. Perhaps it was my inner voice which said, 'The symbiosis of a story and (hi)story is the most enigmatic.' With this, the elegant bird crowed once more and flew off towards the Byzantine dungeons nearby.

The Byzantine monuments, which I was sure I was seeing for the first and last time, existed in symbiosis with their environment. They took a step forward to today while their neighbors took a step backward to yesterday, both of them meeting at a central point in time, looking like they were all wearing the same pale, faded clothes. For the time being they enjoyed the pleasures of quietude, but they were waiting for a sign. The few cars passing through the crooked streets did not honk and no children's cries echoed. On the faces of the oldsters walking hesitantly along was satisfaction, something between happiness and unhappiness. It was clear that they were well aware of the fragrance of fig trees emanating from the overgrown gardens, the small Ottoman cemeteries which suddenly sprang up at the end of streets that curved about like narrow streams, and the barely standing wooden houses incongruously harboring pharmacies.

There were no traces of pretense in the stance of the

off my shoes and go in. The mosque, as a church, was thought to have provided the last resting-place of Constantine XI. In front of me was a group of lively and aged American women. A female passer-by wearing a villager's baggy pants, who had probably never been to Taksim Square – the center of the city – in her life, observed unforgettably that, 'These days you see crazy old women wandering around here all the time.' The lack of proportion between the square footage of the floor and the height of the ceiling was impressive. I could believe the story that the floor of the ninth-century building shrank over time while the ceiling grew higher. For Cevat Mert an additional feature was that the church had served as an arsenal for the Ottoman navy after the Conquest.

The Pantocrator monastery – Zeyrek Mosque – was closed to visitors because of a wide-spectrum renovation project. But I walked decisively to an adjacent building, which had been built by the empress Irene, of the Comnenus family. The monastery, looking from the outside like a caravanserai, contained the tombs of Michael VIII, founder of the Palaeologus dynasty; and of Manuel II, Constantine XI's father. The complex included a hospital, a retirement home and a small cemetery. I parted from my guide in front of a cistern wall that stood like a lacey screen between the city and Zeyrek. The guide believed that without knowing the life story of Fatih Sultan Mehmet, the conqueror of Constantinople, no one could understand the finale of Byzantium. The wooden houses on my route looked frail enough to blow away in the first strong wind. But those houses, now the color of coal, had survived who knows how many powerful earthquakes? It was odd that the most important monastery of the city was shrouded in sack-cloth for its restoration. I only hoped that it would not come out on the other end looking like a boutique hotel. In the annex was a café with more cats than customers. From the farthest table it was possible to watch the parade of Byzantine and Ottoman monuments; and impossible not to come eye-to-eye with the Galata Tower. I was a bit irked by its innuendo.

I drank two glasses of tea while going over my superficial notes and then ambled down to Atatürk Boulevard to catch a taxi home. The street nearest the Boulevard appeared to be an open-air ethnology exhibition. A row of butchers from Siirt, a region in the southeast, were busily cutting up sheep carcasses for local kebab, and a mélange of charcuteries offered delicacies exclusively from Siirt. Customers sat on low stools in teahouses conversing in Kurdish and Arabic in low voices and laughing in loud bursts. In the last one a rooster strutted about nervously.

On my right, a thousand feet away, the Valens Aqueduct shimmered like an oasis. We began to gravitate toward each other. This half-mile-long and ninety-foot-high structure straddled the avenue like a science-fiction giant, supported by six arches through which vehicles passed with appropriate respect and fear. Eugenio said about this fourth-century work that it had 'broken away from the walls and marched into the city to hunker in the middle and serve as a warning'. Spying a couple of boys playing on top of it, I was spurred to exercise my right to walk across it. Where the aqueduct started up it was closer to the ground. Moreover, a small abandoned shack had been put there by fate. I worried that I would raise a laugh from the claque of nearby tire repairmen as I clumsily climbed first onto a garbage can, then the roof of the shack, and finally up to the aqueduct. It was slightly less trash-filled than urban beaches. I started off, swaying like an inexperienced tightrope walker. As I climbed upward my body cooled down. It was like being on a Ferris wheel; I was astonished by the feeling of spaciousness. In a small nook overlooking the boulevard two boys about ten years old were smoking cigarettes and throwing rocks at the cars below. They were surprised to see me.

'What are you two doing on my grandfather's aqueduct?' I said half-jokingly.

'I swear we didn't know, sir,' said the one wearing a T-shirt with 'F.C. Köln' written on it.

I attempted to befriend Sadun from Silvan and Hamdullah from Eruh, both eastern towns with beautiful names. All at once I felt sleep overcoming me, and suddenly decided to do the weirdest thing of my life. I informed the boys that I would give them twenty liras each if they watched over me while I had a nap. Their eyes brightened. One said, 'God give you rest'; the other said, 'May your life be long.' I made a bed for myself out of the newspapers and plastic bags strewn around. When I go down in *The Secret History of Byzantium* as the first emperor to sleep on the Valens Aqueduct, I hope it will be noted that I had two guards, on my right an Arab and on my left a Kurd.

The one with the T-shirt that said, in English, 'The limits of my language are the limits of my world,' woke me as the evening *ezan* was just finishing. I gave them fifty liras each and they insisted on kissing my hand, then ran off in the direction I'd come from. I stood and started walking in the opposite direction. I was disillusioned at coming away empty-handed from this safari that I'd embarked on without knowing what I expected to find anyway. The descent from the Valens Aqueduct, which I'd climbed purely for the sake of climbing it, reminded me of Aztec temples where the stairs extended farther and farther as you went down and down. Just as I began to think that I was stretching my imagination, my feet touched the ground. I found myself in the rear courtyard of the Kalendarhane Mosque, once the Akataleptos Church. I'd visited this monument, which served as a dervish lodge during Ottoman times, on the first day of my safari. I felt a warm glow, as though I were back in a sympathetic labyrinth. Serendipity?

*

The common conclusion reached by history books, encyclopaedia articles, and internet sites was that Constantine XI was quite a liberal and straightforward emperor who became a martyr by heroically defending his capital city from the powerful Ottoman army. Yet there were others who were also instrumental in the fall of Constantinople: the Pope, who pretended to provide aid, and the Venetians and Genoese who offered symbolic support.

The Immortal Emperor squeezed the life story of Constantine XI into 128 pages and listed 200 works in the bibliography. For the sake of being academic, the author, D.M. Nicol, was apparently determined not to deal with his inner world at all. I thought I should read this book exactly the way I would observe a game of chess.

... Emperor John VIII had no children. He had in mind that the oldest and most talented of his three brothers, Constantine, would succeed him. But on the day he died the other two brothers, Thomas and Demetrius, made moves of their own to take the crown. Thomas, the younger, reached the palace first. Demetrius, the Selymbrian despot who opposed the Orthodox church's joining the Catholics, had a fighting chance as well. But Constantine was the favorite son of Manuel II's widow Helen. She persuaded the avaricious younger brothers to yield, and succeeded in having Constantine installed as the last emperor of Byzantium. She informed Murad II, the Ottoman sultan, of this step and obtained his assent. Between Constantine and his brothers there always remained a chill. When the emperor was desperately defending his capital against Mehmet II with limited resources, his brothers were nowhere near him; and after the Byzantine defeat they continued as despots in the Morea by the expedient of paying taxes to the Ottomans. Over time the waning of their power kept pace with the waning of their honor.

Thomas's son Andronicus, the legal heir to the Byzantine throne, sold his rights to King Charles VIII of France. I couldn't help thinking that if Mehmet II had been in my far-off grandfather's shoes, the first item of business would have been to have his two brothers strangled for the sake of efficiency and the prevention of dishonorable intrigue.

... Constantine's paternal grandmother was Italian, and as a prince he'd married – without love – two noble Italian ladies, both of whom he lost to sickness. On becoming emperor, he sent his confidant Sphrantzes to friendly neighboring kingdoms in search of potential wives. He wanted to counter the empire's gradual loss of power with a majestic marriage. After two years of fruitless searching, the matchmaker thought about Fatih's stepmother Maria Brankoviç, daughter of the Serbian despot George Brankoviç. After the death of Fatih's father Murad II, Maria had gone back home to Serbia (Fatih was the son of Murad by a different wife). Constantine's mother Helen was also related to the Brankoviç family, in fact. But this attempt failed too, and the emperor ended his quest for a wife.

... It seemed as if my many-times-great-grandfather had spent his whole life doing homework and standing guard. I don't think he ever tasted the pleasures of power. Although he was quite just and generous, he lacked the full support of the church and his people for siding with his father and older brother. They felt that uniting the Orthodox and Catholic churches under the hegemony of the latter was not a bad idea. For Constantine, who was fond of philosophy, the reasons behind the quarrel between the churches were insignificant. Union would win the support of Europe in the event of danger from the East; and furthermore Byzantium, as the inheritor of the Roman and Hellenic cultures, would find a way to bring the callow kingdoms of Europe to accept its superiority. Unfortunately this goal was embraced neither by the church nor the people. Loukas Notaras, who was the equivalent of a prime minister and was thought to be supporting the emperor's efforts from behind the scenes, uttered a sentence for the history books: 'Better the imam's turban than the bishop's hat.'

DM Nicol wrote that Constantine XI was born on February 8, 1405, whereas the pedestal of the statue on the book's cover proclaimed February 9, 1404, as his birthday. To me this ambiguity, with the second month the only common denominator, was typical of the Byzantine destiny. I liked the book. What I read in *The Immortal Emperor*'s conclusion lent support to Askaris's hypothesis: that my many times great-grandfather had not died fighting on the walls, and that six Palaeologi were on the passenger list of the last Genoese ship to leave the battle …

Constantine XI, who assumed his rightful throne only with his mother's help, and was helpless in finding himself a wife, tried always to do good for his people but could not avoid fatal mistakes. This situation suddenly brought someone else to mind – me! I remembered so many instances of exemplary behavior, like not running red lights even at midnight on deserted streets, never cheating on exams, and as for girls – well, let alone accosting one on the street, I never even raised my voice around them for fear it might be misunderstood. I rushed to a phone booth and called my tenured pimp.

ZETA

Washington DC was 2,400 years younger than Istanbul, and although I thought that a population of 600,000 was rather insignificant for the capital of the great USA, I appreciated the symmetrical avenues laid out by letters and numbers. It reminded me of Ankara with its gloomy official buildings, unsmiling civil servants, and military officers roaming the streets in shifts. I was a university sophomore when I first saw the concrete-hued Potomac River, and I thought it added some color to the city. Spring was coming to an end and the humidity was terrible. I visited the museums, took the train back to New York, and put Washington on my list of cities not worth seeing twice.

This time I was surprised to notice so many brick buildings erected at strategic points, as if a nearby brick mine had nourished the city's architecture here and there until it petered out. The Four Seasons Hotel's suit of brick armor annoyed me too, but the luxurious interior was soothing and the staff spoke like they were crooning lullabies. My suite was on the second floor, with a view of the Rock Creek Park so calming that it put me to sleep. Maybe my settling into this hotel on Askaris's recommendation was a plot to get me used to luxury?

Dumbarton Oaks was a private mansion before it became a research institute. Its brick walls looked as if they were waxed every month and in its well-tended gardens the birds sang carefully. Its major research areas were Byzantium and pre-Columbian America. That these two fields were not in symbiosis was clear from the museum section, where the busts were challenging the masks and vice versa. To bolster the image of the library, which resembled a bomb shelter, it was emphasized that it accommodated 200,000 books and documents.

'Two days at Dumbarton Oaks will complete my personal education,' I told Askaris. 'And then I'll drop in on a few American friends and relatives. You won't need to see me for ten days.'

'Yes, Excellency,' he said. As he diverted his eyes to the floor I knew he'd already drawn up the list of men he would put on my tail.

The summer lethargy at the library expanded my lack of energy. I wandered aimlessly through the stacks. I grabbed a heavy tome on the statesmanship of Manuel II, the model Palaeologus, and seated myself at a remote table. On one of the pages I flipped through was a photocopy of the conclusion of a Venice-Byzantium treaty. Manuel II's signature on the document, dated 1406, filled up a whole line and spilled over – it contained more than fifty letters. I couldn't help laughing. It was as though the large ornamental letters had righted a wrong. I took two history books from my bag, one in Turkish and the other in English. I was going to read the biography of Fatih, the executioner of Byzantium, here in the most important Byzantine library on the planet.

According to our school books Fatih was a leader of genius who opened and closed an era; a bibliophile and art lover; and a peerless sultan who would have conquered the rest of

Europe had he not been poisoned by Western schismatics. His contemporaries in the West, on the other hand, knew him as a deceitful bisexual and ruthless enemy of Christianity and civilization, who was poisoned by his son Beyazit II.

He was a polyglot in command of eight languages. He was an aesthete who loved philosophy and the arts and who absorbed the classical literature of both East and West. My partiality for him, caused by his secret talent for poetry, became respect when I realized how he'd ruled the Empire like a chess master to improve and expand it. He drew lessons from the palace intrigues he'd witnessed as a boy. He placed spies in countries he was interested in, Byzantium above all. And he always based his actions on the intelligence he received from them. He was ruthless towards his family when pre-emptive action was needed, and towards even his favorite pashas when it was necessary to punish a lack of success. Historians who had difficulty accepting the Conquest of Constantinople exaggerated the number of soldiers in the Ottoman army by a factor of three, and disregarded the presence in his camp of the vizier, Halil Pasha, who was actually a Byzantine spy. Halil Pasha passed along tactical plans to the Byzantines and tried to demoralize the Ottomans by spreading rumors such as that a huge Hungarian army was about to engulf them from behind. At the proper time he was beheaded.

Fatih Sultan Mehmet benefited from both the right and wrong of Byzantium. He avoided the trap hidden in the Pope's honeyed words: 'Your mother was a Christian; so join us and rule the whole of Europe.' Intelligent and philosophical, he was playful but haughty. His goal was to surpass what Alexander the Great had done in the East by seizing control of the West and holding onto his power.

He was forty-nine when he died, either from poison or from a kink in his intestines. Wasn't Constantine XI also forty-nine at the time of his pseudo-martyrdom? It's no surprise that history has missed this coincidence, since it prefers inventing to decoding. Askaris declared that my distant grandfather made the arrangements for Fatih to be poisoned at the age of forty-nine. I'm waiting for the moment when I'll hear the story of this impossible-to-prove irony in detail. As the portrait of the mysterious sultan came to life in my mind, it dawned on me had Byzantium a leader of Fatih's caliber at the time of the Fourth Crusade, Europe today would have a less checkered map and the globe a less irritating balance of power. But I'm sure Samuel Beckett would have scorned this view and said, 'The gods enjoy chaos.'

Whenever I went to the library I ran into a certain South American historian. He had a body at the uppermost limit of dwarfism and a thin high-pitched voice. He was sure the history books would need rewriting when he finished his research on Theophilus II (829-842), the aesthete emperor. He took me for a British academic and I was too lethargic to correct him. He once asked who was my favorite Byzantine emperor. The name of Constantine XI popped out of my mouth at the last second instead of Fatih.

'But why?'

'Because he was my great-great-great grandfather,' I said, and we both laughed merrily.

*

The University of Virginia is in Charlottesville, which was a three-hour drive from my hotel. To prevent Ed, the talkative driver of my rented limo, from disturbing me with any other royal statistics, I was prepared to read *The Washington Post* down to the most minute advertisement. I was looking for an adjective combining apathy and irritation to define my feelings towards history.

'Charlottesville owes its population density to the presence of the university and its many rich retirees.' Ed's murmur of a sentence equipped me with the good news that we'd reached Charlottesville. The brick buildings scattered across the university campus looked like scattered flocks of sheep, and the Jeffersonian stone buildings among them like exhausted shepherds.

At the Information Center I was surprised by the officials' lack of surprise at my interest in old student records and where they were kept. They directed me to the Alderman Library. Alderman Library was a five-story brick building that impressed me. The pillars in front seemed to be made of material left over from construction of the stone buildings and didn't seem out of place. As I passed through the door I momentarily wondered what the School of Architecture must look like. Although it was still the summer holiday there was some kind of liveliness in the library and suddenly I missed my students, almost to the point of regretting that I was here.

What I wanted was quietly to trace my father by look-ing through his graduating class's yearbook. These collections usually listed the home addresses of graduates at the back to make it easier for alumni organizations to contact them.

I thought I might contact a family member and find out whether the handwriting sample was really his or not.

My father was born in 1944, so I asked the student in charge for the 1966 and 1967 yearbooks. When she brought them to me I realized that she was a Turkish Cypriot, but I was too preoccupied to say hello in Turkish.

When I saw the picture of my father in his mortarboard cap in the 1966 yearbook I collapsed into the first empty chair. Except for my mother and grandmother, anybody who saw this face – to which the photographer had managed to add the hint of a smile – and me would exclaim, 'But this is a picture of you ten years ago!' Paul Hackett had an innocent charm and could be considered handsome. I could not be considered handsome; though I had his facial features, probably they were positioned somewhat disproportionately.

There were no addresses at the back of the yearbook, but I discovered a mysterious clue next to my father's picture. It was a forget-me-not aphorism from a Greek philosopher written in Latin by Randolph S. Fitzgerald IV. There could hardly be more than one person with that name. I consulted the Internet via my cell phone for information on Randolph IV. It seemed that after graduating from the College of Arts and Sciences at the University of Virginia, this friend of my father's, who had inscribed the esoteric good wishes, completed a doctoral degree at the same institution. He'd taken an editorial job at a small New York publishing house after retiring from teaching at a college I'd never heard of. I sent a note to his electronic address: I was Paul Hackett's son, in Washington on private business, and I would like to meet him.

By the time I climbed aboard my limo for the trip back to my hotel, I'd corresponded with Randolph IV twice. He invited me for dinner at his home and added, 'If you're thinking of bringing wine, I prefer Margaux.' I sent my counter-suggestion: 'If my vegetarianism is a problem, I can drop by for coffee.' I decided I liked this guy when he answered, 'I'll make the necessary changes in the menu but as punishment you may bring two bottles of Margaux.'

At the Richmond turn-off Ed said, 'Could a mystery-novel project possibly be the reason for your visit to Virginia?'

'Is hatching conspiracy theories a regular feature of Washington DC limo-drivers?'

'Well, it's just that I remembered that Edgar Allan Poe was a student at the University of Virginia, sir.'

His remark about Poe brought to mind Selçuk Altun's novel, *Many and Many a Year Ago*. Despite Eugenio's recommendation, I'd never read the book, which took its title from the first line of Poe's sentimental poem. Had it been Askaris, he would have said, 'A prejudice passed through a sieve, Excellency, is the sign of nobility.'

*

I always liked New York twilights. Twilight is the hour when the city surrenders to time, and it's unimaginable that there's not a single poem to celebrate it. I was on the fourth floor of the Four Seasons Hotel, bird-watching in Central Park, as I tried to think of a movie set in New York that did not include the Park. I somewhat enjoyed the quiet of the hotel. After two martinis at the bar I went out to

Lexington Avenue, the city's kaleidoscopic boulevard, but there was something sad about it. Still I kept walking until I realized that I was reciting Cavafy's 'Waiting for the Barbarians' from the end to the beginning. I turned right on Park Avenue to find the wine shop recommended by the hotel. The salesperson, who looked like a nun, attached a holy significance to what she was selling. I endured her exaggerated sales pitch and chose two bottles of a certain label because they cost $150 each.

The worn-out taxi driver was from Bangladesh. I startled him with my 'Selamün aleyküm' and gave him the Morton Street address. In August the New York streets appear to be lying pleasantly fallow. When you go south the town looks like a chameleon that gets cuter as it gets smaller. Randolph IV's penthouse had a plain appearance in harmony with the bohemian atmosphere of the street below. The newest book in his library could have been an Ernest Hemingway novel. I thought the ungraceful reproductions on the walls and the geometrically patterned prayer rugs on the floor might have a secret wish to exchange places.

Randolph IV had white hair, rosy cheeks, and a good deal of surplus weight. He seemed to be challenging the world with a perpetual smile on his face. I managed not to laugh when he asked me to call him Randy. He whistled as he opened one of the Margaux and put a new-age CD on the stereo. We sat next to each other on the sofa while he squeezed his biography into one paragraph for me.

I was first comforted and then worried by his not mentioning how I so resembled my father. His family was old Chicago. His grandfather had lost everything in the 1929 crash. His father was an out-of-work cellist who drowned in Lake Michigan when Randy was four. The next year his mother married a Puerto Rican dentist and moved to San Juan. Randy was brought up in Richmond by his grandmother. He diverted his gaze to the floor and told me that he and my father had shared a flat for three years at the university. He stayed married to a woman of Armenian extraction until he learned how to cook – five months. Randy appeared to be happy with a life shaped by literature and yoga.

When my turn came, I planned to earn his confidence by frankly summarizing my own life, except for the Nomo detail. I was in the US for a business meeting, I said, and wanted to learn what I could about my father and try to meet any relatives who were still around.

I was rising to my finale when the call to dinner came and my appetite fled. But the menu of arugula salad with walnuts, cold tomato soup with basil, risotto with saffron, and profiterole with ice cream was nearly faultless. As Randy encouraged me to talk and repeatedly refilled my wineglass, I realized that he was preparing to deliver a confidential monologue. When he brought in my after-dinner green tea, his face was noncommittal.

'I was never able to learn where your father came from,' was seductive enough as an opening sentence. 'But when your grandfather, First Sergeant Patrick, came home from the Korean War and retired on disability pay, the family moved to Santa Teresa in California. Your grandmother – I've forgotten her name – was an immigrant housewife. Paul's sister Emma was six years younger and wanted to be either a nurse or a nun. I once spent Thanksgiving holiday with the Hacketts. To me it was like the house was wrapped in an atmosphere of eternal mourning; the grandfather seemed to be making the rest of the family pay for an injustice done to him.

'Paul Hackett always played it close to the vest – I don't know any other way to describe him. He had the attitude of someone who'd been forced to grow up suddenly without living the joys of childhood and youth, and probably that's why his classmates treated him as if he were older than them. He was intelligent and reticent. I was sure that his goal was to seize the past as he was seizing the day. Although he had a special talent for science, he chose to study history. When he wasn't working mathematical puzzles he was breaking the codes of equations, and he never took his nose out of the historical atlases he found in the library. He compared the maps of Greece and Italy to abstract sculptures and that of Turkey to a mass of clouds about to rise. We never had a conflict but we never became soul-mates either. He would disappear sometimes for a day or two without telling anybody where he was going. He tutored foreign students and flirted with Asian girls. I wasn't surprised to hear that he'd married a Turk. The year we graduated I learned by chance that he'd received a grant to continue studying at a governmental institution.

'The most media-prone intelligence agency – and also a government scapegoat – is the CIA. Years later I heard also about the DIA, INR, NIO, NRO and other exotic small agencies. The elite agents in those places probably do nothing but read and write reports. Your father could not reveal which of these he belonged to. After graduation he worked for five years out of an office connected to the State Department.

Then, at least ostensibly, he retired and became the division's Istanbul representative. In reality he was probably being sent to the front lines after completing his education at the base. In any case he was happy because he was going to live in the ancient center of Byzantium and would get to travel in the Middle East. After that our correspondence was reduced to Christmas cards.

'Two summers later we met in New York. He was quite changed. His anxiety was less pronounced, and he had self-confidence. He looked tired but happy. My curiosity was piqued by his expensive clothes and gold watch. I imagined that he wanted to create an image like, 'I might get a cable at any minute summoning me to an important meeting in Washington.' When we parted, although I was prepared for something weighty like, 'Life is more complicated than it looked from the university campus,' he didn't go beyond expressing regret that he couldn't invite me to Istanbul, even for a few days.

'We never saw each other again, but we wrote once or twice. Not to go into detail, it was obvious from his announcement of it that his marriage wouldn't last long. In his last postcard he reported the happy news of your birth and added that your mother had given you a Turkish name, but that he would call you Adrian. His favorite personality was always the Roman Emperor Hadrian.

'I never heard from Paul Hackett again. I wasn't surprised, actually, by the break in our relations. Seven years went by. I was in Charlottesville for a class reunion on the fifteenth anniversary of our graduation. A South Korean classmate of ours named Yun swore that he'd run across Paul in Toronto two months earlier. He had a beard, said

Yun, and he was in the middle of the street shouting at the young and beautiful woman with him. These circumstances made him hesitant to walk up and greet Paul. Yun could be considered one of his closest friends, and was not likely to be wrong.

'Seven more years went by. This time I read in the alumni magazine that Paul had died in a traffic accident. A very brief bio said that on leaving the media sector he'd taken a PhD in Middle Eastern history from McGill and was teaching at a university out on the Canadian steppe. In the 'survived by' part there was only the name of an Anglo-American woman.

'As I read the news it occurred to me that he'd lived his forty-four years as fully as possible, in his own way. Your father was a man worth tracking down. I believe you should fly to Santa Teresa the first chance you get. Your aunt would be fifty-eight by now if she's still living. Even if she's moved away it shouldn't be hard to find out where she went – when I was there it was just a quiet town of 40,000. Emma and Paul were quite attached to each other ...'

I decided not to show Randy the two photocopies I'd brought along when I heard about the 'secret agencies' in my father's past. Maybe I could ask my Aunt (?) Emma about the cryptic handwriting. We said good-bye and I told him I would go to Santa Teresa the next day. I added that I'd be happy to host him if he ever came to Istanbul – but felt a pang of regret as soon as I said it.

My mood improved as I walked toward Seventh Avenue. As I passed a lonely Greek restaurant I called Askaris in Istanbul on my cell phone. He was relieved to hear that I would be back in a week at the latest. I made him write down in detail the features of the two South American girls I wanted him to send to my hotel in an hour and a half.

*

I didn't like Los Angeles, either, when I first saw it. It looked like the city planners forgot to put in a center, nor do I think a first-class poet ever came out of L.A. To avoid shallow tourists and pretentious urbanites, I rarely left the Four Seasons at Beverly Hills. Ensconced in the lobby, I observed the flow of rich patrons, then parked myself at the bar and refused to budge until I'd read John Ashbery's last book, *A Worldly Country*, from cover to cover. The waitress who brought a dry martini to me four times told me she was studying literature at the local community college in the evenings. She confided that this was the first time she'd ever seen a book by this master of American poetry in a customer's hands. I was touched. When I finished the slim volume I slipped a hundred-dollar bill into it and left it for her as a tip to my cup-bearer.

Next morning at Union Station I asked for a first-class train ticket to Santa Teresa. A *zaftig* woman was handing out tickets like wages to slave laborers. She was appalled. Not only did she question me about why I wanted a first-class ticket for a two-hour train trip, but she fixed her baleful bug-eyed glare on me until she received an answer.

'Did your boss order you especially to ask this question?' I said. She burst into laughter, her giant breasts lifting and lowering like a barbell.

There were four of us in the carriage. The mother who kept telling her small son to stop picking his nose took me back to my childhood. According to my grandmother, whenever I was caught in the act I would say, 'I'm not picking my nose, I'm taking out mucus.'

The Pacific Ocean was on our left and the Sierra Madre mountains on our right. Yet after a while the trip grew dull. We stopped at stations with beautiful names like Olvidado and Perdido and I thought about my excommunicated middle name, which I'd learned only two days ago, along with my difficult-to-pronounce five-letter name, and smiled. But what made me laugh out loud was the honorific bestowed on me by the least-known agency on earth. My grandmother used to take my strange sense of humor to heart, saying, 'When he grows up this boy will be a clown, but he won't get that right either.'

The Santa Teresa train station looked like a relic from the town's pioneer days. The train passengers, perhaps out of respect for the ancient building, exited without haste. Juanito, the elderly driver of my taxi, seized the first opportunity to mention that he was seventy-two years of age. It would clearly have broken his heart not to be told, 'You don't look your age.' When I said my destination was the Edgewater Hotel he replied, 'You got two and a half hours before check-in. Want to take an orientation tour?' I'm sure he made the same proposition to every customer who arrived on the 11:33 train and probably never received 'No' for an answer.

We began our tour at Ludlow Beach. The street names of this town of 85,000 were distributed equally to the Spanish and English languages. I was familiar with the old Spanish architecture of the public buildings from cowboy movies.

Rich retirees lived in Victorian English villas. Palm trees and masses of bougainvillea gave the place a canvas-like charm. Nobody was in a hurry; they seemed to belong to a more lenient time zone than L.A. Maybe because of a wish not to miss the concert offered by the ocean's assortment of tones and colorful waves, an ad-libbed silence ruled in Santa Teresa. By and by I began to feel alienated from the shopping mall that looked like an air-raid shelter and the empty streets piercing Cabana Boulevard, which ran along the coast, like arrows. This deserted town was a postcard beauty that could easily serve as a mock-up stage set. In those squat finance centers and desolate villas quite a few crime-novel plots could be hatched, whose anti-characters could water the thirsty soil of the dead city in a short chapter.

Edgewater was more like a feudal castle than a two-hundred-room luxury hotel. As well as giant palm trees in the garden there were short ones in the restaurant. The patrons lurking in the commodious lobby seemed to conspire against the pianist by talking all at the same time. I took my key and went up to my second-floor room with ocean view. I opened the window and waited. Despite a polite wind escorting the playful sound of waves, there was something missing in the mise-en-scene. For a good while I enjoyed sensing but not knowing what it was.

According to the telephone directory and the Internet there were seven Hackett domiciles. I would have been quite surprised if among them had been the names of my father or grandfather. Moreover, the possibility of our kinship with these Hacketts was remote since, according to Randy, my grandfather did not come from Santa Teresa. On top of everything else, it would hardly be wise to carry out a thorough survey of the town if there was a Nomo agent at my back. No alternatives came to mind other than gazing at the ocean out of the open window. I called room service for a vegetarian sandwich and a glass of grapefruit juice. I think, after going through the minibar and drinking up the little bottles of cognac and vodka in a sip or two, that I went to sleep expecting a prophetic dream. At 3:22 I woke up without a plan. I went down to the lobby, taking with me the latest book – *Averno* – by poet Louise Glück. It was quieter now, with a more pretentious musician at the piano. He was in his mid-sixties and had the look of an alcoholic, moving his hands in circles, hitting the keys slowly and singing songs of sorrow.

The obese uniformed man behind the desk attracted my attention. He was enthusiastically assisting the picky patrons, using body language like an energetic policeman giving directions, making marks on their tourist maps and writing addresses on little slips of paper. As soon as he got rid of the last old couple I popped up at his desk. The name tag on his jacket pocket said 'Jesus'; I tried not to smile. Before the saintly man could say 'How can I help you?' I laid a crisp new twenty-dollar bill in front of him. He abstained from seeing it.

'In your opinion, Jesus, what would be the best way to track down a relative of mine who lived here thirty years ago?' I took care to pronounce the first letter of his name like an 'H'.

Jesus continued not noticing the twenty-dollar bill as his left hand moved toward the phone. He spoke to someone in a scolding tone of voice and then handed me a name and phone number on a slip of paper.

'Kinsey Milhone is our pianist Daniel Wade's ex-wife. Once upon a time she was said to be the best-known private eye in Santa Teresa. Nowadays she works as a security consultant for the finance companies. If she can't help you, she'll point you to someone who can.'

I scrutinized the phone number digit by digit like I was looking for an alibi. When I lifted my head to thank Jesus, he was giving the address of the golf course to the rotund man behind me and there was no sign of the twenty-dollar bill. I went back to my room to call Kinsey Milhone's office. Unlike in detective novels and movies, my luck was no good – I dialed the number seven times and got no answer. I left a polite message and focused my attention on the latest TV adventure of the easy-going Simpsons. I was on the cusp of boredom when Madame Milhone called. She had a self-confident and sultry voice; I noticed that I was buttoning up my shirt. I summarized my request with the sentence, 'I'm looking for my Aunt Emma Hackett,' and a big laugh crackled back over the phone.

'I'm sorry, young man,' she replied, and I felt a bit more comfortable. 'But solving this case will make my reputation as the speediest detective in the history of detective novels and put me in the Guinness Book of World Records. Emma Hackett was my classmate from grade school through high school. We lost touch when she moved to San Francisco thirty years ago, but I know she's running a nursing school there. I'll get her phone number and address from a mutual friend. Meanwhile I should express my sorrow over Paul's death. He was a genius for some of us, and for others he was nuts.

'Look, let's meet at 7:30 in the Edgewater lobby. If you're really Emma's nephew, I'll tell you her whereabouts. In return, I'll expect a perfect meal at the hotel restaurant.'

Before saying hello to Kinsey Milhone, I observed her from a distance. As if her worn-out blue jeans and faded rose-colored T-shirt weren't enough, she made no attempt to hide the gray in her hair. She had a pert turned-up nose and cheerful eyes. She walked like a retired model despite her aging looks. She looked a little over fifty but didn't seem to care about that. This plain but attractive woman had fallen into the luxurious lobby like a ball of light. I moved toward the female detective, whistling as she waited, trying to visualize her in her younger days.

As soon as she saw me she raised her right hand and said, 'No need to show your passport – you're a Hackett.' We proceeded to the restaurant, which was more like a palace. Kinsey persuaded the waiter to ask the chef for a salad not on the menu, and ordered Chilean sea bass to go with it. She left the wine selection to me. She observed me like a psychologist with a sense of humor, working up, I supposed, the outline of her report.

'Your grandfather was a neurotic war hero. He took special pleasure in his retirement, but he treated his family like prisoners of war.' Perhaps this sentence was formulated beforehand. 'Your grandmother Mara was Serbian I think, an immigrant and a quiet but sagacious woman. We were the diffident witnesses of her endless struggle to protect her children from the caprices of her fascist husband.

'Your father was regularly the most successful student at

school, but a little odd. He never came to parties and he liked to flirt with immigrant working girls older than himself. During summer vacations he would go and visit Mayan and Aztec ruins or else bury himself in the public library. He acted like he was superior to his own age group. He constantly tried to create the impression in his circle that he was an enigmatic character. I would have bet money that Paul would become a bloodless academic.

'Emma, on the other hand, was a good-hearted and lively friend, mature and intelligent. Since she never complained, we called her 'Saint.' She did well in high school – her brother helped her – and got a scholarship to San Francisco State. In her third year there her mother went nuts and ran off to Florida with a Korean mechanic twelve years younger than herself. Her father had a partial stroke and she quit school to look after that bad-tempered man. He died two years later and they sold the house to pay off a bank loan. There was some money left, and with that your aunt finished school, took up another academic career, and married a widowed academic when she was pushing forty. At that time I'd just divorced my second husband. I told you on the phone that your aunt heads a department in a San Francisco nursing school. Before we leave, I'll give you some phone numbers and addresses that I got from a friend still in touch with her.

'Emma kept up with her old friends in Santa Teresa for a while. Whenever I saw her I thought she was trying hard to act like a businesswoman to avoid revealing her inner world. But I never understood why she wanted to hide her brother's death. Off and on I go to San Francisco on business, but usually I'm just grateful to get back here in one piece, let alone have time to visit old friends.

'Young man, instead of a long-winded conclusion let me just tell you one thing: You're lucky to have an aunt like her. You won't be sorry you met her.'

Kinsey professed to love the Napa Valley wine we drank, so I had two bottles gift-wrapped for her and we walked to her car, a twenty-year-old Volkswagen. I felt certain that her previous car was a thirty-year-old version of the same. She pinched my cheek and gave me her card with Emma Hackett Green's address scribbled on the back of it. I don't know why I didn't watch her car rattle out of the parking lot. I felt a strange emptiness after she left. But when I turned to the inviting ocean breeze I felt relieved, as if I'd solved a thorny equation: Santa Teresa was a giant stage set erected for Kinsey Milhone's scenes.

Back in the lobby a Maxi girl in a miniskirt approached me with a telegraphic sentence: 'The restroom on this floor is out of order; may I use the one in your room?'

'If you have a friend with the same problem I can help her out too,' I said.

Later, after sending the pricey prostitutes away, I pressed my nose against the ocean in my windowpane and shut my eyes to intensify the pleasures of midnight. It struck me what was missing in this 3-D postcard. The aroma of citrus fruit?

*

San Francisco! At first sight I declared it my favorite town in the USA. (I gradually dropped the habit of collecting a harem of cities. Now there's one city on earth that makes my heart leap, and it's not Istanbul.)

The minute I walked into my ninth-floor suite at the Four Seasons I cheered up. I wondered when I would have had enough of this marathon hopping from one luxury hotel to the next. The greenery that came closer as I moved closer to the window was called the Yerba Buena Gardens. When I was a student I would go to the park and occupy the bench nearest the entrance as if I were standing guard. I loved to watch the toddlers beam with happiness as their small hesitant steps led them to the grass. Despite my anxiety – 'Does this indicate an incapacity to become a father?' – I never tired of this amusement. If one of the kids began crying I was hurt to the quick.

I asked room service for a salad, sandwich and grapefruit juice. My order was brought in with Fellini-like flamboyance. They must have been rewarding me for choosing the worst menu in the hotel's history.

'3333 B Geary Boulevard, Florence Nightingale School of Nursing.' There was a quizzical note in my voice as I read the address; the taxi driver comforted me. 'Could be worse,' he said. 'I've seen 8300 Geary.'

In order not to start a useless conversation I didn't ask why a city of 800,000 should have such a long non-boulevard. The hospital looked like a dead whale. The nursing school was an annex and belonged to a nonprofit foundation. In front of the main hospital gate stood a bust of the founding elderly lady; in front of the nursing school that looked like a fitness center stood one of Florence Nightingale. I wanted to believe that sculptures embody the personal marrow of the people they honor. I couldn't walk by the symbolic nurse without my shoulders straightening and my feet falling unconsciously into step.

There were two bulletin boards in the hallway. On the first was the nursing profession's oath; on the second a notice politely requested donations and drew attention to the resulting tax deductions. The information desk was manned by a black guard who was born to play Othello. I knew I would not be scolded if I approached him with the deference ordinarily reserved for a judge. Since it was still summer vacation, my aunt was not at school. It happened that the security guard's father had served in Turkey in the 1960s at a radar station that was then an American base. He gave me Emma Hackett Green's address and phone number without hesitation when I disclosed her Turkish connection. I had a fifty-dollar bill in my right hand just in case. We were both astonished to see that I put it down on the left end of the counter. He pushed the bill away with the back of his hand and I threw myself out of the place apologizing profusely.

My taxi driver was listening to classical music and I paid no attention to his boasting. When I told him 'City Lights Bookstore', he informed me that it belonged to Lawrence Ferlinghetti, the last poet of the Beat Generation, who had just entered his eighty-ninth year. He enunciated his words one by one slowly, as if he had a half-retarded passenger in the car. We started off and I asked him to turn down the radio. 'If you like, I can recite one of the master's poems for you,' I said, and without waiting for an answer began declaiming *'Two Scavengers In the Garbage Truck, Two Beautiful People in a Mercedes.'*

The fifty-five-year-old bookstore had a certain charm. The only prose work among the dozen books I carried to the cash register was a biography of Hadrian. I couldn't bring myself to correct the talkative check-out girl who thought I was a literary scholar.

Even if the bar next door to the bookstore hadn't been Jack Kerouac's favorite watering hole, its beautiful name – Vesuvio – would have lured me in. It looked as if the all-embracing gloom of this claustrophobic den had gone unchanged for the last fifty years. When the three senior bohemians at the bar looked at me questioningly, I felt obliged to seek their approval by nodding hello. I regarded with envy the junior poets at the crowded tables behind us, with their beards and granny glasses and grungy girlfriends. After my second martini I called my aunt. Her voice was gentle but tired. We arranged that I would bring her the package from Kinsey Milhone tomorrow at two. I would try my surprise announcement face-to-face.

After four drinks I managed to stand up without swaying. I walked down Columbus Boulevard with numbers and words crashing into each other and washing over my mind. I hoped that walking would sober me up. Coming across a 24-hour striptease club, I greeted it with a stanza from Karacaoğlan:

At dawn I stopped at the beloved's village
Welcome, my love, she said, come in
Putting her rosebud nipple to my mouth
You're tired, my love, she said, take this in.

Is every suburb in the world half an hour away from its town?

I feared I would fall asleep the moment I set foot in Alamo, that quiet district of the rich. As I stopped people on the street to ask the whereabouts of Emma's address, I wondered about the residents of the charming villas. The natural flora framing the deserted streets looked like it would quit the scene when the photo shoot was finished. I queried a paper boy who stammered, 'The street across from the shopping mall that looks like a sleeping dinosaur.' I mildly enjoyed Stone Valley Way for its lack of postcard glossiness. Its houses were not engaged in a gaudiness contest. The mailbox hanging from the second-last house said, 'Emma H. – Albert Green.' The modest house had a miniature garden and an old Nissan parked in front of the garage.

I whispered an Arabic prayer and rang the doorbell. The door opened instantly and I was facing my aunt for the first time. Emma Hackett Green looked about sixty-five and the shirt hanging out of her jeans failed to conceal a few excess pounds. She was outgoing and instantly charming in a thoroughly natural way. It didn't surprise me to see her take a startled step back. She covered her mouth and chin with her left hand. (I'm left-handed too.) I stood there hoping she would retrieve her brother's face from memory and recognize me. I couldn't bear her trembling, however, and said, 'Instead of a package I brought greetings from Kinsey Milhone. And a surprise from me. To use the name I never used, I'm Adrian Hackett.'

I imagined that she would shriek and rush to throw her arms around me, but in fact she turned her back and burst out sobbing. Before long she pulled herself together

– after all, her life had seen plenty of ups and downs before this. Wiping her face with a tissue, she moaned, 'I knew it, I knew it,' and then did throw her arms around my neck. Her living room was airy, but I felt that the furniture there was not begotten with the joy of life. Prints of local birds and butterflies hanging on the wall did not soften the room's rectitude. On the end table next to the leather armchair in which I sat was a framed picture of my aunt, her husband who appeared about fifteen years older, and an underfed little girl. Al, a retired academic, looked like a scarecrow. I was glad that he'd gone to Sacramento. The shy girl looking distrustfully at the camera was their adopted Tibetan daughter. The picture was taken nine years earlier when she had come to live with them, with Virginia as her new name. My honorary niece was now a high school student and due home from summer camp in Costa Rica.

My green tea came in a giant cup. Clearly my aunt was settling in for a long conversation. I went first. It was the third time in five days I had to supply my autobiography and I was getting tired of it. The more I talked, the more I bored myself. As though under an obligation to seek forgiveness, I listed all the prohibitions my mother had imposed on my father's memory. My voice was louder than I expected as I declared, 'I've never even seen his photograph, much less a line of his handwriting.'

When my aunt's turn came, she cast her eyes to the floor, a gesture that foreshadowed a concise and political talk.

'Probably Kinsey already told you that our family life was short on love.' Her voice cracked as she said this. 'My mother met my father in Cincinnati where she was working at a bar. For the need of American citizenship she tricked my father into marriage. You know what I mean. Poor woman, she made a terrible choice of victim. My father was talented but neurotic, hard-working but unlucky. He was wounded in the Korean War essentially because of inaccurate information, you might say. He could never accept that he was forced to retire with what they called a physical disability, while his commander was given a medal. He turned into an angry man and a near-alcoholic. Torturing us was his main pastime and of course my mother was his number-one victim. I think all of St Teresa was surprised that she put up with it for so long before she finally ran away.

'Paul strove hard to keep our family intact and helped me survive that period with the least possible harm. He was not only a model student but at the same time a man of good sense.

'I'm sure he tried to compensate for his father's notoriety with his own academic success. Paul tried to open up to life by reading history at the public library and, in his words, dueling with mathematics. Every new act of helplessness by my father was a multiplier of Paul's resistance. I figured he would end up a good liberal academic because he loved listening to jazz.

'He was as happy as a child when he got the job in Istanbul. I wasn't surprised that he married an Istanbul girl, only that she wasn't an Istanbul Greek. They only had a civil ceremony because of the ruckus in your mother's family, but they came to America on their honeymoon. My sister-in-law and I weren't crazy about each other. I didn't find either her face or her disposition pleasant. Paul said she was a noble and mysterious Easterner and it was only natural that I should fail to grasp her superiority.

'The next thing to be surprised by was not the divorce but the reason for it. If Paul had to find a lover, and so managed finally to find his soul-mate, it was because of his wife's capricious ways. When the news hit the papers he lost his job. Muriel was Canadian; they moved to Montreal. After taking a long time to get a PhD there, he started teaching at universities I was hearing the names of for the first time.

'Our correspondence fell off after my brother moved to Canada. I met Muriel twice. She was a beautiful and naive person. She treated Paul with a blown-up respect, like he was the greatest scholar in the world. I heard about their marriage two years after the event. They didn't have money problems. Your father resigned his jobs often and went through long periods of not even looking for another one. Yet he was always irritable. He seemed to be waiting for bad news and nobody dared to ask him why. Muriel called me for the first and last time to give me the news of her husband's death. They were living in Vancouver. As Paul was leaving a bar suddenly a jeep came out of nowhere and hit him and then vanished. My brother had a drink now and then, but he couldn't really hold his alcohol. On the night of the accident he was apparently drinking with a middle-aged man that nobody else knew. They left the bar separately.

'You were very precious to your father, Adrian. Your mother used a bag of tricks to prevent you from getting to know each other. When you grew big enough to go out and play in the street, he used to come and watch you from a distance. In the second year of this your mother sent her men to give him a bad beating. He always had your baby pictures in his wallet and in his house …'

At this point in her monologue she leaped up and fetched an album with photos of my father. Trying not to see his sad face, I turned the pages quickly. Suddenly a five-by-seven inch picture fell out. The man trying to smile at the camera eye was my father, and the startled baby holding his hand was me. On the back of this photograph, taken on my first birthday, was written:

Dear Em,
Adrian is one year old. He started walking a month ago. He will come and visit you one day.
With all my heart,
P.

My aunt was enjoying the situation's implications, while I was astonished. If it was indeed my father who wrote those lines, I'd found the answer I was looking for. The handwriting was identical with that of the photocopies. I knew I should not be too hasty to invent conspiracy theories. This probably wasn't sufficient evidence to associate my father with Nomo, I told myself.

To make my aunt happy, I took the picture. We said goodbye to each other and promised to get together again but neither of us believed it. A taxi waited for me in front of the house. As I got in, it occurred to me that the men who attacked my father in Galata could also be working as secret agents put on my own trail by Nomo. I felt I should properly introduce myself to this organization that might one day be my savior, and the next my executioner.

I read Hadrian's biography on the San Francisco-New York and New York-Istanbul planes. If you omitted the religious factor, he and Fatih might have been (up to and including the whispers about their sexual preferences) soul-mates who ruled the greatest empires of the world like chess masters.

ETA

With the approval of the Doge of Venice, Enrico Dandolo (1107?-1205), the army of crusaders who had lingered in Constantinople for ten months instead of continuing to Egypt commenced to plunder the town. Historians, noting their extreme violence, have described how the pious looters who set out on their crusade for the love of God ended up plundering the houses of the poor and killing young and old without exception, even raping the nuns. At the end of the third day the 900-year-old capital of the world lay in ruins, and the magnificent complex called the Great Palace was totally destroyed.

The puppet Latin Empire founded by the crusaders would limp along for fifty-seven years. Michael VIII Palaeologus, the usurper of the Byzantine throne in exile, expelled them from Constantinople in 1261. He then settled into the Blachernae Palace that butted up against the land walls, away from the city center. Because it had been built in the twelfth century and was now the home of an emperor, he had it remodeled. The Ottomans called it the Tekfur Palace, a derogatory appellation since 'tekfur' meant feudal lord and that was no way to address the emperor of Byzantium.

I remembered these details as I walked along the street of the Chora Monastery – now the Kariye Mosque – toward the palace ruins. I was satisfied with the quietness of the street. I refrained from asking the precise whereabouts of this 800-year-old legacy of our (?) family. Later in the morning I heard first a rooster, then a jackhammer, but there was neither chicken coop nor construction site to be seen.

The improvised duet continued until the palace walls rose up before me. I went up a short rise near Hoca Çakır Avenue, afraid I might miss an important clue to the puzzle if I skipped any part of the walls. The crude restoration work made them look like patched clothes. It didn't upset me to see that, as a reaction to this barbaric enterprise, the symmetrical indentations had been turned into toilets and garbage pits. Two recesses that looked like caves had been transformed into makeshift warehouses by a carpenter and a greengrocer. I wondered who on earth the moustachioed men working there paid rent to. In front of the walls was a barricade of garbage containers. As I walked by, some street cats jumped in and out of them in panic. I climbed a rickety staircase to the top of the wall. On the plot of land between that point and the E-5 motorway was only one building: the Tekfur Palace. The rest of the space was dedicated to a children's playground, a car park, and sports fields.

From a height of sixty feet I surveyed the movement on the motorway. The hum of a flood of motor vehicles swelled like a chorus, then receded as if it had hit a breakwater. I was satisfied with the music, and resumed my stroll toward the Golden Horn to see the palace up close. The highway curved in parallel to the curve of the walls. Between them was a park containing a kiosk that looked like a dead bull. A few puny olive trees grew in front of it and I was reminded that an olive tree could live a thousand years. Maybe these saintly-looking trees had breathed the same air as my ancestors. Where the park ended I saw the gate to the palace. It had bars like a prison and a sign on it that said: 'Restoration in Progress. No Trespassing.' In truth there was no restoration in progress and I was certain that nobody knew when or if such work would ever start. From outside the bars the palace at first glimpse looked like a mammoth skeleton. Looking at the façade more carefully, I noted a kind of ornamental symmetry. I shut my eyes to imagine how glorious it had been in its heyday, but the image lasted no longer than a sonnet. When I opened my eyes, I was appalled by the sight of a palace that looked like a nun who'd been stripped of her garments, raped, then beheaded.

I wondered about the last hours of Constantine XI at the palace that now served as the base for an army of pigeons. I continued my descent toward the Golden Horn as the noon prayer call began to rise in unison from the city's 3,000 mosques. Bushes grew on these jaded walls, and small trees grew in the gaps. Neither history nor nature could complain of this symbiosis. A small but neat Ottoman cemetery nestled on Eğrikapı Street where the walls ended. I made a note to myself to come back and read the epitaphs later. Cars and trucks were passing beneath an arch that divided the cemetery into two; I made this my landmark. At the time he settled into this palace on the edge of the city it was said of Michael VIII – who stole the throne from the seven-year-old emperor he was supposed to protect by putting out his eyes – that he would flee 'at the first chance'. But he turned out to be a leader who fought for his country; and when he died, his burial without a funeral ceremony was an oriental irony.

I retraced my steps, observing the odd neighbors of the walls frame by frame. All those streets bearing spiritual names were like huge maquettes drawn without rulers. I saw women leaning from the windows of their miniature houses in startling postures and locked in a studious chorus of gossip. The lady of a house painted in a hue of green I'd never seen before was scolding her son – 'My worthless fucking offspring' – while her husband sat like a chieftain at the window counting his beads. Young men about to begin their military service strolled up and down the streets holding cell phones like bombs. The colors of the clothes worn by the carefree, jobless neighborhood crowd and of the aging cars they drove faded at the same rate and met in the same hue. A robed *imam* approached me with a folk song on his tongue. I felt a kind of test in his greeting; he was surprised by my reciprocal sincerity. As he pranced off I wondered if he knew that most of the words in his memory were borrowed from the Old Testament.

A coffee-shop entrepreneur had set up a few small tables and chairs in the shade of the walls, and sidewalk pedestrians had to detour around them. I sank into one of his chairs next to a group who spoke in whispers, perhaps in Kurdish. The young waiter seemed surprised by my question: 'How old are these walls?'

'How should I know?' he said, almost scolding me. Then he reported me to his boss and had him laughing too.

Down from the arched gate was a row of one-storey houses that were perhaps attached to the walls. It looked like they would fall down if they were separated from one another. I crossed to the other side of the street and looked at the fourth one from the left. Its windows were paved over. Anyone would think it was a small innocent warehouse. Not very much later I would show up at its door full of curiosity about the trials I would meet inside.

*

At midnight the following day I rang its doorbell, three long and two short. (I'd rehearsed in advance to prevent possible rhythmic embarrassment.) I knew that I would find Askaris and his two assistants bowing and scraping the instant the door opened. If I said 'Good evening', they would cast a respectful glance or two at me. I was becoming accustomed to the dichotomies of the period. Two of the rooms were full of large cardboard boxes: a successful camouflage. In the room on the left Kalligas moved one of these boxes, stepped on a spot just beneath it, and stepped back. There was a faint mechanical whine, then a black rectangular opening appeared. We descended as a team and as we did the room darkened and the basement we stepped into lit up. I must admit that I was stunned when, after twelve steps, we entered a salon. The ceiling was painted with colorful icons and along the walls in glass cases were marble busts of the Byzantine emperors. Had I failed to scrutinize the ten-inch-high busts one by one, I would have insulted the Nomo representatives. Constantine the Great, Theodosius II, Justinian I … it was embarrassing to see myself commemorated there along with the others. But I was relieved, as I passed Fokas, to realize that I was not the ugliest link in the chain. My many times great-grandfather's expression carried the resignation of an old Casanova constantly rebuked by his wife. The bust of my own majesty, Constantine XV, had perhaps only been brought yesterday. In it I tentatively confirmed the condescending features of a young man listening to someone else.

In the middle of the salon was a huge white marble table, and on it a large ivory model of Constantinople. I almost expected to find a button on this splendid toy city that I could push to start up the life within. I wanted to caress the figures belonging to the palace, the hippodrome, the aqueducts. I inspected the model for a long time, monument by monument, magnifying each at least 200 times in my imagination. I could not have cared less whether the Nomo representatives might think I was putting on a show. When I looked up I felt mentally exhausted, and wiped my forehead weakly. I heard someone say, 'Excellency, would you like a glass of water?' I turned and with an effort stammered out, in every language I knew, 'Mankind is a worse plague than natural disasters.'

It was odd of me not to have noticed earlier the bitterness in the Byzantine emblem on the black lacquer table between my bust and the model. The purple double-headed eagle glowering at East and West simultaneously was a true mirror of the Empire's fatal dichotomy. They invited me to be seated in the most ostentatious leather armchair in the room. The team, with Askaris in the middle, sat opposite me on the edge of their chairs, after of course asking my permission. They clasped their hands and bowed their heads. Askaris first expressed Nomo's gratitude to me and then began to explain the nature of the examination.

He took a two- by six-inch silver box from a purple leather bag and pointed at a not-quite-antique mechanism just under the lid. It was stamped with a royal seal. This he slowly raised. When he held the box upright you could see, on the left side of an aluminum panel within, six small empty squares lined up equidistant from one another. And at the very bottom was a one- by two-inch rectangular glass surface that was gray in color. On the right side of the uppermost square was written, 'Antioch Museum'. What I had to do was go to that museum and find a half-inch by half-inch piece of magnetized purple metal hidden in one of the objects on display, then place it in the first square. When this was done, the name of a historic site would appear on the right side of the second square. I was then expected to look for a second piece of metal at that venue. The last item in Constantine XI's will was concealed in the artefact that I needed to find as the sixth step. I had a year in which to do all this. Either my great-grandfathers had failed to find that final item or else they could not decode its meaning. If I were successful – and Askaris could not enunciate this possibility in a tone indicating confidence – Nomo and I would together formulate a plan to carry out the will's last instructions.

After all this there was another, second, round. If I happened to succeed in this too I could discard Nomo, whose mission was accomplished in any case, in whatever manner I wished. In that event, 'You will control a fortune whose size cannot even be estimated,' said Askaris in a trembling voice.

But if I was unable to get beyond the fourth or fifth square, Nomo would evaluate my 'transcript' and, if possible, award me 'selected' status. I could then join Nomo's three-person Board of Directors as President. It seemed a bit weird for Askaris to tell me that if the Board got stuck two-to-two on an issue, the President's vote counted double.

I wondered to myself, as I listened to the recitation of rules and regulations, about how many rounds of testing I could complete. Askaris didn't ask if I had a question. He gave me all the information I needed, and I felt sure he wasn't holding back anything. My inner voice told me this was not the first time he was going through all this, but there was no way to know for certain. It was the 500-year-old Nomo tradition to say little and ask no questions.

The reality, which required no question or answer to confirm, was that I was underground at a point not far from the old palace. I would definitely be surprised if the door behind the bust of myself did not open into a tunnel and end somewhere in the Tekfur Palace. I thought it the better part of valor to let myself go along with the excitement of playing the leading role – in a historical TV serial. I thought about the people in the neighborhood above me, living like actors in a Fellini movie. Some were probably fast asleep, others watching shallow television. Maybe one or two were making love. Were they in my shoes, they might start contemplating how to reduce all the billions that would potentially be in my hands. In my case, I could have a glass building built in the shape of a book in the city center. I could establish the greatest library in the world for dictionaries and poetry. At night a laser show on the front of the building would project, in rotation, the letters of all the alphabets of the world. On another wall a new poem would be illuminated every night. The building would be my shield from the world's ugliness, and also my grave. The rest of my fortune I would leave to the most beautiful creatures in this world: poor children.

THETA

The town of Antioch (the present-day Antakya) was founded in the fourth century B.C. on the curving banks of the beautifully named Orontes River, known in Turkish as the Asi. It was there that early disciples of Christ adopted the title 'Christian' and founded their first church in a cave. Antioch grew to be the third-most important city of the world, after Rome and Constantinople. No doubt this is why the evil eye fell on it more than a few times. First, in 525 A.D., precisely when it had become the apple of the Byzantine eye, it suffered a great fire. Then in 526 A.D. an earthquake hit. The earthquake struck on May 29 – the same day of the month on which Constantinople would later fall – and brought total ruin to the city. The historian Procopius claimed that it killed 300,000 people. But Antioch rose out of its own ashes, mainly because Justinian I wanted it rebuilt. It was the massacres by the soldiers of the First Crusade in the eleventh century, followed by a twelfth-century earthquake that killed 80,000 people, which ultimately did the city in. After that it would be little more than a nostalgic point on the map.

These headline topics were followed by a virtual fashion show of antique engravings of Antioch. In every frame I sensed the magic of a lost fairy-tale city. I murmured to myself Cavafy's respectful lines on Antioch. I needed such poetic therapy as I walked along the Orontes in the center of the city, for the magnificent river had become a puny creek, prostrate in its concrete bed, a hopeless trickle of brown water.

Was it the final mission of the Orontes to divide the town into two? The rich had moved to the north. (For some reason, the north is mostly the superior.) It might have been the lack of architectural detail in the buildings I encountered on my way, or a certain kitschiness in everything around me, but I was irked. I liked the Savon Hotel, a 200-year-old converted soap factory, because it was in the south. Besides, it had a spacious courtyard that gave it the magnanimous air of a lord's manor. South and north seemed to live in different time zones. In the September afternoon the south, emanating aromas of citrus and spice, was charming.

My orientation tour began with Kurtuluş Avenue, which was busily filling the hotel with noise. I soon found myself surrounded by run-down buildings left to fend for themselves. (They had managed to survive a few earthquakes, after all.) But their looks revealed the charm of good craftsmanship and they seemed to enjoy the taste of being left alone. The tiny streets were hardly wide enough to accommodate two people side by side. In the market there was a barber, a mosque, a glassware shop, a bookstore and a bakery shoulder-to-shoulder. In rows of jars on shelves in the grocery shop the only product I recognized was olives. Lined up next to them was a pair of tired-looking slippers. Taped to the window of a jewelry store, a flyer conveyed the good news that spectacles might be mended inside. Although nearly all the shops were empty, the shopkeepers weren't aggressive. They spoke Arabic among themselves but would resort to Turkish for an unfamiliar customer.

Since nothing in this town required haste, they were quite good-humored.

I'd taken a Mediterranean tour ten years earlier with Iskender. We stopped at Antioch on that trip but had to pass up the museum because it was closed. I remembered that we had a samovar picnic at Harbiye, called Daphne in Roman times because of the nymph's encounter with Apollo there. I also remembered the embarrassment of several youths at being chosen for the task of answering our questions about an address. Antioch, boasting two of the oldest and most significant mosques of the Islamic world (and a rare sight: their main gates were just below their minarets), was a visual pleasure that wouldn't escape me this time.

*

The Antioch Museum was limited to a single floor. There were five exhibition salons and a small courtyard. The way it reminded me at first sight of a run-down school was of a piece with its faded glory. The salons and courtyard were full of colossal mosaics. I wondered where new ones from local archaeological excavations could go. I knew I wouldn't find a catalogue in the building – regarded as the most important mosaic museum in the world – which was why I'd brought along a photocopy of an old museum guide borrowed from Selçuk Altun.

In keeping with rules and regulations of Nomo, Pappas and Kalligas stayed in the courtyard for security. Askaris would accompany me as an observer but of course would not participate in the (re)search. According to a faded sign at the museum entrance, Kemal Atatürk, founder of the Turkish Republic, had declared 'The foundation of the Turkish Republic is culture.' (I began my first test with a smile.) Askaris was kind enough to say, 'Excellency, I've visited this museum quite a few times. If you please, I'll be glad to wait for you at the entrance to the first salon.' Obviously he didn't want to annoy me by hovering over me like a proctor. Maybe it was he who had, within the last two days, delightedly stuck that small purple square in some awkward corner.

In the museum were Roman and Byzantine mosaics along with Greek and Roman statues, reliefs and inscriptions. Were I writing a mystery novel, I thought, I would hide the purple square in one of the giant mosaic panels occupying the walls. The arrangement of the art was consistent with what my veteran guidebook informed me. In Salons I, III, and V were fifty-three mosaic panels, all from the Roman period. Those in the second-century group called 'Sweet Life' were more attractive and humorous than the later ones.

In Salon IV, fourteen of the forty-five mosaics dated from the Byzantine period. I had the whole place to myself as I studied them one by one. The security guards were off conversing with themselves in the morning quiet. I stood before each of the fourteen nominees, viewing and reviewing them from different angles and secretly expecting them to emit signals. I retreated to the center of the room and rotated in order to view them all from the same perspective. I was happy with the alertness overtaking my body. I remembered documentaries I'd watched on television about lions setting off on hunting trips as a family. Instead of diving into a whole herd of antelope, they saved their energy for the victim, which was chosen according to criteria known only to the lions. By and by I better understood the priority they gave to the weak and the small. By contrast, I had no criteria to go on other than a few scraps of information posted next to the panels. I narrowed the field to four candidates. 'Ananeosis' ('The Awakening') was an inviting title for the beginning of an examination. I approached the seven and a half feet by fifteen feet piece with suspicion. The surface of this fifth-century mosaic comprised probably 125,000 small squares, which formed an odd portrait of a Byzantine woman. Was one of her eyes filled with fear, the other with hope? I noted the dichotomy as, beginning with her chin, I moved my gaze in zig-zags across her face. It was like counting stars and I stopped lest I fall asleep. But was there a little something extraneous on the tip of Sister Ananeosis's nose? The salon was still empty as I made a furtive grab at that dark patch with my left hand. The touch of metallic cold thrilled me from the inside out. I felt like I was caressing the breast of a naked Byzantine beauty lying on the beach.

The purple square clung to my fingers like a small bird, and I was a-flutter with excitement. We assembled in the courtyard in front of the Double Lion statue. I was expecting applause for my early goal. As they listened attentively to the account of my search strategy, Pappas and Kalligas wagged their heads and Askaris looked at the floor. I took the silver box from the briefcase in Kalligas's hands. I almost muttered a prayer as I placed my catch in the topmost recess. As soon as the two squares met, a mechanical groan rose from the box. The window that suddenly opened next to the second recess said: MISTRA.

IOTA

I tried to maintain the fiction to my family that I was working for an international company by spending the month of September abroad. In the distant metropolises of Europe I visited zoos, museums and antiquarian book and map dealers that I hadn't been to before. I participated in erotica auctions and chess tournaments using a code name (Bizansov). I read the biography of Constantine I and the history of Mistra. I looked for good poets and generous prostitutes and had better luck with the latter than the former.

When a plane ticket to Athens arrived for me with departure on October 6, I would have surprised Askaris if I hadn't found a hint of mystery in the date. It turned out to be the eighty-fifth anniversary of Istanbul's liberation from the occupying forces.

My taxi from Venizelos Airport smelled of lemons. The aroma produced a good feeling in me. I completely relaxed when the sullen driver neither turned on the radio nor asked where I was from. The autumn sun enveloped the taxi and suffused a sweet itch in me. As we neared the city a kind of excitement of seeing the fatherland for the first time swept though me. It was a bit disturbing.

Athens! The city that 4 million out of Greece's 12 million people have made their home. I didn't feel estranged by the traffic jam that we plunged into, nor by the duel between vehicles and pedestrians. Was the common denominator of the latter their exasperation? Greeks seemed to be perpetually quarrelling either with their cell phones or with each other. I felt like I knew these feeble people with their rich body language and vivacious step. The city where aestheticism had begun was now besieged by buildings with no architectural presence. Maybe when the Athenians left their city at a second command, this conglomeration of ugly shacks would be razed.

Askaris referred me to the Hotel Grand Bretagne as the Pera Palace of Athens. I was absolutely certain that the suite reserved for me would have a full view of the Acropolis. The bellboy who took me to my room said, 'Do you have any other questions?' though I hadn't asked any. He appeared too young for a query like, 'If you want to name a hotel Great Britain, why do it in French?' Steven Runciman's *The Last Byzantine Renaissance*, which takes up the cultural flowering of Mistra during the Palaeologus period, had my full attention as I stretched out on the bed big enough for three people.

By four o'clock I was in the downstairs lobby. When I stepped into the café where the Nomo team awaited me, all three jumped up from their table. Luckily, in the hubbub of the café nobody noticed. The place was dim and packed with everybody speaking at once. Those with cell phones in hand, instead of cutting their conversations short, spoke louder, as if this would prove them right. The fat man at the next table, caressing his moustache with one hand and counting his beads with the other, served as a natural metronome against the roar of the crowd behind him.

'Askaris,' I said. 'Did you prepare this scene for me so that

I wouldn't miss my own country?' I regretted the question immediately: the team hadn't yet learned quite how to take my humor.

I broached my wish to stay in Athens for two days. My plan was to tour a few museums and historic sites before setting out for Mistra. But before everything else I had to investigate something that had bothered me on the street. I almost said as I stood up, 'Let all those who favor me rise and follow,' but refrained. I felt the urge to clasp my arms behind my back as we walked toward Syntagma Square in the rays of the late afternoon sun. The street consisted of modest shops whose owners stood outside and waited for evening to come, meanwhile smoking and yelling rudely at noisy, helmetless motorcycle riders. We didn't stop until we came to the Güllüoğlu Baklava shop. I had the odd feeling that if I went in to buy sweets for the group, I would devour somebody else's share. Just as I dove into the nearest street a *simit* peddler appeared before us with a tray full of the circular Turkish pretzels. I felt impelled to buy one. He gave me two banknotes in change. One had an arithmetic problem written on the back, the other was mended with sticky tape. Askaris said, 'Excellency, come November there will be *salep* peddlers shouting "Salepi!"' (*Salep*, made of hot milk and powdered orchid root, was an inescapable feature of Istanbul winters.)

I was as excited as a child let loose in an amusement park. I created my own labyrinth by rushing down nearly every street we encountered. I was in a hurry to discover a new sight, sound or smell with each turn I took. Nothing was strange to me though – the houses with their curtains of old lace, the shops with wrinkled flags in their windows, children clumping around in slippers, and boastful cats. Despite the cool evening, nearly all the customers at the coffee shop where we took a break preferred the outside tables. They seemed to be peacefully awaiting an order. In front of the building next to the café, a few people in a ragged queue began exchanging words. Would they dance shoulder to shoulder if somebody struck up a *sirtaki* tune?

The building looming up at the square to which Askaris led us was the Orthodox cathedral. It took me thirty seconds to turn to him and say, 'Are you trying to tell me that this is the most glorious holy building of the city and therefore the city doesn't really have a glorious holy building?'

'Excellency, may I trouble you to walk toward the statue at the end of the courtyard?'

I turned to look behind me; the courtyard looked like a disused ice rink. In the center stood the statue of an archbishop who was a secret hero of World War II. It seemed odd for him to have the expression of a pompous chieftain. Was that another statue behind his, between the cathedral and the square's perimeter? As if hynotized, I walked slowly toward the massive object that seemed to be signaling like a lighthouse. On a pedestal of ordinary marble, the kind used in bathhouses, stood a bronze statue of my ancestor Constantine XI. He wore his commander-in-chief uniform and in his right hand was a miniature sword. He looked old and tired, as tragicomic as Don Quixote setting forth on his last journey. If the sculptor wanted to carve a noble, scornful face disgusted with treacherous allies, he'd certainly succeeded. The figure had a long nose like my grandfather Yahya, high cheekbones like my mother, and a long face like mine. Despite the poor lighting I could sense his presence, cell by cell, and feel him like a human soul. As I slowly circled him, I seemed to feel the weight of our shared history passing into me. I chased away the birds perched on his head and cleared away the leaves heaped on his feet. I paced briskly and purposefully before him as though I were on guard duty. I was the helpless, neglectful grandson who returning after a long absence finds his mythical grandfather on his sickbed. Evidently I was under the influence of a trans-generational blood tie. I turned to the team who stood watching me, stunned, and said, 'This statue of Byzantium's last emperor is a size smaller than that of a nameless archbishop and is moreover hidden in its shadow. And this is the very Constantine XI who supported the union of the Catholic and Orthodox churches. The people who put this statue here have insulted Byzantium and its memory. Is Nomo unaware of this scandal – or have they not seen fit to correct it?'

In touristy Plaka, a town about to begin its winter hibernation, I chose a tavern called Byzantio for dinner. What was positive about the place was that it resembled a simple Anatolian restaurant and was music-free. I was alone with Askaris and about to hear him hold forth on Mistra. There were three tables in the tavern. Just behind us an old Greek was showering compliments in rudimentary English on a Japanese girl young enough to be his granddaughter. The girl focused her gaze on the plate before her. I was willing to bet that she would make her escape as soon as she finished eating. It was embarrassing. I tried to shame the shameless rogue with my stares, to no avail. But I relaxed as I drank more and more of the white wine. Askaris was unable to add

I didn't feel like telling Askaris that I was moved by what he said. We left the restaurant when my eyelids grew heavy, but we stopped by the cathedral courtyard again. I knelt down with my back against the statue of Constantine. No poem suitable to the occasion came to me. Since sweet sleep was about to seize my soul, the team members in unison took me by the arms and helped me home.

Next morning I jumped out of bed with a faint feeling of guilt. It was 6:33 a.m. and it occurred to me that I could view the town from my window. The sky was changing from dark to light gray. Atop the Acropolis the Parthenon grinned like a tenured ghost. I took a meditative shower and after read Seferis. When I made a second move to the window the sky had decided on a gentle blue. The Parthenon was shining in its eternal glory while the squat buildings of the town bowed in respect. I was as excited as if I was the first beholder of a freshly completed painting. I threw the window open to discover the background music of this panorama; I would scarcely have been surprised to hear the sound of an *ezan* rising from a remote corner.

The existence of ordinary tourists at Athens' most historical sites was a bore. They were only there to take pictures; their *joie de vivre* was just a show. The National Archaeology Museum was full of people, whereas there was no one except me in the small Museum of Byzantium and Christianity. (Its two most prominent pieces were pilfered from Edirne and Side, in Turkey.) The team was tense – apparently they thought they would be scolded because of the museum's deep silence.

'If you arranged to have this museum closed and reserved for me so that I could visit it properly, kudos to you,' I said.

Towards midnight Askaris sent two prostitutes to my room. The jingling of their gaudy jewelry recalled to me the grace of the 5,000-year-old necklace I saw at the Archaeology Museum. I was embarrassed.

*

The next morning we headed for Mistra in two limos. Complying with the rules meant staying in separate hotels and traveling in different cars. I was always with Askaris. I'd become somewhat accustomed to this clever and – even more than me – ugly fellow. The deserted road from the Corinth Strait to the Peloponnesian peninsula made me drowsy. The battlegrounds of antiquity that we'd studied and forgotten in our history classes had long lain fallow – hadn't they? All those mountains that played roles in various Greek myths became a size smaller. Were they waiting for the end? It was belligerent Sparta that surprised me, though. It was now a town of green trees and a population of 20,000. I likened it to a rebel once sentenced to life in prison who now took up gardening.

Mistra, a seven-minute drive from Sparta, had lapsed into a small village. Although it was established by Latin invaders during the Palaeologus period, it became the Byzantine capital of the Morea, the last piece of territory to remain in the hands of Constantinople. The heirs to Byzantium underwent their training here. Why the region was given to Sparta after Greek independence is unknown.

Mistra was a holy place, as holy as a village on Mount Ida. I could hardly believe my eyes when I saw the statue in the miniature agora. Except for being a size smaller, it was identical to the statue of Constantine XI in Athens. Was this an allusion to my great-great-grandfather's apprenticeship period? One of the tourist signs pointed the way to Steven Runciman Avenue. Runciman (1903-2000) wrote the only thorough book on the Morea. He was high in my esteem because he characterized the Crusades as 'invasions of barbarians' and moreover was a lover of Istanbul and Seferis. Also, he had never married.

We started up the hill on the right and I smiled at myself as I said a prayer in Arabic. We'd just rounded the first curve when Taigetos, the center of the Byzantine archaeological site, rose up in our path. This conic hill was 900 feet high and I felt like hugging it. All lined up as residents of the upper town were the blasted Latin castle on the peak, the church of Haghia Sophia a stone's throw below it, the Despot's Palace holding the center like a caravanserai, with an Ottoman mosque for a surprise neighbor, and finally the Pantánassa Convent under the protection of the cypress trees. I'd memorized them all from my maps, books, and engravings. At the top of the mist-shrouded hill a range of relics from the Middle Ages welcomed me. I had an idea where I would find the second purple square. But first I needed to familiarize myself with this social complex that was resisting the notion of turning into a ghost town. (This was probably Nomo's real intention.)

We abandoned our grandiose automobiles in the hilltop parking lot. Untended goats were grazing atop collapsed sections of the old walls. The bees were performing their final duet of the season with the goldfinches. Rain had fallen before our arrival and the earth smelled of the joy of life. I wanted to climb to the top and inhale a deep breath stretching from Galata to Mistra. We walked carefully along the paths that seemed designed to discourage people from coming to visit – and to annoy them if they did come. Our first stop was Haghia Sophia. The church was ready for a Mass, if only it had had doors and windows. There was a sad harmony between the frescoes on the walls and ceiling. Maybe it had taken 700 years for the figures to achieve the correct pastel tones. The Pantánassa Convent was the only building still performing its original function. The merriment of the tourists who clambered up to it in single file annoyed me. We were casually herded into their line. I don't know why, maybe it was the glasses she wore, but I was surprised by the young nun who passed us by, eyes cast to the ground. The group of locals invading the convent couldn't keep quiet – they were experiencing the bliss of setting a holy picnic table. I couldn't eat the hard candy I took from a bowl proffered by an elderly nun.

'It's spoiled because of unheard prayers,' I whispered, as if the team could hear me.

The convent's spacious balcony reminded me of the timber summer houses perched in the mountain pastures on the eastern Black Sea. As the fog began to thin, I sensed the luminous glow of a caravan of light made of mosaic squares heading toward the east. I shut my eyes to better hear the hymn that accompanied this timeless phenomenon. When the caravan visually reached Antioch I opened them. Somehow I was disturbed by the team hovering behind me and had a sudden urge to tease them.

Without turning my face to them I asked, 'Do any of you know the ancient poet of this land, Hegesippos?'

Silence. 'Congratulations,' I said. 'I'll recite a stanza from him to you:

Nettles and camel thorns on four sides of me.
Be gone, traveler, or you'll get scratched.
I'm Timon the misanthrope himself.
Hurl your curses however you like, feel free.
Just get the hell away and be gone!

And now it's time for us too to leave. We have work to do.'

With that I turned and charged into the Despot's Palace through the Monemvasia Gate. Mistra was a mosaic puzzle laid down on an uneven plot of land. In a way I enjoyed not being sure whether the buildings, the youngest of which was 500 years old, were a question or an answer. I was fairly confident that I would find the second clue in the room where the Despot once held court. But I had a present-day obstacle: the palace was closed to visitors because of restoration work supported by the European Union!

Kalligas had a word with the guard, who gave us the good news that we could go in if we received permission from the construction superintendent. With a hand that he lifted in three movements, he pointed to a young woman standing in the middle of the courtyard under a Panama hat. The chief of restoration wore boots, trousers and sunglasses. It looked like it might not be easy to get a 'Yes' from her. Using body language for emphasis, she was raining orders on a team of workers arranged in a half-circle before her. I approached with curiosity. Her voice was seductive and the hair springing out of her hat was blonde. If she weren't speaking Greek like a machine gun I would have thought she was Scandinavian. I wondered why everybody laughed when she came to the end of her melodic sentences. When she clacked her boots with the metal ruler in her left hand, she reminded me of those ranch owners' daughters in the Western movies who scold their servants, jump on their horses, and ride off into the sunset.

Her team dispersed and I moved towards her. I caught her eye and assumed my most appealing attitude. I stated, in English, that I was a scholar from Boğaziçi University and an amateur historian addicted to Byzantium. Having come as far as Athens, I did not want to leave without visiting the Despot's Palace. I succeeded in getting her attention when I added that I could pass as Greek on my mother's side. I refused to give up when she replied, in fluent English, 'I only have authority to offer privileges to bona fide Byzantine scholars' and rattled off the names of those Byzantine historians to whom I gave credence. Then I mentioned my personal research at Dumbarton Oaks and New Chatham House.

'If you like,' I said, 'you can ask me about the false eunuchs at the Great Palace, or I can enumerate for you the emperors who've taken naps on the Valens Aqueduct. But, please, grant me this favor.' I was begging, surprised at the meekness in my tone.

Her glasses were like a mask covering her face, but when I noticed the young woman's cheeks lifting, if only slightly, I relaxed somewhat. She brought the ring and index fingers of her left hand to her lips and whistled sharply. (I always envied people who could whistle with their fingers.) She nodded in my direction to the guard who leaped from his chair when he heard the shout, 'Akiii!' Then she took a penlight from her pocket and handed it to me, saying, 'Here, you'll need this. Please bring it back to me in an hour at the latest.'

The Despot's Palace was in fact a building that lacked aesthetic distinction. It had been the residence of the district governor and therefore was meant to be as large and pretentious as possible. Strangely enough, it seemed to have something of the soul of a Seljuk caravanserai. I found the hall that the old map in my hand said was the 'Throne Room'. Restoration had not yet penetrated this space, which was dim and austere and seemed to have been left empty for generations. I identified the prevalent aroma – wet hay. When I pressed the switch on the penlight, no pigeons or bats took wing and no bugs began to chitter. Something must have altered the atmosphere not long before. There were mosaic compositions in the center of the stone floor. The most prominent featured a half-naked philosopher warding off a monstrous tiger with the scroll in his hand. This part looked slightly less dusty than the rest. I used the penlight to scrutinize the mosaic square by square. And there was the purple square, in the holy man's beard. It stuck to my hand the moment I touched it. Was it a laughing matter that the person who'd hidden the second clue might be in charge of the Mistra restoration team?

I didn't want to show rudeness by exiting the building too soon, so I remained in the meditative atmosphere and reflected on the Palaeologan tekfurs who consorted with philosophers.

In particular Manuel II, a man of wisdom and an aesthete, had made Mistra the center of the last Byzantine renaissance. There enlightened priests, scientists, philosophers, scholars and selected artists had gathered. Churches and palace were transformed into colleges. Classical philosophers were studied and criticized; new philosophies were born. And so Mistra attracted the attention of Europe and became the target of Vatican suspicion. In my sources thus far, the reasons why a small rural town was chosen for this melancholic renaissance remained vague. But in my opinion the Palaeologoi simply felt hopeless about their swiftly crumbling Constantinople. They depended on this site – now an archaeological park – for the same reasons that Constantine I, fearing Rome, had founded Constantinople. My eyes focused on the cobwebs dangling from the corners of the walls and ceiling. Perhaps they were still holding for safekeeping the unrecorded words of wisdom uttered under their roof 600 years ago.

Neatly wrapping the new clue in a paper napkin, I murmured my favorite prayer and left the building. The restoration chief sat under a portable sunscreen at the edge of the courtyard. Feet stretched out on the small table in front of her, she continued to shout orders in English and Greek at the walkie-talkie in her hand. Her legs were long and shapely. Next to her boots lay a copy of Javier Marias's *When I Was Mortal*. She shut off the walkie-talkie and lowered her feet to the ground. I was curious about the face that she kept concealed behind her hat and sunglasses. 'I suppose you weren't too impressed with what you saw?' she said.

I handed back her penlight while I lined up a few sentences like, 'I conversed in a time-tunnel with the philosopher

Plethon and Byrennius and Bessarion. Those great halls are imbued with their presence. I'm grateful to you for enabling me to enjoy this pleasure.' Behind my generous expression of gratitude might have been my easily found second clue.

The young woman sat still for a short while, perhaps because she wanted to think about the words I'd just said and those I was about to say. She began with, 'Well, I'm glad to meet a Turk without a moustache who loves Byzantium,' and continued with, 'I'll be in Istanbul in December to deliver a lecture. If you're interested, I'd be happy to invite you. If you'll leave your e-mail address, we can notify you.'

I scribbled my e-mail on my card and gave it to her. 'May I ask the title of your paper?' I said.

'In short, I'm claiming that Manuel II was the most superior but unfortunate Byzantine emperor.'

'H.G. Beck offered the thesis that Manuel was one of the most sympathetic emperors, appreciated even by his enemies. Steven Runciman seems to agree with him. I'll definitely come and listen to you.'

'So is there a marginal Byzantine emperor that you like a lot?'

'I've always liked the Palaeologus dynasty. If I had to choose one emperor among them, that would be Constantine XI.'

'Should I ask why?'

'I could reel off a dozen reasons, but the best one is probably the instinctive one – blood ties.'

The young woman started to laugh. In all this time she was the first woman – except for the prostitutes – I was able to make laugh, and she was an academic whose full face I couldn't even see. (I wondered what color her eyes were.) As she handed me her card, her cell phone rang. I understood from the fact that she began speaking Italian coquettishly that it was her boyfriend. Soon enough I was sorting out the mystery of Dr Mistral Sapuntzoglu. She was an assistant professor in Classical Archaeology and History at Stockholm University, and either her father or her grandfather must have belonged to one of the families torn away from Anatolia, as I inferred from the adaptation of her last name, 'Sabuncuoğlu' ('son of the soapmaker' in Turkish) to the Greek alphabet. Dr Sapuntzoglu's phone conversation was not long. When I mentioned my surmise she said, 'Yes, you're right. My father Costas was a native of Edremit. And my mother is Swedish. But my name has nothing to do with Mistra.'

'Don't I know! More precisely, I know about the winds that show up in poems. The mistral is a cold and obstinate wind that blows from northwest Europe down to the Mediterranean. It's a nice poetic word, though. I once bought a book of poems by Gabriela Mistral for that reason, and then learned that she won the Nobel Prize in 1945.'

As one of her assistants hove into view, we were shaking hands with the prospect of meeting again in Istanbul.

*

As a team we walked to the neighboring church of Saint Nicholas. I wanted to see how Nomo would react to my choice of the Santa Claus church as a venue for deciphering the clue.

The third stop would be Sumela Monastery. I'd never been to the monastery, which was carved out of a mountain outside my ancestors' home town, Trabzon. The Sumela that I'd seen on postcards and in documentary films looked like a cartoon mansion. When I was in middle school I once begged my grandmother to take me there. She said, 'Son, are you crazy?'

We'd finished early in Mistra. But at the last minute I was inspired to drop by the Church of Saint Demetrius, where the coronation of Constantine XI took place on January 6, 1449. It gave me a thrill to be inside the small holy place: to be crowned emperor in Byzantium was synonymous with receiving an open-ended death sentence. I gave the team one hour to visit their monuments of choice. Pappas and Kalligas preferred staying with me. Askaris wanted to see two deserted churches on the southern edge of town.

We stopped off in Sparta to take a break at the Palaeologus Café – the name was enough for us. The place looked like a bomb shelter. The TV was set to a fashion channel, and it was amusing to watch the male customers ogling the swimsuit parade. Had I seen more men with moustaches in the crowd, I'd have sworn that I was in Tire or Bergama on the Turkish Aegean.

'Pappas, call the waiter to take our order,' I said. 'And ask him if they have a discount for family members.'

We all had a good laugh.

KAPPA

At one time, if I felt assured that the word 'Laz' – the name of a regional tribe prey to national jokes – would not come up, I would admit that I came from Trabzon, which was founded by Miletus in the seventh century B.C. as Trapezus. On any antique map or chart, I knew I would find Trapezus on the Black Sea. (When I first separated it into two words, 'trapeze' and 'us,' I felt fulfilled, like I'd solved a tough puzzle.) After the Latins confiscated Constantinople, 'Pontus' was the name of the rump empire whose capital was Trabzon. It sounded like a password. Its fierce independence, which lasted until 1461 when the Ottomans finally took it, was a constant irritant to Byzantium.

After my grandfather had settled in Galata even to utter the name 'Trabzon' was forbidden. Ten years after he died I went with my grandmother to the city that he'd abandoned because of financial disaster. Trabzon was sandwiched between two hills and the Black Sea but had begun seeping out of this enclosure toward the south and west. In place of the family mansion, which was neighbor to the Atatürk Museum and had a birds'-eye view of town, now stood three apartment blocks. Had Eugenio seen them he would have said, 'Only King Kong could have been the architect of this tragedy.' In the dazzling green and purple of the exterior plasterwork I found only the mirth of caricature.

I could barely endure a week of hospitality at my grandmother's cousin Samiye's house. The childless widow's parlor was a field of potted plants; moreover, she owned an ill-tempered cat named Cimcime. She was constantly offering food to everybody and if they declined she was hurt. My head ached every time she attempted to sprinkle cologne on our hands. She spoke to her plants and her cat in different tones of voice and belched loudly before going to bed.

During that first visit I decided proudly that visiting Trabzon was like being back in ancient time; it had fortifications from Miletus, an aqueduct and church from Byzantium, and a mosque, baths and several mansions from the Ottomans – none of which I was ever taken to. Samiye and my grandmother were not aware that such monuments existed. I imagined that the Tabakhane and Zagnos bridges were markers that divided the town into upper and lower, and I conveyed to them salutations from the Galata Tower. I went there to sit and watch passersby. I assumed that half of the males in the population of 200,000 had gone fishing. The shopkeepers who perpetually dozed off while on duty would perk up when they strutted the streets and puffed out their chests in greetings to each other. The funniest of all were the bowlegged guys with noses like eagles' beaks. I kept a daily record of these sightings. From the vantage of the Atatürk Museum the thin sound of a *kemençe*, the small violin that was a folk instrument of the region, would occasionally rise and grow until all Trabzon would link arms and dance the *horon* together. Such was the video clip in my mind on my way back to Istanbul.

The summer of the year I entered high school, Eugenio presented me with a monograph on Trabzon. I read this encyclopedic book like I was studying for a final in an elective course. The Trabzon of nineteenth-century engravings was not much different from a fairy-tale city. The tombstones in the Imaret cemetery stood up like dervishes preparing to whirl. In the panoramic photographs shot from the seaside, the melancholic atmosphere of the city was obvious. The Trabzon folk in these faded pictures looked as if they had all assembled for a masquerade. Frame by frame I observed my fellow citizens staring at the camera with distrustful eyes. The procession of images took me back to the bridge memories of my childhood visit. Just as every nation that had once ruled the place left behind stone monuments, so also they left traces in the people still drinking from the fountains. Among these were men and women with long faces. I thought I knew them from Byzantine frescoes. The common feature of the men was the stubbornness in their eyes. And I knew where I'd seen that attitude of casual challenge: in the figure of Sultan Yavuz Selim – Selim the Grim – who served his apprenticeship as governor of Trabzon.

Sumela Monastery was carved by hand from the side of a mountain. Construction began in the fourth century and lasted a thousand years. I used to push the limits of my childhood imagination by studying postcards of Sumela: if not as brave as an acrobat walking a tightrope, it was as sublime as a romantic chateau on a cliff side. I told myself that one day I would fly to Trabzon to get to know it and would come back without going into the city center here. I didn't want to hurt the feelings of my grandfather – I liked him a little more with every prayer that his wife and daughter offered for his damnation.

*

Now after twenty years, again for the sake of not hurting the soul of a forefather, I was in the skies over Trabzon. I told my grandmother I had a business meeting in Ankara; she would have been suspicious if I'd asked about her Trabzon cousin. As we came into the city from the airport, words like 'balaos' (mad), 'kambos' (bug) and 'zazal' (bald) were dancing in my head to a melody that united the Pontus Greek language with Samiye's Turkish. If I were writing a novel, my protagonist would likely not be captivated by the woman in Samiye's role. But I was getting a little worried about my own life, which had already slipped beyond the borders of a novel.

If I needed to convince myself that I wasn't dreaming all this, I could turn around and look at Askaris following me like a languid street dog – I found him so strange that I didn't want to know anything about his private life. I understood from his behavior as we neared Trabzon that he was not very familiar with the city. His heavy beard put me in mind of my grandfather's last photograph in the family album. I was sure he grew it to camouflage his nearly bald head and long nose. His frown and the disapproving gaze he turned on the camera with his large eyes – these were perhaps also signs of his charisma.

When my grandfather ran into difficulties at the University of Paris, he moved on to the Department of Economics at a college for immigrants in Geneva. His daughter considered him a lazy dreamer and failed businessman. His wife thought he was a man up to no good, who dropped in and out of clubs and restaurants and went on 'business trips' abroad at every opportunity. On the other hand, Galata denizens knew him as a gentleman and a philanthropist. I'd forgotten which Joannes my grandfather Yahya was, but it was perfectly clear from his way of life that in the eyes of Nomo he was not one of the Elect. I suspected that Nomo had provided a certain standard of living for him and thus had exempted him from either the fortune or misfortune reserved for me.

Downtown Trabzon stopped progressing 2,700 years ago and now looked like the River Ganges. Even a little fender-bender meant enormous traffic chaos. The increased number of women in headscarves caught my attention. They looked like a collection of young and eloquent girls with ivory complexions who would abandon their scarves and leave the set as soon as the movie was shot.

I liked my hotel just fine, with its rose-colored atrium that looked like a sheik's tent. It was a mild November day. After lunch I visited the Haghia Sophia of the Pontus with Askaris. As we entered the church courtyard the roar of the Black Sea came at staccato intervals. I recalled the majestic Sea of Marmara. If it had a message to impart, it would deliver it in squiggly lines accompanied by imaginary musical notes.

The front of the plain thirteenth-century church had become a storage place for archaeological fragments. A tombstone next to the ladies' room bore the name of Kamer Sultan, daughter of an Ottoman emperor. I saw a family resemblance between the building's design, the color and cut of its interior stonework, and the Armenian and Georgian churches and Selçuk mosques of the region. This sense of collaboration impressed me. The ceiling frescoes offered the pleasure of viewing a painting. I felt the warmth of wandering through a naïve art exhibition in provincial Byzantium as compared to Constantinople. I called Askaris' attention to the deficiency of expression, as well as the translation-cum-printing errors on the descriptions posted in the church and said, 'If I were an emperor not in exile, I would know what to do.' I thought that I would get used to the roaring as we moved closer to the spacious windows on the north side. I was wrong: the Black Sea was like a restless tiger that sensed its master being threatened.

Pappas and Kalligas were waiting in the courtyard. I set them free, telling them I wanted to explore Ottoman Trabzon. But since Askaris wanted to linger at Haghia Sophia a little longer, my bearded guards had to go with me. We went straight to the Ottoman bridges that divide the city between north and south. Those monuments, which in olden days had served as escalators to the time tunnel that carried me away to the Ottoman city, now looked a size smaller. I enjoyed the prospect a while, scanning the town for traces of the Trabzon that Sultan Yavuz had governed for twenty-two years, and where his son Suleyman, the future Magnificent, was born.

First I watched the commotion enjoyed by a group of ten- or twelve-year-olds joshing with each other on their way home from school. What was musical about them was their shouting at each other all at the same time in their accented Black Sea Turkish; what made it really dramatic was how they used their accents to demonstrate superiority. A little later began the promenade of older youth. It was odd how I couldn't predict whether they would finish their sharp-edged conversations in a quarrel or a laugh. They pronounced each word with a special lilt and only when they came to the end of a sentence did they decide on the intonation. Then there were the young girls – their procession over the bridge was a folkloric fashion show. They would appear in small clusters and ritualistically divert their eyes to the ground as they passed in front of the boys. I didn't want to think about how Pappas and Kalligas, walking like puppets on either side of me, would – if necessary – sacrifice themselves to save my life; but also – if necessary – would sacrifice me just as quickly for Nomo. For now they didn't look much different from minor characters in a comic book.

We passed into the Ortahisar neighborhood together with the late afternoon *ezan*. A feeble autumn breeze caressed my face, which I took as a sign. I started to chase it, without asking where or why, when I suddenly felt my feet nailed to the ground. It was like I was wearing kaleidoscopic glasses. I stood, squinting. If no password was demanded of me, did that mean a message was forthcoming? My head began to hurt and a weariness crept into my cells. Then the thin curtain of fog facing me slowly lifted. There before me stood a row of Byzantine, Ottoman and Republican buildings shoulder to shoulder, resisting time and humanity and apparently issuing a challenge.

In this neighborhood squeezed into a confined and hilly plot there were other venerable structures showing respect for the topography. The faded pastel exteriors of picturesque houses that I wanted to call 'little mansions' recalled the ceiling frescoes of Haghia Sophia and the calm hotel atrium.

I felt more rested as I strolled those narrow paths, occasionally passing a dry fountain with an inscription like 'Every death is an early death'. I had street dogs for company and the paths usually ended in a cul-de-sac of wild fig trees. On these cool nameless streets I savored duets of silence and serenity. The sky grew darker but I felt that every corner had its own light to emit.

Poking my head into the Ortahisar Mosque, I watched the people at prayer. During the thirteenth century, when this mosque was the Church of Panaghia Chrysocephalos, the Pontus kings had held their coronation ceremonies in it. In the row of seven- or eight-year-old children at the very back, a faded and illegible message in English on somebody's sweater briefly aroused my curiosity.

We then took a break at a café for retired men, where whoever wasn't duelling with his cigarette was counting his prayer beads very slowly. I was a bit abashed by their universal chorus of 'Welcome' when we came through the door, as if they were saying 'Amen'. Those with prayer beads appeared to be linked up to something between happiness and its opposite, and expecting news. On our way out I saw flyers for a *horon* dance in the window of a CD shop next to a print shop that declared its establishment in 1901 like it was sending an SOS. A young man in the doorway looked at me with eyes that said, 'Mistakes will not be forgiven.'

I could express the lightness of being I was feeling in one sentence: 'I was taken by a royal boat to the monastery complex.' And a warning that Nomo would not have liked was whispered into my ear: the true task is to master the achievements of both the Byzantines and the Ottomans.

In Trabzon I was halfway there. Yet if I was undergoing a test, I was beginning to grow curious about the examination committee. It would be a very Byzantine business indeed if Nomo was trying to wear me down in a duel. It was said that 'Sumela' derived from 'melas', meaning 'darkness' in Greek. I like darkness: every hue of it has a different taste. I know this from poetry.

*

I declared to myself with a sigh that, if I were writing a novel, whenever I heard that Altindere National Park was half an hour from Trabzon I would write down forty minutes. I felt like I was pursuing a protected species when I read that Sumela Monastery was situated inside the park.

I like words made of five letters, and I was curious about Maçka because it was both on the Silk Road and in Xenophon's *Anabasis*. I'd forgot that Altindere Park was actually in the Maçka district. I was with Theo Pappas in a two-car convoy driving through the sunny autumn morning. I'd begun to sympathize with this wrestler-like guard who was never offended by my jokes, perhaps because he didn't get them. I decided not to tease Askaris and so I didn't say – yet – 'Was this man hired to unguard me?'

The way was charming: full of joy, full of green, under open skies with groups of clouds posing patiently. We saw buildings flimsy enough to belong to a cardboard stage set; maybe they grew out of seeds carried by the wind. We passed a middle-aged village woman with a pile of brush on her back and a bony cow on either side of her. The three of them walked with the same gait and swung their heads to and fro in the same rhythm. They were probably all thinking the same thing too.

As we headed south, the altitude and the quiet both increased. I greeted the sovereignty of silence with respect. I found the ticket-seller's affection at the park entrance slightly out of place, however. If Askaris had been beside me I would have said something like, 'This man is like a caregiver who demoralizes the patient.' We climbed a curving road that grew more ruthless as it rose and came finally to a parking lot. Parked there was a tired minibus from the neighboring town. Altindere was shaded by colossal oak trees. We were caught in a stand-off between massive green and enormous silence. It was thrilling to feel that I could fly if I shut my eyes. Surely the park was the monastery's terminal of eternity. Just then I came face to face with the mountain itself, rising 4,000 feet above sea level. Sumela shone like a giant painting suspended from the peak. I couldn't take my eyes off it; was the monastery growing larger, the longer I stared?

It was an architectural work fifty feet high and 120 feet long, with a Gothic aesthetic that harmonized with the environment. Once more I found myself wondering how this structure got itself built on the edge of a cliff over the course of a thousand years; it made me ashamed of my puny diplomas. I knew that I would find the third purple square in one of two venues when I went inside the complex in another half an hour. I'd done my homework. I was coming to better terms with myself as I thought about how the human race, with faith and nails, could remove forty feet of a mountain. If by this means I was receiving some kind of spiritual training, I owed a debt of gratitude to the examination committee.

According to generally accepted myth, the Virgin Mary appeared in the dreams of two Athenian priests and ordered them to establish a sacred site in the Black Mountains of Trebizond. (Whenever Mary's name is mentioned, it makes me think that Paul of Tarsus, from Southern Turkey, the flag bearer of Christianity, has not been properly honored.) The two priests, who were relatives, were brought by destiny to the foothills of these mountains after a tiring and tortuous trip. There they carved a small church out of the monumental rock and remained there until the end of their lives, dying on the same day. The local monks then took over, and the remote church gradually grew into a regional center. In the sixth century the Byzantine Emperor Justinian threw his support behind it. The period of difficulties came to an end in the fourteenth century with the help of the Pontus emperors. By now Sumela was a worldwide religious center. In the sixteenth century, when Governor Yavuz was injured while hunting in the nearby mountains, it was the monks of the monastery who healed him. From then on Sumela came under the protection of the Ottomans. With the declaration of the Republic in 1923, however, it lost its relevance and the monks moved away. It was natural for it to be forgotten on its mountain until the 1980s, when the beginnings of restoration got underway.

The artisan of the path to the monastery was nature. We headed up in single file, listening to the sound of a spring. It echoed like a warning signal and changed tones with each bend. The path was secured by enormous trees. Their dramatic roots, gripping the earth like octopi, seemed to say, 'Traveler, every step you take is under our protection.'

I found myself in the Middle Ages as soon as I stepped through the main gate. To the left of the monastery was an open space like a courtyard, and around it were a dozen small buildings in addition to a church and chapel. I could believe that they were constructed out of stones plucked from the bosom of the mountain. First we went into the monastery with its five floors and seventy-two cells. Up close it looked like a small hospital, yet it was not without a library, wine cellar, and prison. With a little investment it could have become the most enchanting mansion on earth. When you looked down from the terrace a thousand-foot drop-off winked at you. No doubt every visitor exclaimed, 'This must be heaven,' on seeing the pellucid blue sky under which the sweet symphony of a running stream serenaded the virgin forest.

The passengers of the minibus, whose bumper sticker read 'Don't tailgate! You'll regret it!' were gathered in the courtyard. They were elderly and white-skinned and not happy with the tour. One of the women was berating her husband for bringing her here. My own short tour started at the chapel and ended at the rock-cut church. There were a total of seventy-two frescoes in the church and twenty more in the chapel. The cramped space meant that they covered the entirety of the two buildings' stone walls, inside and out, plus the church ceiling. In the course of a thousand years the artists had illustrated almost the whole Bible, like a graphic novel. I stood in the deserted place and studied the images with the pleasure of viewing an art exhibition. They reflected

also that by finishing off my dream journey in Trabzon, my grandfather's home town, Nomo was playing their own little joke on me. It was time to end my unpaid leave of absence and get back to my students. And so Emperor Constantine XV, unelected, in exile and exhausted, left the rock church.

Waiting in the courtyard, the team was in an anxious state. I'd already telegraphed the bad news with a head-shake as they swept towards me. On Askaris' face was that upset expression common to teachers whose students have failed their mid-terms. I said, patting him on the shoulder, 'We'll come back tomorrow, but I don't think my luck will improve.' Pappas kept his eyes on the ground and looked like he was trying not to smile. I tried to lighten the mood by grabbing his beard in both hands and saying, 'Hey Theo, did you ask Nomo to disqualify me in my grandfather's home town?'

After lunch in Trabzon I decided we should drive up the coast and return by way of Artvin, on the Georgian border. I planned to use this Eastern Black Sea excursion to pull myself together. I would review my notes when we returned. But first I wanted to drop by the hotel to freshen up and get rid of my briefcase. When I opened the door to my room and saw the small purple envelope on the night stand, my heart skipped a beat. To my shock and surprise, the purple square was inside! Stashing the envelope in my briefcase, I rushed back down to the team waiting in the lobby. I told them what had happened. We all decided to keep it a secret from hotel management, considering the possible risks. To assess the seriousness of the situation I took the silver box from my briefcase and placed the square in the third slot. There was a click and ten seconds later, in the opposite rectangle, the words popped up, 'Palace of the First Ecumenical Council of Nicaea, Iznik.'

Was this a royal joke or a trap? I turned to Askaris and said, 'I won't go to Iznik, nor even Izmit, until I speak with Nomo.' It made me nervous to see him exchange meaningful glances with Kalligas. Scolding both of them, I said, 'I don't know who you should call, Askaris, Nomo or your master; but I know well that I want some kind of answer right now!' The horse-faced man clutched his cell phone and walked away from us in order – probably – to talk to one of his superiors. He obtained a reply that somebody would get back to me in an hour. We climbed into a rented van and turned toward Artvin. Just as we hit Hopa we got a call, and Askaris told the driver to pull over. He got out and spoke on his phone briefly. He looked relaxed when he came back.

'Excellency, they're asking you to continue. Unfortunately no further information was given to me to pass along to you.'

Seeing my lip curl, he felt the need to go on.

'Excellency, will you permit me to offer a brief explanation of my own?'

'If you leave out the phony answer you got from the phone and compress it into forty words, all right.'

'Excellency, this is my personal evaluation. In my opinion, you've been put through a test of character. If you wished, you could have hidden the fact that the envelope was left in your room and you could have taken us all back to Sumela and pretended to find the purple square there. Nobody could have claimed that you'd done wrong. But at the cost of being disqualified, you disclosed the truth.'

'Askaris, you've already said enough. Do you even believe

what you're saying? My reasons to drop out of this game are stronger than those I have to stay in. But I'll stay, maybe just because I refuse to walk out in the middle of an exam. And maybe too because I wouldn't mind seeing Iznik.'

I relaxed on our return journey. The mystery of the envelope would be revealed, I supposed, either in due time or by way of a leak from Nomo. When I noticed the team also relaxing, I said, 'Friends, I want you to hear a poem by Karacaoğlan, who happens to be the greatest poet – past, present, or future – this soil has produced. Askaris will translate it into English, then Kalligas into Greek. And Pappas will summarize what he's understood. Whoever screws up will find himself in the Black Sea.'

LAMBDA

One issue that vexed me in elementary school was the failure of the seasons to keep up with the calendar. For me it was a scandal that in the northern hemisphere winters did not begin on December 1 and end on February 28. When I made the mistake of asking my grandmother the reason for this, the reply was, 'These things are decided by the Almighty, not by the calendar.'

In our neighborhood, according to Eugenio, the four seasons consisted of yesterday, today, daytime and night time. Anybody cooking up a theory like this would have to be a dyed-in-the-wool Galatian, of course. But I knew that with this line of thought he wanted to put me in the mood for an exam. And that's exactly how I started to tackle riddles and puzzles, with myself as my own rival and judge. If our winds had gone nervously slaloming around, I wouldn't have liked December. But when I was a child, that muttering wind used to be my number two confidant. Naturally I didn't admit it openly, as Tristan would have been envious. In one of the dreams that I hid from everybody the mother of all winds was the sea and their father was the shadow. The jealous shadow was the love child of the sun and the moon. He repeatedly abandoned the sea, yet he wouldn't let the wind stay with her either. Yes, they were immortal as long as the sun continued to rise.

Winds were the carrier pigeons of time. They took messages from lakes to deserts, from forests to mountains and, most important of all, from one ancient building to another. As I descended from Galata to Eugenio's museum-like house my mind was buzzing with these things. The Tower looked a little disappointed because I hadn't got close to any buildings older than it on my journey.

'Well, Reverend,' I said, sidling up to it. 'Things aren't how you think. I'm in the middle of a test made up of six questions. The first two were so easy they were a joke, and on the third they forced me to cheat.'

I objected to being put through a stress test, if that was what Nomo had in mind. To get away from it all, I declared December a month-long holiday. The team's response was something between joy and surprise. I would devote my time until the end of the year exclusively to my hobbies and the town prostitutes.

*

On the night of December 8 I was enjoying a pleasant tiredness after Hayal's birthday party. 'You're the best big brother in the world and you deserve the best girl on earth!' my sister had squealed as she embraced me upon seeing the Chopard wristwatch I'd bought her. My own stoic inability to feel euphoric was always a humorous contrast to her exuberance. I remembered the night I'd found Hayal, half-naked and crying on the street, and carried her home on my back. The olive-eyed girl had become my daughter and sister both and helped me retain my self-respect. I felt an inner glow as I gave her a hug. And to maintain that warmth I could think of nothing better than a vodka on ice.

Before climbing into bed with Michael Palmer's *Collected Poems*, whose cover featured two lions about to cry, I checked my e-mail. Dr Mistral Sapuntzoglu was inviting me to a talk that she would give at the American Research Institute in Turkey on 12.12.08 in the evening.

ARIT was founded by a consortium of a dozen American universities. Its respectable library held 12,000 volumes in English on Byzantium. More than the half-hearted promise I'd given to Dr Sapuntzoglu, it was this library that drew me to ARIT before the appointed hour. The modest mansion in Arnavutköy, without a view of the Bosphorus, was probably the legacy of either an inefficient or unfortunate Ottoman bureaucrat. I spent forty minutes in the quiet library on the top floor and felt relieved to find no notes from my father in any of the forty books I scanned. Boredom struck as soon as I pulled *The Oxford Dictionary of Byzantium* off the shelf, so I went down to the lecture room. There were seventeen minutes to go before the talk. About fifty people stood around in small groups chatting and waiting. The male-dominated, middle-aged audience darted surreptitious glances at the young blonde woman in front of the lectern whenever they got the chance. She was conversing with a bearded foreigner and Selçuk Altun. I was still in the phase of surprise when Eugenio's old friend beckoned me over with an insistent gesture.

In his bookish English he said, 'Evidently you've already met Misty, in Mistra of all places. This kind of pleasant coincidence only happens in novels. And you still continue to insist on poetry.'

As I listened to him ramble on about how he had worked with the speaker's uncle at the London office of an international corporation and how their friendship went back to the 1970s, I studied Mistral Sapuntzoglu with new interest. Apparently the blonde woman who'd assisted my research in Mistra had blue eyes and a pert nose. Her high forehead was a sign of intelligence, according to my grandmother. When I joined the conversation I saw that she was not in fact a cold Scandinavian beauty. She was self-confident and relaxed, like somebody from the Mediterranean. I figured that men put up with her conceited ways because of her beauty. Me, I never did like those 'Grace Kelly' types. I planned to sit in the back and sneak out at the second paragraph.

The bearded American academic who could tell jokes in perfect Turkish must have been the head of the Institute. It was an annoyance when he invited me to join their small group at a fish restaurant after Mistral's talk. He only smiled at my lame and panic-stricken excuse. Just at that moment Selçuk Altun came out with his statement: 'Just so you know, Misty wants to see some of the neighborhood Byzantine churches during her two weeks of research in Istanbul. I know you carried out a similar expedition not long ago, and besides, you have some spare time. I already told her, in your name, that you would be glad to show her around.' It was odd that this writer, whose works I never read, was manipulating me as if I were one of his characters. But I couldn't say no. Smiling at the speaker, about whose talk I had no curiosity whatever, I said, 'Well, I owe Doctor Sapuntzoglu a favor.' I took a seat in the back of the room close to the door and prepared to listen to how wonderfully one of my ancestors,

Manuel II, performed as an emperor.

From the monotonous introduction by a female academic we learned that Mistral took her PhD at Cambridge after graduating from the University of Stockholm (which would make her about two years younger than me). To warm up the audience Dr Sapuntzoglu said, 'You can understand from my last name that my father was a Greek man with Anatolian roots. But I can't do much with the Turkish I learned from him except swear at your forefathers.' This brought a laugh from the majority. I stayed until the very end of the paper, which was called 'Manuel II Palaeologus: Statesman of Genius?' The doctor was not only a good speaker, she had a good command of her subject. She captivated the audience in her third sentence by reading a note that Manuel II wrote about the Mevlevi Sufi order. (I wondered how many of her male students fell in love with her as they listened to her lectures.) While emphasizing the accomplishments of Manuel II as statesman, commander, diplomat, scholar, writer and theologian, she ignored his underhanded treatment of Venice. She spoke about Manuel's daughter Zampia and her marriage to a respectable Genoese man, and I imagined Sapuntzoglu as the mistress of a semi-potent married professor.

Over the next three days I took Mistral to a total of twenty-two churches or ruins of one kind or another. Trying to keep to a schedule, I picked her up at ARIT in the morning and saw her off to Arnavutköy again in the evening. The first day we visited the churches converted to mosques that I'd explored in the summer. We had help in finding other places on her list from the guide Cevat Mert and various neighborhood informants. Even I got excited when we went looking for the Church of St. George, which was built by Constantine IX as a place to meet his lover and was burned down by his wife Zoe after he died. And the Church of Soteros Philantropos, where Princess Irene took refuge upon her husband's death. And the Church of Our Lady at Blachernae, where the Blessed Virgin's garments were kept. Mistral was a woman at peace with herself, who whistled a tune whenever she found the opportunity and never uttered a word without a reason. I carried one of her two bags, performed translation duties, and hosted her at little neighborhood restaurants. I was irritated by the obnoxious stares of thick-headed men wherever we went. I prayed for God to give patience to guys with good-looking girlfriends. Since it was against my nature to flirt, and anyway I didn't want to cause any misunderstandings, I refrained from asking her any personal questions.

I found Dr Sapuntzoglu's working style somewhat unusual. She hauled out her Leica and started shooting dozens of pictures as soon as we hit the first church on her list, then furiously scribbled notes with a pen that sported an erotic puppet on its cap. Her pace reminded me of a junior war correspondent; later on I compared her to a doctor administering to a hopeless patient as she ran an expert finger over a wall surface. I attributed her lack of reaction to the texture of sights, sounds, people and color in the vicinity of the churches to her familiarity with such things from rural Greece. There seemed always to be some kind of oriental music in the background at the ancient sites we visited. Whenever those anti-musical melodies rose from the half-open window of a worn-out house or a dilapidated shop or a passing taxi,

Miss PhD would wink and shimmy like a belly-dancer.

We said good-bye with the cliché, 'Let's get together in Stockholm some time.' So I was surprised by next morning's e-mail: Mistral was inviting me to dinner to say good-bye properly. To my response – 'All right, as long as it's on me' – she said, 'I knew that was coming.' We met at a dimly lit fish restaurant on the Bosphorus. The waiter laughed when she knocked her head on the table three times to underline her embarrassment on remembering that I was a vegetarian. In short, over the course of the dinner, which encompassed a lot of white wine and some custom-made vegetarian *meze*, the formality between us evaporated. She was twelve when her parents divorced and she moved with her Swedish mother from Athens to Stockholm. Her mother went into the tourism business, but died when Mistral was still at university. After that she made up with her father. Perhaps to console her, I told her about my own family drama. She left out her love stories, and she did not show me a picture of her boyfriend.

Mistral planned to stay in Istanbul until December 29, without an intense working plan. I took her the next day to visit Galata and we had lunch at the Tower. Discovering that she was a good listener, I showed her the sights of the dis-trict point by point from the Tower's panoramic perspective, as if I wanted her to get to like the place. I was certain that the small-time shopkeepers were whispering that I'd found another expensive prostitute, and the neighborhood women were gossiping about how the cat at last had caught the mouse.

On our way back from the Samatya neighborhood, whose name was unchanged since the foundation of Byzantium, she said she wanted to meet my family. She managed to impress everybody – kissed my grandmother's hand, made my mother laugh with something she whispered in her ear, and teased Hayal in German. I knew what I would be put through after this short visit. Straightaway, my grandmother issued her orders: 'This girl is an angel, my son. Marry her as soon as she converts to Islam and changes her name to Ayşe,' and Hayal teased me, saying, 'The woman of your life came to your feet.' I squelched her, however, with my reply, 'She has a boyfriend, I believe.'

Mistral and I met every day. I took her to the Princes Islands and Yoros Castle, to second-hand sellers of history books. I was never bored when I was with her. I moved past her physical beauty and was overwhelmed by her inner world. I assumed that she knew how I felt. I narrated scenes from my travels to her, and in return was treated to obscure Palaeologan anecdotes. We conducted 'irony competitions', watched movies and documentaries at my apartment, cooked and washed dishes together. We were as relaxed as two people with no expectations of each other could be.

On the morning of the 29th of December I took her to the airport. The day before that we'd wandered around the Covered Bazaar at Selçuk Altun's suggestion and stopped in at a place called The Blue Corner. In this mysterious little shop I caught her looking at an antique gold Ottoman necklace called an 'Armudiye', for the pear-shaped gemstone on it. I bought it secretly, and gave it to her as she was about to board the Stockholm plane. Her eyes opened wide and she said, 'What are you, some kind of aristocratic character escaped from a romantic novel?'

MU

Although there were lots of weighty books on Iznik ceramics – an overrated topic in my opinion – there was no comprehensive history of Iznik itself. Established as the capital city of Bithynia in the fourth century B.C., it served later as capital of the Byzantine Empire in exile, not to mention its role in the Seljuk and Ottoman empires. The city was enriched by monuments memorializing five civilizations and was shaped like a helmet turned toward the East as if its feelings were hurt by the West.

The basic tenets of Christianity were first laid down in Iznik – which was then Nicaea – when the Roman Emperor Constantine I called the First Ecumenical Council in the year 325. My sources did not go into detail about the precise venue of the Council, the more sensitive ones merely speculating 'perhaps the emperor's palace was used for the meeting.' Although various authors referred to Samuel settling in Iznik because of its nice weather when he stepped out of his father Noah's Ark for a break, nobody even hazarded a guess about where the emperor's palace might have been. Those experts I asked for help found my questions out of place. The most tangible assistance came from a second-hand bookseller named Püzant (in Armenian it means 'Byzantium'). I met him through Selçuk Altun. After speaking with some officials at the Patriarchate, he informed me that the palace had stood on the south shore of the lake and was probably now beneath the waves.

I once visited Iznik with Eugenio when I was at high school. It was a one-day excursion on a calm Sunday in November. For the three miles of ancient walls Eugenio used an archaic Turkish word, *mukavim*. I was then too shy to ask what it meant, which was something like 'robust'. Eugenio not only spoke Turkish better than anyone else, he used to show off by embellishing it with old but meaningful words. I liked the walls because they turned the city into a toy town. The intense greenery, however, was about to take over the historic texture like an undefined brush stroke. I liked the persimmons, too, that hung like lanterns on the short trees surrounding the houses.

When I combined what I read in the books with my impressions from that early trip, I conceived the idea that any clue I might find at the Haghia Sophia church or the Nilufer Hatun *imaret* – mainly a soup kitchen for the poor – would lead me to the palace. We climbed into a minibus as a team. To Askaris, who was hunched over beside me, I said, 'For this fourth clue I'm supposed to find a place that's not even mentioned in the history books. I hope Nomo hasn't screwed up.' All he did was to bow his head.

We pulled into Iznik on a misty January morning. (What I first liked about the city was its population of only 22,000 souls.) Although it was a weekday, there wasn't much action on the streets. The town looked like a quiet park, with the inhabitants trying to conform to the image. I got out of the vehicle now and then to make little discovery tours, but it wasn't clear whether I benefited from them: was my motivation the pleasures of tourism or a semi-conscious expectation?

The buildings still standing inside the walls were in dimensional collaboration. None of them threatened the town's panorama. Among all the churches, fountains, theaters, cemeteries, mosques, tombs, hamams and medreses, I was most impressed by the minarets. Since they were not in competition to see which could be tallest, they avoided scraping the sky and were holier for the fact. I learned that originally the town and the lake did not bear the same name. Lake Askania resembled a blue-gray blanket on a deserted piece of land. The cool serenity proceeding from the thick green canopy of the town reminded me of Sparta. I thought that owing to all the historical turbulence it had to endure Iznik had been endowed with a long term of living in a cocoon. I hesitated a while and then decided that the aroma dominating the atmosphere was that of burned fig. The silent men who filled the low-ceilinged coffeehouses looked like they were expecting news. If someone told me that they were agricultural extras in a 1980s soap opera, I would have believed it. They appeared totally unaware that they were citizens of one of the twenty most ancient towns on earth. But if they couldn't name the three historic churches within walking distance, they at least maintained an upright posture. This refinement, stemming from simplicity, was also a characteristic of the inmates of the local monasteries before corruption set in.

Nilüfer Hatun, a noble lady of Greek origin, was the mother of Sultan Murat I. The *imaret* he built in her name had since 1960 hosted the Iznik Museum. The way they displayed artifacts of civilization from prehistoric to Ottoman times was so perfunctory that it killed the appetite to see any more of the museum. The Islamic tombstones and Roman sarcophagi in the garden impressed me, however. I watched a small mob of children playing hide-and-seek among them and thought that if I could record this on video, I could show it in every biennale around the world. As I expected, there were no clues awaiting me here. Feeling like the first man in history to leave this charitable institution empty-handed, I rejoined the team and we continued on to the church of Haghia Sophia.

When an earthquake demolished this ancient church in the sixth century, the Emperor Justinian built a new one in the same place. All the Byzantine emperors-in-exile were crowned here, in this place that looked to me like a giant prayer room. Some time after the Ottomans conquered Iznik they converted the church to a mosque; the conversion was carried out by the master architect, Mimar Sinan, on orders of Sultan Süleyman the Magnificent. The building was now a skeleton, playing the role of a boutique museum. My point of reference in this isolated place was the mosaic floor. The two-thousand-square-foot stone creation bore an interesting pattern of geometric figures in pastels, dominated by the color purple. As I pored over the kaleidoscopic work stone by stone I recalled the reference books I'd read. Nearly all of them just recycled quotations; none presented any original findings. I needed new sources, not those old constipated histories. (Hadn't I learned a lot about the Ottoman world from reading Karacaoğlan's poetry?) The guard in the booth unwillingly gave me the phone number of a guide named

Sedat Engür. But Engür came readily when he heard that I was going to pay him a hundred TL an hour for his services. We met on the minibus. He was a retired history teacher but looked like a character out of *commedia dell' arte*. I asked a few questions to test his knowledge as well as to help exhaust his desire to talk.

If one ignored his mispronunciation of proper names, what he told me was more or less analogous to what I'd read. He narrated history with the sincerity of a storyteller, and in a musical tone besides. He squinted his eyes and his paragraphs grew longer and he rocked his upper body to and fro like a Koran reader. When I asked where the First Ecumenical Council was held, he was startled. I almost heard him say, 'Are you the police?' It was clear that he did not accept failure in the event of being asked a question to which he had no answer. 'People talk about a "council palace" or "council church" but nobody knows the address of such a place,' he said curtly, and mentioned disparagingly a local character named Üstat Reha.

The person he referred to belonged to an old Iznik family that had eventually moved to Istanbul. Reha read history in England and became an academic overseas. When he retired, he came back to Istanbul. But he always spent spring and summer in Iznik. He was a confirmed bachelor. Because of his claim that when it came to Iznik's history he was the most knowledgeable of all, the townspeople nicknamed him 'üstat', or 'master.' He swore that he would one day write the definitive history of the place, but since he was an alcoholic nobody took him seriously. As Sedat Engür rambled on about where the First Ecumenical Council might have been held, I cut him short and said, 'Will you please give me Reha Bey's address?' With a hint of gloating in his tone, he replied, 'He died two months ago.'

I went to the motel where Master Reha camped out when he was in Iznik. Had someone told the receptionist, Recai, 'Smile constantly!'? If I spent a night at this moldy motel, I could probably squeeze some information about Üstat Reha out of Recai, who had the looks of an accomplice. Motel Askania was an ugly three-storey building on the southeastern coast of the lake. It appeared to have been erected to sabotage the charming harmony between lake and nature – which was also true of all the other buildings thrown up in haste over the past fifty years. The old fellows in the lobby playing with prostitutes young enough to be their grand-daughters must have arrived in the jeep with Bursa license plates parked in front. Askaris and I rented two rooms; in keeping with Nomo regulations, the bodyguards and driver would stay at a neighboring hotel. We'd come to Iznik prepared for eventualities, with a suitcase each. Askaris said he was tired and took to his room, so I approached Recai.

Tucking a fifty-lira note into his jacket pocket, I said, 'My curiosity is aroused – they said that if you want to get to know Iznik, you can't do it without Üstat Reha.' He was probably arranging his sentences in his mind as his left eye took in the cash.

'Who doesn't know Üstat Reha?' he said. 'This is my thirteenth year at Askania. Reha Bey first stayed in this motel the autumn after I started. He usually remained from May to September. When he was sober he wouldn't talk, and when he was drunk nobody listened to him. If he was in good health he walked around the lake in the mornings and around town in the early evening. He drank at night and sometimes wouldn't emerge from his room for two days. He was a gentle man and they say he saw and knew a lot. He was always on medication of some kind – he told the waiters in the lobby that he was paying for the sins of his youth. At the end of last summer, before he went back to Istanbul, he gave a bag to me to keep. Inside it are notes on Iznik. I planned to pass it on to somebody else one day if I found anybody to take it.

'Hamdi the taxi driver was Reha Bey's regular chauffeur in his commutes. Hamdi came in November with an aluminum box in his hand; Üstat Reha had died in a European city I never heard of. In his will he asked to be cremated and his ashes cast into the lake. Right after that event a myth went around town. It seems that the ninety-year-old ancients who'd never opened their mouths before now began to claim that Üstat Reha's forebears were not really Muslims but Christians who converted.'

This exposition was followed by two shallow anecdotes about the Master's scholarliness and generosity. Likely Recai was after another tip as well as getting rid of his custodianship of the bag.

'Do you want to see the bag?' was his question, as I expected it would be.

'Yes, okay, why not?' I said, trying not to appear too eager.

Inside the green cloth bag was an Aquascutum briefcase that contained two folders and a thick Venetian notebook with an ornamental cover. On the first page was written REHA EKIN in black ink. Two arrows drawn over it intersected in such a way as to say: Read this in reverse. NIKE AHER. The words moved me. 'Nikea' was the Greek form of 'Iznik', and 'Her' was a shortened version of the town's first known name, 'Helikore'. Even if Reha Ekin was not a real person, or if he failed to present a useful clue in the thick journal, I was sure to find an intriguing life story. One of the folders contained maps and pencil drawings of people and historical buildings; the other contained notes in English and the chapter-by-chapter outline of a proposed book. My soul was overwhelmed with a near-orgiastic excitement. I respectfully closed the briefcase and slipped a hundred-lira note into Recai's pocket that he pretended not to notice.

We went to the nearest fish restaurant as a group. To annoy Askaris I invited our driver to join us. All four ordered catfish. I called them sharks with feet. It was amusing to see the Laz driver gazing at me with piteous eyes as I ate my vegetarian meal of salad, yogurt and toast. When our coffee arrived I said, 'Gentlemen, I'm going upstairs to review a couple of local sources, but we all know that's not going to be much help. My feeling is that this may well be our last supper together.'

*

I knew Recai would give me Reha Ekin's room with the lake view. Quickly I laid out the contents of the capacious briefcase on the table. The notebook was more of a yearbook than a diary. The ex-resident of this soap-scented room, after offering family information on the first six pages, gave a condensed narrative of each of his years in three pages or less.

Every ten years he stuck a photo of himself to the top right corner of the related page. (I compared him to the young Franz Kafka and the old Constantine Cavafy.) The yearbook was written in black ink and fluent English. But his language, which he'd perfected at university, began falling apart in the last fifty pages. I finished the notebook, after two tea breaks, at 2 a.m. (I read once in somebody's diary that this was the hour when most people died.) I mentally summarized what I'd read.

When the Ottomans finally captured Iznik, the Vatatzes, the city's most aristocratic family, converted to Islam. (According to the Byzantium family tree, we could actually be relatives.) But it was a false conversion. Their aim was, first, to preserve their wealth and, second, to preserve the town's Byzantine heritage. (I learned incidentally that people who were Muslim in name but Christian in essence were called crypto-Christians.) The last of the Vatatzes, Sefa Efendi, moved to Istanbul with his wife and daughter in the twentieth century because he feared developments in the War of Independence. His son Reha was born in the winter of 1932. He had great expectations of this fragile boy. On the advice of his favorite teacher at the English High School, Reha went off to Scotland to St Andrews University, which was founded forty years before the Fall of Constantinople. He planned to study history in accordance with his father's wishes.

During his early days at St Andrews, his depressed sister committed suicide. His discovery of his homosexuality the following year was the first breaking point in his life. His demanding father expected him to marry and continue the

Vatatzes bloodline as well as to write a book on Byzantine Iznik. Sefa Bey learned that his son was a homosexual the year the boy graduated from university, and kicked him out of the house. Reha pursued a PhD with the secret support of his mother, and worked in London at the Research Institute for Byzantine History. He failed, however, to complete his doctorate and lived through several short-term unhappy relationships. The day before his thirty-fourth birthday he received news of his father's death, which was synonymous with financial relief.

The second breaking point of his life was the moment he met L., five years later. L. was as handsome as the Roman Emperor Hadrian's lover Antinous of Bithynia, and fifteen years younger than Reha. And fond of luxury. To make him happy Reha started selling off the Byzantine icons and jewels that were considered the sacred trust of the Vatatzes. Without his mother's knowledge, of course. L.'s wish was to live like a princess in the fleshpots of the world. Suddenly one day, leaving his older lover behind, he ran off to Nice with a new boyfriend. Reha Ekin was unable to cope with this and took to drink. Three years later, when L. came back, Reha was so ecstatic that he didn't much mind that L. had AIDS. To pay L.'s medical bills Reha sold off his priceless manuscripts of Iznik history to the Research Institute, for which he still worked. His method was first to make photocopies of critical documents and then show them to trusted friends. L. in the meantime was deteriorating rapidly and began pressuring Reha to kill him. One night in the sickroom, when Reha had reached the bottom of a flask of cognac, he smothered his lover with a pillow. Then he fell into severe depression when L.'s family, conforming to their son's wishes, buried him next to his French lover, who had himself died just after transmitting the AIDS virus to L.

The next year Reha retired and returned to Istanbul to live with his mother. When he was sixty-four his mother died in her sleep, leaving him all alone on earth. He tried to rearrange his life on a London-Istanbul axis. He also went into rehab and managed to reduce his alcohol intake somewhat. If, as the last Vatatzes, waiting for death was his destiny, his one wish was to write a book titled *Byzantium in Iznik*. He had done the research. But whenever he tried to start the book his hands shook, his head hurt, and his struggle with his memories began anew. He had an army of chronic illnesses to contend with, led by congestive heart failure. His summers in Iznik were therapy, but turning into the town fool was the last straw.

At seventy-seven he had nothing left to sell except the house in Şisli where he lived. He sold it to a man from Azerbaijan and went to stay with friends in London. On his last visit to Iznik he became erratic in taking his medication. The four final sentences of the thick notebook were in Turkish: 'I will go to Nice. I will visit L.'s grave every morning. I have no friends except exhaustion. A meaningful end is my right too.'

I read the Turkish paragraph twice; the certainty that it was written in this room disturbed me. I stood up. I needed to strip away the exhaustion caused by reading something that was autobiography, crime novel, travelogue and erotica all at the same time. I went out on the balcony – which made me think of a pilot's cabin – and focused on the lake, with odd expectations. From the vantage point of a curtain deliberately left open I had peered into a secret chapter of a life that ended in suicide. I could not respect the love affair of Reha Ekin, who savored the pleasure of deceit up to his last breath. On top of everything else he had, for L.'s sake, become a murderer – though I had some doubt whether the motive was wholly love. I changed my mind about drawing an analogy between Nice and Nikea.

I took only the map of ancient Nicaea from the files, which were a researcher's treasure chest. Reha Ekin had enlarged the map and included the modern name of each monument as a subtitle to the original Latin. On this map the 'Council Palace' was situated between the lake and the restaurant where we'd dined. Which meant that the twelve-foot-high pillar still standing at that point on the shore was not a part of the city walls, but perhaps the last remnant of the palace. This clue jibed with Sahaf Püzant's information. If they were not intending to wreck things, Nomo, as the last owner of the Vatatzes manuscripts, might have placed the fourth square on that column.

The next morning as I paid the bill I gave Recai – who did not ask for the bag – the tip of his life. After breakfast we walked along the coast road to the pillar. The team had probably noticed that I was in an expectant mood from the expression on my face. But what about the lake, whose waves were gradually growing larger. Was it becoming worried? I felt my way stone by stone around the weary ruins of the palace that was acknowledged as one of the most sacred sites in Christianity. Then I carefully reached for the fourth purple square that awaited me high on the eastern face of the pillar. I knew Askaris would be happy to see me come back with something in hand. I reminded myself of my decision not to be curious any longer about who put the magnetic piece there.

The team was as excited as a gang of roulette players as I inserted the purple square in the silver box. The fifth stop would be the Tokali Church in Cappadocia. They applauded like they were cheering a winning amateur bingo player. I shot them a dark look. Their company was beginning to bore me. I released them until the end of March, using the harsh weather of Cappadocia as an excuse.

I put Reha Ekin's journals into a plastic bag as soulless as a shroud, added two good-sized rocks, and tied it tightly. As I hurled them into Lake Askania, in the wake of their author's ashes, I composed a cheap graffito: 'Passion isn't deathless, it's lethal!'

NU

Back at home I had an uneasy feeling. Was something out of place in my house or missing from it? It looked like somebody had trespassed while I was gone. I squeezed some grapefruit juice for myself and collapsed on the couch I'd inherited from my grandfather. I forwarded greetings from their Iznik cousins to the Byzantine and Ottoman buildings standing shoulder to shoulder in the panorama before me. While cracking the last ice cube between my teeth, the identity of the anarchist messing with my life dawned on me. It was Mistral Sapuntzoglu, who had left behind her a bouquet, of whistles, fragrance and warmth. When I realized this, fresh memories of Mistral rolled over me. I began reliving the hours we spent together and searched for hidden messages in every sentence of hers that I could remember. I was starting to miss this young woman who could effortlessly attract any man she wanted at first sight. Had a fit of sluggishness overtaken me? I found myself dozing off at every chance, or else sitting alone for hours with the melancholy pleasure of yearning.

When my family began to treat me like someone with latent depression, I decided to share my secret with a person of experience. I met Madam Olga, my knowledgeable procuress, at the Londracula Bar. I might have compared her to a high-school principal except that she was counting her prayer beads. To gain citizenship she had married her Turkish assistant. She spoke fluent Turkish. From her authoritative treatment of the waiters I deduced that she at least partially owned the dimly lit place. It made her happy that I wanted to share my troubles with her. I told her my story, concealing only Mistral's name and profession.

'Madam Olga,' I said. 'There's a young woman I can't get out of my mind. I don't know whether she has a lover, though I assume she does. This crisis commenced two weeks after the girl, who thinks of me as a friend, went back to her home country. She's got a beautiful face and an inner world too. If I had to choose between them, it would probably be the inner world.'

She answered in the comfortable tone of a fortune teller. 'Beautiful women with real personalities are lonelier than men usually think they are, my sultan. So if you're looking for a cure, go after her. Even if this young lady's got a regular boyfriend, maybe she can be rescued from a boring relationship by that thing called love.'

Had I not listened to her I would have been sorry to the end of my life. A winter trip to Stockholm might just add a new dimension to the excursions that Nomo kept assigning me. Before making reservations I went to the Internet, where I learned that Mistral still lectured in the Department of Classical Archaeology and Ancient History at the University of Stockholm. It didn't occur to me until I sat down to reserve a seat on the Stockholm flight for February 14 that it was Valentine's Day.

There were a total of three people in business class. I was glad to see so many empty seats. For four days I'd had a runny nose and a cough. Despite all the medicine and vitamins my cold was not improving. I slept until we landed at the airport with a poetic name, Arlanda. The taxi driver who took me to Stockholm, twenty-five miles away, was named Nedim Arapoğlu and he came from the small town of Kulu in Central Anatolia. In his mid-forties, he had the physique of a retired wrestler, was moustache-free, and chatted cheerfully in accent-free Turkish. After the army he'd married a relative's daughter and moved to Sweden. They went back to Kulu to pay their respects to the old folks every summer. He was a regular at Friday prayers and fasted during Ramadan, but was faithful to his drink as well. His daughter worked at a hair salon and his son Muharrem – who would kiss my hand out of respect when we met – was in high school.

I'd noted that the university campus lay between the airport and the city, so I told Nedim of Kulu I wanted to stop by the Archaeology Department on the way. The harmony between the horizontal brick school buildings and the woods in which they were scattered pleased me. The Archaeology Department, which we found after questioning three passers-by, looked like a chemistry lab. Nedim knew that the giant fruitless plant in the garden was actually a wild cherry tree. It was Saturday and there was no security guard at the entrance, not even one. I strolled quietly through the deserted building. When I came across Mistral's name on a list pinned to a bulletin board, I caressed it.

A light snow began to fall as we left the campus and headed to the city. The car's thermometer registered an outside temperature of twenty degrees Fahrenheit. While driver Nedim droned on and on about how 20,000 of the

30,000 Kulu natives who'd emigrated to Sweden settled in Stockholm and how the city's population was now up to 2 million if you counted the suburbs, I was hatching an action plan. He did not fail to add that the Turkish colony called him 'Arab'. As I stepped out of the taxi in front of the Sheraton I said, 'Brother Nedim, I want to discuss a personal matter with you, tonight if possible.' I knew my homely sincerity would surprise him, like an unexpected gift. We agreed to meet at eight o'clock in the hotel lobby. The snobbish receptionist gave me a room on the fifth floor with a lake view. It was a relief to find that none of the buildings in the panorama filling my large window were constructed during the recent century. Another pleasure was the difficulty in determining whether the body of water bracketed by bridges was river, lake or sea. I swallowed the last of my medicine and crawled into bed. At seven I woke up and went down to the soulless restaurant to fill my stomach.

Nedim Arapoğlu arrived on time and all dressed up. We sat at the bar and I talked about Istanbul and myself until he grew used to the environment, then I plunged into my request.

'Nedim, my friend, I came to this town because of an ache in my heart,' I said to this nice man who avoided asking personal questions. Looking at his face, I realized that I was probably exaggerating Mistral's positive qualities, but I went on. I needed to profess my feelings for this girl. But I didn't know whether she already had a lover, and it was against my principles to ask her this question directly. I could have tried doing a bit of research at that small university building, but there was the risk of running into Mistral herself. And besides, I had no energy because of this wretched cold. Now, if I gave him her address, could he possibly do some checking around for me in her neighborhood and get back to me with the vital information? That is to say, I was prepared to pay him one-and-a-half times his normal daily earnings if he could reserve Monday for this job.

'For work leading to such an obviously auspicious conclusion, I would not ask for more than I deserve, my friend,' said Nedim. We planned to meet again on Monday evening at six o'clock in the lobby to assess the situation and then proceed to his house for dinner.

I was gradually pulling myself together. While eating breakfast on Sunday morning I observed the American and Japanese tourists, who accepted no boundaries in their sight-seeing. While the Americans were living the pleasure of each moment, the Japanese appeared to be dutifully carrying out their jobs as tourists. It wasn't snowing and I toured the city in the taxi of Tarik from Sarajevo.

I imagine one of Stockholm's missions is to imply that heaven may be a boring option. Its buildings were not engaged in a contest for beauty or size. Winter precautions were in force on the streets; no traffic jams were to be seen nor car horns to be heard. I saw no queues, either on the streets or in the buildings. Needless to add, there were no beggars anywhere. In this city exempt from visual pollution, I didn't see even one partially rusted garbage can. The designer's touch was revealed in the weekend dress of these urbanites who moved, annoyingly, as if they were models prancing down a catwalk. I wondered about the incidents that caused them to burst into laughter – maybe the flawless mechanical order of which they were components honed the edge of their responses. Meanwhile I thought about how Istanbulites refreshed their joy of life by fighting against a new and different kind of infrastructure problem that popped up every week. My Sarajevo taxi driver, who had read every Yashar Kemal novel translated into Swedish, informed me that in order to deal with the monotony of life in Sweden the Stockholmers took refuge in detective novels. I was delighted indeed not to find any global masterpieces in the city's museums: thus the imposition of fashions and names upon the people was avoided.

A couple passed by me arm in arm as I ducked into a coffeehouse for a break. The tall beautiful girl walked triumphantly close to her shorter, unhandsome boyfriend. I took the sight as an auspicious omen. I had dinner at a pizzeria close to my hotel. Later, as I sat in the hotel bar with a Sudoku book in my hand waiting for sleep, an immigrant prostitute approached and suggested a massage in my room. I sent her away, this hustler who was trying to tempt me into betraying Mistral. Ten minutes later I saw her walking to the elevator with an eager Far Easterner. I laughed at myself; Mistral could be in her lover's arms at that very moment.

The next morning I went to a second-hand bookshop with a skeleton in reading position in its window and bought Freya Stark's *Rome on the Euphrates*. After that I stayed in the hotel until my private detective showed up. Nedim began his report with, 'My friend, I have not brought you bad news.'

'I found somebody I knew on her street and asked questions of somebody who knows somebody who knows her. Your lady does not have any boyfriends so far. People say good things about her. She lives alone, and for the last ten days she's been hosting her father who is visiting from Athens …'This news gave me the reassuring feeling that I'd covered half the journey.

As for Nedim, he lived in a suburb whose name I couldn't remember, near the airport. Having agreed to meet his family, I arrived at his house on a street that looked so portable as to make one wonder if it was real. The neighbors were mostly from the Balkans and Somalia. His wife had a name as complicated as mine and worked at a bakery. I presented a bottle of perfume to his ceremonially dressed daughter and pressed a hundred-euro note into his son's pocket as he kissed my hand. The claustrophobic living room achieved a kind of primitive kilim design out of the fusion of Anatolian and Scandinavian furniture. I was apparently a good reason for the Arapoğlu family to cheer up, for they exhausted me with their hospitality. We laughed throughout the night and exchanged big hugs on parting.

I asked Nedim to keep the next Tuesday open for me too. According to his intelligence, Mistral's father dropped in at the Butterfly House café in Haga Park every morning at eleven o'clock. This botanical garden was situated across from the university and not far from Mistral's house. I needed to meet Costas Efendi from Edremit.

My tour of the 230-year-old park was cut short by the Imperial Cemetery, which reared up like an oasis of ice. Among the small buildings the most charming, according to Nedim, was the tent that was the Ottoman Pavilion. The Butterfly House, wherein a tropical climate was re-created, looked like an aquarium made of sailcloth. Inside it hundreds of butterflies freely and amicably came and went among the guests, perching on them at will. All manner of beautiful native bird and fish species were displayed there also, like objets d'art. I was sure they resisted eye contact with humankind.

The one customer at the Butterfly House café was Costas Sapuntzoglu. He looked like Omar Sharif. It may be that he was trying to balance his eighty-year-old looks with his youthful beige suit as he disinterestedly turned the pages of a magazine. I gravitated toward the table next to his while Nedim went out to ring my cell phone once or twice and hang up. I took a peek at Costas as I supposedly talked to my mother – loudly – on the phone. I cut my imaginary conversation short; Costas looked up and said, in Turkish, 'Hey, son.' Two words in Turkish were enough; we pulled our tables together. My cap and reading glasses were a kind of disguise.

I started off by giving my name in reverse, and told him that I lived in Hisar and taught at Boğaziçi University. I was in Stockholm for research. It was clear from the way he chewed on his lip while listening that he was eager to spill his life story. Although he understood Turkish, he preferred to tell it in English.

His question, 'What was the most grievous mistake that Atatürk ever made, in your opinion?' startled me.

'Dying too soon?'

His voice shook.

'The population exchange between the Greeks of Turkey and the Turks of Greece.' He used the Turkish word for the exchange – 'mübadele' – and as he did, he sounded like a small child unable to say 'bogey-man' without trepidation.

'After the Holocaust, the greatest crime against humanity is to compel people to leave their homeland. Nobody had the right to uproot us from the Aegean that was bestowed upon our ancestors 3000 years ago!

'I was born in Edremit the day before the Republic was declared. I wasn't even a year old when we got to Athens in 1924. In those days the Greek situation, like that of the other Ottoman minorities who were involved in business, wasn't so bad. We spoke both Turkish and Greek at home, like with the other exchange families. I was the spoiled boy since I came along after three girls. Until my father's stroke, the whole family would visit Istanbul every other year. We had Turkish and Armenian friends there, in Pangaltı and Büyükada, who were closer than relatives. The yearning of my father, mother, and two oldest sisters for the homeland lasted all their lives. My youngest sister and I respected their feelings. Our trips to Istanbul would not have ended if I hadn't lost her last summer.

'I graduated from a California beach city university in six years and started working at a maritime company in Piraeus. My life was pretty irresponsible; I had a weakness for women. My mother pressured me to marry the flighty daughter of a hotelier, but it only lasted a year. I was fifty-two when I married Anna, my daughter Mistral's mother. She was twenty-four years younger than me and working as a guide at the Mediterranean branch of a Swedish tourism company. She made me chase her quite a long time. But I wearied her. We divorced when Mistral was finishing middle school. The two of them moved to Stockholm. My daughter visited me in Athens sometimes during the summer holidays, and it was always agony when she left. She was at university when her mother died of cancer. After that she went to live with her pianist grandmother, who died four years ago. After Anna died, my relationship with my daughter improved. God be praised, she's turned into a lady and a very bright scholar. It made me happy that she broke off her flirtation with that widowed professor. Now my one desire is to be able to love my daughter's children when they come along.

'I live in Athens with my middle sister's widowed daughter and spend summers with Mistral. Winters, if she calls, I come. She says her work-related stress dissolves when I'm around. It's like a joke, to know you're good for something after eighty ...'

He enjoyed the attention, and asked questions about my parents. When I said that my father was an American and my mother a Turkish-Greek-Georgian combination, he said, 'Well, kid, it seems that you're a less pure Anatolian than I am.'

He asked if I would sing an Istanbul song for him before he left, but said okay when I proposed a poem instead. I picked a section of Bedri Rahmi Eyüboğlu's 'Istanbul Epic' that I especially liked:

Just say 'Istanbul' and I think of
A basket full of reddish-colored grapes
On a fine evening at Şehzadebaşı
A girl walks by, ruthlessly female
Three candles on top of the basket
I would kill myself for her attitude
Taste of grape honey on her full lips

Desire filling her from top to toe
Willow tree, summer breeze, harvest dance
Surely she was born in a wine cellar
On a fine evening at Şehzadebaşı
Once more the keel of my heart
Runs aground on the rocks
Just say 'Istanbul' and the Grand Bazaar
Comes to mind the Algiers March
Arm in arm with the Ninth Symphony
A perfect bridal suite a splendid dowry
Only the bride and groom missing
For sale cheap cries the auctioneer
And in the corner a pot-bellied oud
Bedecked with mother-of-pearl
Tamburî Cemil Bey on old 78s …

As I came to the last two lines Costas of Edremit grabbed my arm and said in Turkish, 'For God's sake, stop.' He stood, took his coat and cap with the initials AEK written on it, wrapped his turquoise scarf around his neck, and left me sitting there. Just before the door he stopped, flung his right arm up and, without turning back, walked out very slowly. It was pure drama.

*

At the end of the street that ran in front of Mistral's house Nedim and I kept watch in his beloved Volvo, which he called 'my little black donkey'. It was seven in the evening and a reluctant snowfall had begun to fall, the kind my grandmother used to describe as 'sifted through the finest sieve'. A minibus pulled up before the three-storey house and an old man emerged from it. A *sirtaki* tune wafted from the open minibus door as Costas came through the garden gate to welcome him. The two laughed and embraced and danced briefly to the tune shoulder to shoulder. This little scene lasted three minutes, during which the deserted street seemed to warm up a bit. The minibus drove off and the two old Greeks continued to sing.

We were eating our sandwiches when a small jeep pulled into the spot the minibus had vacated. Mistral climbed out from the passenger's side and I tried to shrink down into my seat, dropping my water bottle. Both of her hands were full. Whatever she said to the woman in the driver's seat made her break into laughter. Ten minutes later, when the lights on all three floors had come on, I asked Nedim to call her cell phone, say 'Wrong number,' and hang up. I wanted to be sure she had it close to her. Then, simultaneously invoking the names of all the Byzantine emperors in turn, I composed a text message for her:

> You swept into and out of my life like a comet and my head is still spinning. I missed you so much I followed you here. At this very moment I'm across the street from you in front of the florist's shop. I'll count to 1001, and if you will come down to me, I'll whisper to you the words I've been saving for the woman of my life …
> H.A.

I read over what I'd written twice and felt embarrassed both times. I was sure my head would begin hurting as soon as my hesitant finger hit 'Send'. I waited in the snow, but Mistral did not even bother to come to a window and look out to see if I was really there. Nedim understood that my gambit had failed from the way I stalked, sulking, furled umbrella in hand, back to the car, mortified as a host shamed in front of his guests. On our way back to the hotel he said, when he'd finished grumbling, 'Listen. If this girl of ours is as perfect as you've painted her, maybe she's a lesbian.' I had to smile. At the hotel we exchanged addresses. He spoke first.

'It's not without reason that they say something good always comes out of something bad. You're a fine gentleman. I hope it's your fate to be happily married to a good Turkish girl. I haven't yet seen a Turk marry a Swedish girl and be happy.'

'If I hadn't come to Stockholm and declared my feelings for that girl, I would always feel like something was missing,' I said. 'I thank you for your help and hospitality, Nedim. It was a good side effect of this visit to get to know you. Please pass along my regards to your family. I'll call when I get my return flight straightened out. If you're free, you can take me to the airport.'

I didn't go in immediately but stood in the freezing cold weather for some time as if, I suppose, I was taking a meditative shower. Then a voice from inside me warned, 'Come on, don't show weakness, Your Excellency Constantine XV. A more majestic finale awaits you.'

XI

When discussion turned to my sensitive skin and nature, my grandmother never failed to say, 'Just like his grandfather.' If I changed my shaving cream my cheeks would turn red; and every feeling that I bottled up inside me would turn into a sore in my mouth.

When I got up the next morning I had a sore the size of a baby aspirin on the tip of my tongue. Just drinking water was painful. Actually this was the first time the condition had surfaced since I'd made up with my mother. Now I felt stunned, like a victim running into his torturer again. It was probably because of shame over a move seriously unbecoming a chess master. If sending a syrupy melodramatic message to a woman newly met was what was called love, well, I could deal with that. Besides, I had a ready-made excuse for why I could not seduce women. It was because my forefathers married according to order; that is, if somebody caught their eye they only had to issue an order, and voilá! With this sentence I suppose I've accounted for why I hired expensive whores for my lovemaking.

If Karacaoğlan were in my place he would say something like, 'We had nobility when we set out / But we lost it on the way.' I had to smile. I decided to drop in on Elsa in Venice. I hoped that she would say, 'So are you an unmitigated blockhead, or what?' when she heard what had happened to me. It wasn't enough to change my mind when I learned that she'd taken off for Melbourne to celebrate her father's seventieth birthday; I determined to fly to Venice anyway the next day, via Rome. I'd already made reservations for five days at a hotel with a long name.

After breakfast I went to the Stockholm municipal aquarium to rest and watch the big fish peek out and sneer at mankind. And I wanted to have a look at those buildings stacked up like barricades on either side of Gamla Stan, which refused to abandon the Middle Ages, before going home. I made a move to chase some accordion tunes wafting through the deserted street, wondering who was the musician. But I turned tail and went straight back to my hotel when a platoon of aged tourists walking like wound-up toys hove onto the scene.

Feeling a great sleep coming on, I focused on Freya Stark's Anatolia-loving historical travel book. That night I brought in two immigrant prostitutes to give me a massage. In the morning I set out for the airport without calling Nedim from Kulu.

*

I found the Westin Hotel Europa and Regina an appropriate name for a hotel that was born with difficulty out of the merger of two private palaces. I didn't smile when the receptionist, a friend of Turkey, said, 'We saved the best room for you.' Suite 106 overlooking the Grand Canal had a noble ambiance. I remembered the aphorisms I'd written in honor of Venice during my student days when I was trading winks with my neighbor across the way, the Church of Santa Maria della Salute. I'd never shown them to anyone, even Elsa.

If you say, 'Venice is the earthly corner closest to heaven,' you may be doing it an injustice. Are you sure that heaven has mystery?

Do you wonder why the protective water encircling Venice evokes glass? If so, it means you didn't notice that the city is inside a glass jar.

Every year 14 million tourists pour into Venice. Only five out of a thousand visit the Museo Correr and its original art works. The other 99.5 percent beleaguer the city with pollution of sight and sound. The city may be paying for its past sins.

Will you go out at night to explore the streets of Venice? Can you slip between the fog and the echoes with the agility of a gondola?

Venetians never take off their masks. They laugh secretly at the tourists who think they wear them only at carnival.

I spent a while thinking that the best thing to come out of the mess Nomo had made of my life was meeting Mistral. The next morning I set out on a tour to renew memories and strengthen old ties with Venice. What immediately struck me was how I had gradually become an advocate of Byzantium. In the architecture of palaces and other landmark buildings on the water the Byzantine influence was obvious. I tried to visualize similar buildings on the shoreline between Sarayburnu and the Golden Horn. They had nearly all been destroyed – with Venetian support – by the hooligans of the Fourth Crusade. My feet took me to the Church of San Marco, the garish copy of Haghia Sophia. At the top they'd put the Quadriga, the Four Horses sculpture stolen from the Hippodrome at Constantinople. I went up close. A plate beneath read, 'Brought from the Conquest of Constantinople.' In fact the Venetians worked hard at their plunder, stealing whatever was light in weight and heavy in value. I had an odd feeling, here before the most famous horses in the world. It was like running into some of one's own people now forced to work in an international circus. Their innocent looks hurt my heart. They seemed to know who I was, and expected me to take them home. I wondered what punishment Constantine XI had thought fit to mete out to the Venetians in return.

The last charismatic European emperor, Napoleon, deemed the San Marco Piazza the most beautiful living room in Europe. There I visited the Museo Correr. The Marciana Library enjoyed the glories of both a palace and a temple and boasted ceilings as ornate as a church's. The bibliophile and collector Cardinal Bessarion (1403–1477) donated to the Marciana all the manuscripts and rare books he'd acquired from the Byzantine scholars and artists who scattered across Europe after the Conquest of Constantinople. Basilios Bessarion was a monk from Trabzon whom the Emperor Joannes VIII appointed metropolitan of Nicaea when he was having trouble convincing the Orthodox community to join the Catholics. Basilios took refuge in the Vatican and there was raised to cardinal-hood. But I couldn't bear looking very long at those Byzantine documents collected by that apostate bibliophile. What went through my mind was that I'd paid good money to admire the jewellery stolen from my house and now on display in the thief's window. I withdrew into a dim room full of antique globes of the world. I watched the guard dozing on his chair, swaying like a potential soothsayer who hasn't filled his quotient of prophetic dreams. I circumambulated the spheres until closing time and found my favorite cities hiding in time tunnels. My judgment of Venice: you were the most advanced city-state in the world, but instead of becoming a far-seeing diplomat you devolved into a pocket-picking shyster.

*

The waiters at Harry's Bar played a considerable part in its status as the most expensive bar-restaurant in town. Besides remembering my favorite salad dressing, they were skilful humorists. This time, however, they did no more than greet me. After dinner I went to my room and watched the emptying-out of vaporettos at the stop on the opposite shore. I descended to the dim bar in the lobby. I wondered how many times the pianist had exhausted his routine stock of commercial songs. I intended to read Attilio Bertolucci's *Viaggio d'Inverno* with a dry martini for an escort. The barmaid wore a tag on her breast that said 'Intern' and dropped my drink while handing it to me. I said, 'It's all my fault' to the bartender who came running to see what the crash was about, and the intern looked at me with pity. I will never solve the riddle of women. I was draining my third drink when Eugenio called on my cell phone. Believing I was in London, he asked me to bring his favorite tea, which could only be found at Fortnum and Mason.

'But I don't think I'll be back for three or four weeks.'

'Then you can bring three or four packages.'

The sarcastic exchange raised my spirits. I saw an attractive middle-aged woman approaching. 'When I hear a sentence in Turkish, I greet the owner,' she said, and I invited her to sit down.

Wendy Sade had been a teacher at Üsküdar American Girls' School twenty years ago. She was in Venice chaperoning her cellist daughter, here to play a concert with the rest of her string quartet. I couldn't sort out what Wendy of Boston really did other than work as a freelance translator.

Still, when she whispered, 'Are you abandoned or abandoning?' in my ear, the charismatic woman was almost sure that I would spill my guts to her. I began my narrative like a character in a pop song: 'If a man is going to be abandoned, he first has to have a lover. I was eliminated in the previous stage: the proposal.' Instead of answers or diagnoses from Wendy I wanted to hear comic prognostications, as though she were a crone of a fortune teller who'd chanced to come my way. By rights the night ought to end with a witty remark or two, after which I should go out and hunt up a prostitute.

'Wherever did you get the idea that not answering a text message means "No". The Brazilian soap operas? Believe me, you'd have been rejected with a sentence if she had negative feelings about you. This young woman is quite possibly just waiting for the right opportunity to call you.'

'Wendy, until that development occurs, may I call you Aunt Pollyanna?'

'It's nothing to me, young fellow with the unusual name. But if some day you do manage to marry the girl with the beautiful name, send a plane ticket along with my wedding invitation.'

The card she left on my table said that Wendy Sade was a literature professor at Florida State University. (Did I know this spirited professor, whose name sounded like a pseudonym, from somewhere else?)

I met the morning in Venerotica. To gain admission to this nightclub, where male clients wore masks, I first had to meet a one-legged pimp on the Rialto Bridge, and then follow him for ten minutes.

On the day before carnival began, I moved on to neighboring Ravenna, which had served as Byzantium's representative in Italy from the sixth to the eighth centuries. I stayed at the Hotel Byzantio and visited the churches trying vainly to compete with Haghia Sophia in the field of mosaics. I found traces of Constantinople in the Piazza del Popolo; and I realized that I'd had enough of Byzantine relics here in this town where my fellow citizen, Basilios Bessarion, exhaled his last breath. I don't really know why, but I flew to Nice – the city of Reha Ekin's suicide – and grew bored with its spa-camp atmosphere in two days. I then dropped in on Seville, merely because a retired sea captain said, in the lobby of Le Meridien, 'The worst thing that can happen to a man in Seville is to be born blind.' I picked Lausanne, which was suffering an invasion of aged tourists, by personal lottery. Because the first letter of its name happened to be 'H', I went to Hamburg. The reason for Nantes was its last letter, 'S'; and for Liege, its five letters. I read all six volumes of Edward Gibbon's *The Decline and Fall of the Roman Empire*, and returned to London. There I reunited with my team. Askaris did not find my thesis that historians would make good dream interpreters funny. When my grandmother phoned on the morning of March 6 and posed her sarcastic question, 'Spring is coming and where are you, son of a worthless American?' I was busy making up my calendar of work at the Research Center for Byzantine History.

OMICRON

I felt like the keeper of a lighthouse stuck in the middle of a valley. I was at a rock hotel at Uçhisar, the highest point of Cappadocia. Suite 234 of the Cappadocia Cave Resort had probably been carved out by a Hittite family 4000 years ago. For the umpteenth time I stood by the window to inhale the view of the fairy chimneys filling the panorama. I listened to the silence of the rock and thumbed my virtual prayer beads as I focused on the chimneys one by one.

I don't believe that the conical masses people call fairy chimneys erupted 25 million years ago from the volcanic mountain range thirty-five miles away. That's as dubious to me as all those pages of official Byzantine history. Or maybe the volcanic mountain that threw them out vanished into thin air afterward, like an octopus dying after giving birth?

When I was in high school, the fashion was to liken the fairy chimneys to Indian wigwams. But now I regarded them as shamans assembled to perform auspicious ceremonies. They'd kept their real colors from the photographers, which I thought was an act of poetry. I felt the sun's respect for this melancholy rainbow of colors. The valley imposed its rules of silence on humans, minarets and the zoo of animals in the Hittite reliefs. If I asked, 'Why didn't other volcanoes create such artistic lava?', it would be a trick question.

The valley that from my hotel window looked like a messy

table top, up close looked like an exhibition sculpture. I don't believe either that the word 'Cappadocia' came from the Persian and meant 'land of beautiful horses'. Only a camel would do as a metaphor for this sea of silence.

Cappadocia lay between the first civilization, Mesopotamia, and the city-states of western Anatolia. The Hittites came down from the Caucasus and settled in this strategic corridor. Official history skipped the fact that they were art teachers to the Greeks. It's also interesting that historians cannot agree on the dates of their rise and fall. They rivaled nature in sculpting and were more accomplished in this field than any other civilization. Maybe it was this rivalry that did them in, as they went extinct by famine in the seventh century B.C.

First it was the fundamentalist Christians banned by the Romans, then the eastern Christians fleeing from the Arabs, and after that the Byzantine Christians frightened by the Iconoclasts who took cover in Cappadocia. There, by patiently carving out the conical rocks, they made many a monk's cell, monastery and church. They even hollowed out underground cities where they could hide from pagan armies.

My expedition to Cappadocia lasted two days. The valley was as full of mystery as a chessboard made up of an unknown number of squares and pieces. Here, for mortals, nature modeled the divinity of silence and the wisdom of patience. I felt myself growing lighter as I walked, like a hot-air balloon slipping its ballast. I wondered how many holy places there were thousands of years ago if there were only 300 of them open to tourists today. The biblical stories in those claustrophobic caves were as vivid as if they had been inscribed a thousand days ago. In fact, those dim places didn't need a lot to be ready for an evening Mass. They looked like they might have been sending a message to the massive and over-ornamented churches of Constantinople.

In the Göreme Open Air Museum, standing at the door of the Girls' Monastery, a seventy-year-old American woman ran her hand over the fairy chimney and said, 'Why is the surface of this monolith so soft? It feels like it would crumble if I pushed it hard. Can it really be 20 million years old?'

Her dried-up husband, in shorts and sleeveless T-shirt, who would have been a contender in the Ugly Old Age Pageant, said, 'Well, honey, if you consider that alligators have been having a good time in our fresh water for the last 200 million years, maybe these cones could actually use some more time.'

The million tourists who come to Cappadocia each year prefer spring or fall. They're mostly elderly Christians from all corners of the world, plus a few quiet Far Easterners. Some of them unconsciously want to fulfil a religious duty before passing away. As they zigzagged among the fairy chimneys they lit up like country kids taken to an amusement park in late childhood.

The outskirts of the valley possessed the quietness of a desert or inland sea; in the far corners the calm belonged to a cotton field or an abandoned farm. As the owls saluted the sunset Cappadocia turned slowly into a deserted monastery, and this was excellent.

The Cappadocian grandmother of John Newberry, my neighbor at the hotel, was subject to the population exchange of 1924. When her family had trouble adapting to life in

Thessalonica they emigrated to Melbourne. John was a retiree and a widower. In honor of his grandmother's memory, he sat on his balcony admiring the view of Erciyes Mountain, cracking and eating pumpkin seeds one by one. He expressed amazement that I didn't know the Australian player on the Galatasaray football team, Harry Kewell, and I tried to win forgiveness by reciting a stanza written by his fellow citizen, the poet Les Murray.

On the second day the team and I went to the Ihlara Valley in the hotel van. The driver, Tahir, was a small man with a shining face. If I cracked a joke to him he would lower his head, embarrassed. Maybe modesty was a character trait left behind from the monastery phase of the place. I knew Pappas would be the first to laugh at my theory about the small size of the Cappadocians (so that they could take shelter in the fairy chimneys on the day before Doomsday).

The valley with the lyrical name, Ihlara, was a good thirty miles from the hotel. I was getting used to feeling like our road was taking us across the weary Patagonian plateau. Millions of years ago, when Hasandağ, killer of so many mountain climbers, exercised its right to erupt, Melendiz Creek flooded the fissures and probably prevented a camp of fairy chimneys from forming here. Ihlara was quite a mystical canyon, which was no doubt why, since the sixth century, so many hermit's cells, churches, tombs for nobles, and other structures were hewn from the rocky cliffs rising up from the stream.

We disembarked from the van at a point that rose 500 feet above the valley floor, where we could, as Tahir put it, be in command of the panorama and look down at the creek snaking along like a rope. As I stepped out, a ten-year-old girl materialized in front of me. Apparently her faded T-shirt and cotton trousers did double duty as pajamas at night. The man's black jacket she wore over them – maybe for camouflage – was at least two sizes too big. She had fair skin, a long face, and bright almond-colored eyes. Her ancestors might well have included a Byzantine beauty who sought refuge in the valley a thousand years ago.

'Welcome to Ihlara,' she said.

'Thank you,' I said, 'And is your name as pretty as your face?'

'It's Naile.'

'Naile, what in the world are you doing on top of a mountain all by yourself?'

'I'm a guide.'

This got a laugh, but Naile didn't seem to mind, maybe because she was used to the reaction.

'Well then, our young guide, tell us how the Ihlara Valley was formed.'

Naile brought her two feet together and turned toward Hasandağ. In a charming tone she made an impressive presentation parallel to the guidebook's. Listening to her, I felt at once lighthearted and regretful for my delayed fatherhood, with no children of my own to enjoy. As I rummaged through my pockets for small bills to make up fifty liras, she told me that she would be a fifth-grader next year, and if she won a scholarship for indigent students, she hoped one day to become a teacher. She had some trouble extracting her right hand from the pocket of the big jacket.

'Why are you wearing that jacket in this hot weather?' I asked.

213

'My mother won't let me go around without it.'

'Well, that's curious. Why?'

'Because I don't have an arm below my elbow,' she said, and bowed her head apologetically. I felt a wave of pity for this young girl, who had lightened my spirits, more than for the primitive mentality of hiding a physical disability. I felt like a harsh wind had just stripped the petals from a rare and fragile flower as I stood admiring its beauty.

I had a quick meeting with the team. I borrowed half of all the money they had with them for half a day, added it to all the money I had in my pocket, and put two thousand liras in an envelope. I asked Naile where she lived. Her father was dead; she lived with her mother at her grandfather Hacı Ali's house. I put the envelope in the right-hand pocket of her jacket as we sat on neighboring rocks.

'Naile, please give my greetings to your mother and to Hacı Ali Efendi, and say this: "I helped out four gentlemen today. They liked me very much and sent this money with me for my education." And be sure to tell Hacı Efendi that the money was earned honestly.

'Say "The youngest of them is the boss and he grew up like me, an orphan. He has a small problem and he asked me to pray for him." He said, "Since you're a smart girl with a pure heart, God will accept your prayers." He said he would visit us when he gets his problem solved, and then he will see that my arm is fixed. He said he would pay my school expenses too, until I receive my diploma.'

I made her repeat her lines until she had them down. Pappas took our picture as I held her in an embrace. When I knelt to say good-bye, she put her good arm around my neck and burst into tears. My eyes were wet too. She said 'Thank you' and disappeared behind the rocks, bounding down the path like a young goat.

If I thought that Pappas wouldn't seize the occasion to pile on compliments, I would have said, 'I'll never make an emperor even in exile, will I?' We walked back to the van and I recalled to him the lines by Cahit Sıtkı Tarancı, the poet who actually died when he was forty-six: 'Thirty-five years old and halfway down the road.'

'Meeting Naile was a breaking point for me,' I said. 'It reminded me that I'm thirty-four. It's time for me to get married – by next year – and start loving my own children.'

*

After a long but pleasurable slalom down the hillside, we came to the floor of the Ilhara Valley and sat for lunch at an open-air restaurant next to the Melendiz River, which had been reduced to creek category by old age. The valley had in the meantime become a universally acclaimed hiking preserve. The adjacent tables held European tourists who had just completed their tours. They were mostly middle-aged and wearing perhaps slightly exaggerated expressions of gratitude for 'mission accomplished'.

I started out on the hiking path from the village of Belisirma, a Byzantine leftover. Our destination was the Yılanlı Church. We followed the winding path, keeping the Melendiz on our left. The coyly flowing creek and the birds singing in whispers bolstered the mystical atmosphere. At every step the botanical scene shifted, with a different kind of tree in our path. The braggart poplar and willow trees stood like an army of spears, yet despite them the most attractive plant of the valley was the oleaster trees, which gave off a subtle scent. I felt a lightness in my being as I trailed a flock of butterflies as small as bees. A feeling of peace suffused the place.

The Direkli Church that popped up on our right was not on our agenda, but I couldn't resist its challenge. I gave the order to climb the rocky path. The church, which at first appeared to be a spacious cave, was carved out by exiles fleeing the Iconoclast controversy. The artist who painted the biblical frescoes on the ceiling must have splashed them on in two hours and run away. The thin pillars, narrow chapels, and tiny nooks squeezed in here and there around the place made me feel like I was on a Noah's Ark lowered down below ground level.

I wanted to shout 'Open Sesame!' when I came to the apse with a Judgment Day fresco inside its dome. A little later I felt a sudden trepidation – was the dagger-shaped piece of plaster dangling from the narthex a bad omen? I smiled and moved on, my mind trying to figure out why wild animals didn't move into these untended caves. Heading back down the path, Pappas slipped and fell, and I helped him up, whispering in his ear, 'I'll have to ask Nomo why they put a potato sack like you on my trail.'

We continued walking energetically in an eastern direction. The path carried us along like an anonymous poem, without a single line slipping into the margins. The afternoon was advancing; hardly anybody else was out, only a swaying group of Japanese coming back from their tour.

A lot of churches have frescoes of Saint George slaying the anti-religious dragon or serpent, and so are called 'Yılanlı', 'snake' churches. The reason why I chose the Yılanlı Church in the Ihlara Valley was that I wanted to see the picture of Christ sitting with crossed legs. And I was curious about the twenty-four saints representing the twenty-four letters of the Byzantine alphabet.

We went on walking east. As the afternoon matured, the presence of nature grew less emphatic. We crossed to the left side of the creek over a bridge that resembled an overturned boat. The climb to the Yılanlı Church seemed to be developing into a bit of a challenge for the team. It was actually a cross-shaped chapel cut from the rock in the ninth century. I liked the anarchic feel of it as I wandered around with my flashlight. Christ was not only sitting on the floor with his legs crossed but also had the irritated look of someone caught by paparazzi in an unofficial pose. The twenty-four saints, each representing a letter, looked as perplexed as suspects in a Hollywood movie, put in a line-up to face the victim. The biblical stories on the walls gave off a kind of animated movie warmth. According to my guidebook, the winged devil behind a Christ-figure was saying, 'Son of God, invite me to your holy supper tonight.' The last image carried a warning: it was a woman who would not give suck to her children being bitten on her breasts by two snakes. I said to Pappas, 'Don't you think this place looks like a bar abandoned because the owner couldn't find a bartender to work for him?' He laughed.

I delivered the good news that the expedition was over. We were walking back toward the small bridge when Askaris suddenly leaped on me, shouting, 'Excellency, look out!' We fell to the ground together as a man on the rocks above the church fired three times at us with a pistol. The sound of the bullets sailing over my head was lyrical. Kalligas emptied his own miniature revolver in return, but Askaris opined that by then the shadow wearing a black ski mask was long gone.

I picked myself up from the dirt and said to Askaris, 'I can't extend my thanks to you, Askaris. But I can say that you didn't do a bad job of administering the Nomo test for courage.'

*

My third day in Cappadocia. Three is the magic number in fairy tales. But it was not a good sign that I thought about this. Was something more ominous waiting for me in the land of fairy chimneys? Well, I didn't care even if there was. I was getting bored with this chess game I'd been sucked into. Perhaps the 'Stockholm syndrome' I couldn't get over had something to do with it.

It was impossible to see the sunrise because of the forty or more hot-air tourist balloons polluting the sky. I couldn't imagine the excitement levels of the people in those brightly colored balloons that could hang in the same place for half an hour. But I was sure they cared little for the poetic side of their flame-powered ascension. I took breakfast in my room and waited for the first wave of tourists to clear the churches. I opened *Ba*, by the poet Birhan Keskin.

As the noon *ezan* filled the air we were just about to enter the Göreme Open Air Museum, which encompassed the

Tokalı Church, which resting quietly behind its retaining wall, symbolized the holiness of Cappadocia. Inside the ninth-century space I discovered the mysteries of both a cave and an underground sanctuary. The Tokalı Church frescoes were like oil paintings compared to the etchings and cartoons in the other eight churches. It was almost like the Tokalı art was apologizing to the Bible on behalf of the other stuff. With their lapis-colored backgrounds, the sacred frescoes appeared as if in a divine exhibition catalogue. George Seferis thought they constituted a visual narrative of the whole Christian epic.

Besides me, there was an elderly British couple in the church, speaking in whispers. Like me they were patiently examining the walls and ceilings with their flashlight. I was all alone when I found the purple square. It was waiting for me at the table of 'The Last Supper', in the middle part of the fresco that was just where the church dome met the wall. It was ten feet up from where I stood, but it didn't take me long to find a way to get there. I took the silver box from my bag and held it just below the tableau. It took about two seconds for the purple square to descend, like the word of God, into the box and nestle perfectly into its repository. Across from it these words appeared: 'Haghia Sophia, Constantinople.' I shut the box, muttering, 'Of course it would surprise me if there were no Haghia Sophia in this Byzantine mosaic puzzle.'

I didn't immediately leave the Tokalı Church. I was a little uneasy at reaching the happy ending so soon. Was it the winged devil I'd met earlier in the Ilhara Valley who pointed my flashlight to the supper gone unfinished for the

PI

Did the last square, the one I took from the hand of Judas, contain a message? If there was a traitor on the team, Nomo had a duty to eliminate him. I loathed the idea of drawing up a list of candidates from my closest circle. But long live intuition! I remembered a list my father once made up that I'd seen among my grandfather's rare books. But now I couldn't find the thing, which, as I remembered, looked something like a mosaic puzzle with embroidery. Were I a character in a novel, I lamented with a smile, I could easily find it and extract secret clues from it.

I marked two chess tournaments in the southern hemisphere for the month of April, and I was about to register when Nedim of Kulu called. His voice was tense.

'My dear friend,' he said. 'I have things to tell you, but first you have to promise me you won't get angry.'

'Come on, Nedim,' I said. 'What could you have done to make me angry?'

'Listen, my friend. I liked you from the minute I laid eyes on you. To me you're like an angel. After we said good-bye, I didn't sleep well for two days. I decided to go see the lady professor who broke your heart. I went to her office at the university and apologized for intruding and asked for ten minutes of her time. I told her how we'd trailed her for two days and how serious you were about her. I swore that you knew nothing about my visiting her. "Miss Mistral," I said, "if you think my fellow citizen is not worth his salt because you don't know him well, that would be making a big mistake. You won't find another honest man like that anywhere, not even heaven. If I hadn't come here to tell you this, my conscience would give me trouble every time I pray." I thought she would be surprised, but it was me that was surprised when she started laughing.'

"You have a nice name," she said. "What does it mean?"

"It means 'close friend' in Arabic," I said, "And my last name is Araboğlu, 'son of an Arab'."

'She looked at me and said, "Ah, you Turks." Then she said, "Look, Nedim, I'm a half-fellow citizen of yours by way of both Anatolia and Sweden. I'll tell you a secret if you keep it to yourself. Back in January I discovered that I've got a serious medical condition. While you two were trying to check on me, I was suffering depression because I couldn't find a way to break the news to my father, even though I'd invited him from Athens for that purpose. It's the same disease from which my mother died. From here on, I'm afraid, I'm going to be busy fighting for my own life."

'My good friend, I liked this Mistral for the way she broke this shocking news. The poor girl is brave and mature. I told her, "If your illness is something that you can beat, I'm sure you will, by the way you talk about it. I'll pray for you and if you need a taxi, your fellow citizen Nedim is at your service."

'She called me a time or two and I took her places even if I wasn't on duty. Yesterday we picked up her father at the airport. He broke down when he heard about his daughter's condition, but pulled himself together when we got to the hospital. Still, he cried all the way there. I could hardly hold back the tears myself. Three days from now Mistral is going to have a complicated operation at the university hospital. She's got nobody on hand to help keep her hysterical father calm. Costas Efendi doesn't know Swedish, and his Turkish isn't good enough for me to be of any use. Besides, in Sweden people avoid asking each other even for a spoonful of salt.

'If you're not too busy, would you please pick up and come right away? It will cheer the poor girl up to see you with her father before the operation. Plus, she'll see that you're not just a fair-weather friend … '

I felt worse and worse with each sentence. And I was angry with myself for sending her that message and causing extra pain. I jotted down the details and said, 'I'll come immediately. Meet me at the hospital and meanwhile don't leave them alone.'

For some reason I had the idea to call Askaris. I gave him the particulars about Mistral's operation. Although I'd never spoken about it, it was clear that he knew all about the 'Mistral adventure' – probably more than I did myself.

'What can Nomo do for a Byzantine historian on her deathbed? I would really like to know,' I said and hung up.

*

It was the middle of spring and Stockholm was a dream-like city whose landscape of delicate pastels hues looked as if it might vanish in a cloud of dust if somebody just blew on it a bit. It was nice to think that I could find rest if I walked around the sleep-inducing streets long enough. The inhabitants of Solna had apparently taken an oath to keep silent if only Karolinska University Hospital was put in their suburb. From a distance the complex looked like it was made of Lego blocks. I supposed the interior design would be straight out of an IKEA display room.

Nedim of Kulu and I embraced at the main entrance. 'You've brought good luck, my friend,' he said. 'They've added the country's top surgeon to the operating team.' I had an instant vision of Nomo entering the picture. The team included a nurse named Halime who was, coincidentally, also from Kulu. This *zaftig* woman unaware of recent developments assumed that I was Mistral's fiancé. According to her account, in mixed Turkish and Swedish, the patient was set to undergo an operation of two and a half hours minimum on her uterus. As she pronounced the dark sentence – 'Even if she survives, she'll never have children' – her eyes were touched with pity for me. She repeated my assignment to save Mistral from her hysterical father; she would come in ten minutes to take the patient to the operating room.

I pushed the door of Room 527 open a few inches. Mistral looked pale and exhausted, her eyes fixed on a point on the ceiling. Her father was crying at her bedside. It didn't take long to figure out how to change this tableau: I remembered Costas Sapuntzoglu's fish mania. I whispered two lines of 'Istanbul Epic' in his ear:

When someone says 'Istanbul,'
I think of an enormous fish net.

He looked at me. His weeping stopped and his lips quivered.
I stood and continued reciting lines replete with the Greek
names of Istanbul fish:

> One section a rusty spider web
> Stretched tight at Beykoz
> Another one sagging at Fenerbahçe
> Forty blue tuna in the net
> Turning like forty millstones
> When you say blue tuna you mean
> The king of fish, blue tuna
> Shot in the eye with a hunting rifle
> Trees in the sea turn upside down
> The fish net a bowl of blood
> Clear turquoise water murky now
> In the blink of an eye forty blue tuna
> The fisherman's tongue twisted in joy
> A seagull lands on the mast to swallow
> The chub it caught in mid-air
> And flies away without waiting for more
> Her name he says is Marika
> Like this she always comes and goes.

When I paused Costas threw his arms around me and said,
'Where did you come from, son of Galata?'

'Costas Baba, my business here isn't yet finished. After I
met you I met your daughter and we became almost friends.
I was told that she needed surgery, so I came to see if there
was anything I could do to help.'

Then I took him by the arm and handed him over to
Nedim, who was waiting outside the door. I sank down in

the chair next to Mistral's bed. I wiped the sweat from her forehead with my hand. She was too weak to say anything, but her eyelids fluttered.

'Doctor Sapuntzoglu,' I said. 'You're going to be operated on by the best surgeons in the country. In case you didn't notice, the number of your room is 527, which, let me remind you, was the year that Justinian the Great assumed the Byzantine throne. I'm not leaving either you or your father alone until you get well. And since I might not have another chance, let me apologize for the wrong message I sent you at the wrong time.'

Trying to smile, she lifted her right hand and closed her eyes. Her face was as glorious as a goddess's. I couldn't help myself – I brushed her cheek lightly with the tip of my finger. It would not be easy to remove her from my life. As they rolled her gurney to the elevator, Costas Baba fainted. The doctor revived him and ordered him out of the hospital. I sent him to his daughter's house with Nedim, and promised that I would stay with Mistral until she recovered.

The operation lasted three hours. Costas Baba called me every hour on the hour. The surgeons removed Mistral's uterus and ovaries and decided that was enough. They said it would take a day for her to recover consciousness. I told Nedim to explain the situation to Costas when he brought him to the hospital. As they emerged from the elevator everybody rushed toward each other for a round of embraces.

'I have good and less good news for you, Costas of Edremit,' I said in Turkish.

He answered in English, almost scolding me, 'Don't tell me that my daughter is saved but crippled, Galatian!'

'Your daughter is saved, yes, but she can't have children. But you can accept me as your grandson if you like. I'll be glad to call you Grandpa.'

'I wish I had a son-in-law like you,' he said, loudly, and I put my arm around him again.

'Your daughter deserves a better man than I. But don't let that stop you from loving me more than your son-in-law.'

I sent Costas Sapuntzoglu home again. It was late afternoon and I was sitting in the hallway, about to start Henrik Nordbrandt's *Selected Poetry*, when there was a sudden flurry in Mistral's room. Halime rushed up, saying, 'There's a complication – what's your blood type?' My type was a match, but they needed more. We called Nedim. 'The whole Turkish nation has Positive blood,' mumbled Halime.

For two days I spent half my time guarding Mistral's door. I loved seeing her gather strength. It was like a gardener watching his plants grow. I adapted to the hospital lifestyle, reading when things were peaceful and greeting patients and their kin in the corridors. On the morning of the third day Halime joined me.

'Brother, I was unfair to you,' she said.

'Why do you say that, Halime?'

'I thought you would abandon your girl when you heard that she couldn't have children. One bad side of Turkish men is that they see women as breeding machines. But I see how you treat her. You'd donate an organ if need be. Well, if you're thinking, "Not without a child," you can adopt one. It's a good thing to do; and besides, they're more grateful.'

I was too worn out to explain the real situation to Halime. Or maybe I was afraid she would scold me. Two hours after that the doctor on duty announced that the patient could see visitors. I called Costas, but worried that he might faint again on the way. I drew Nedim aside and said, 'I don't want to be here when Mistral wakes up. She might think I have expectations and feel compelled to reciprocate.'

'What can I say?' he replied. 'You do think about everything. May God give you what you deserve – I hope one day you'll be the president of our country.'

We clapped each other on the shoulders and said goodbye once again. I tucked the equivalent of four days' wages into his coat pocket. I had leave from Costas to go, having told him I would be back after a rest. I paid the miscellaneous hospital fees and had baskets of flowers sent to Mistral and Halime from the first florist I ran into, then went back to my hotel.

The Serbian taxi driver who took me to the airport the next morning told me that the ideal time to visit Stockholm was July. The locals go south to the warm countries, he said, and leave the streets to world travelers. I was about to crack a joke on the lines of, 'Nothing would bring me back here but the Nobel Prize for "Inability to Attract the Woman of One's Life",' but thought better of it. In the first place his English wouldn't be up to it; and secondly I saw that, with his jellied hair, he resembled the bust of Alexander the Great. My unfortunate paternal grandmother was a Serbian, and I didn't want to start a marathon discussion of the ins and outs of my genealogy. My past was a labyrinth trying to swallow its last turn.

*

From London I flew to Sao Paolo, named for Saint Paul of Tarsus, a town in southern Turkey. Guarulhos was not an attractive name for an airport, which was shaped like a somnolent beehive anyway. The taxi to the Intercontinental Hotel smelled of vanilla; I wondered what it was meant to cover up. I was surprised that the driver, Sandro, didn't ask where I was from. When he noticed me admiring the huge and lazy marketplace, he tried to introduce the town to me in broken English.

'Sao Paolo was founded in the sixteenth century … it's the most modern town in Brazil … its population is over 12 million …'

He studied me a while in the rear-view mirror, then started briefing me on the town's sexual offerings. His English improved.

'Mister, would you like to have a girl even better looking than the ones you see in the Carnaval at Rio?'

'If they speak English I would like to have two of them, Sandro.'

I did not assume that the mulatto girls would be familiar with their prominent national poet, Machado de Assis. I was pleased that the one with yellow nail polish asked me where I came from.

'I'm from the country where the saint who gave his name to your country was born.'

The one chewing gum said, 'You mean you're from heaven?'

At the Intercontinental I entered a chess tournament composed of four groups. By beating my six rivals I became number one in my group. Together with the three other group champions I flew to Ushuaia by way of Buenos Aires.

In earth's southernmost town – a quiet place – we took on the champions of an equivalent tournament in Lima. I was beaten in the final match by a retired fireman, Vlad Godunov from Saint Petersburg. Too late I saw through the stammering Russian's strategy, but by that time I remembered where I'd put my father's list.

It was Selçuk Altun who found for me a signed copy, in Turkish, of chess master Garry Kasparov's *My Masters*. The document whose turn it was to be decoded lay between the pages of the chapter on Capablanca. Whenever the topic of genius in chess arose, the name of José Raul Capablanca (1882-1942) was sure to come up. He learned chess when he was five and was watching a game when he died. He never practiced intensely nor cheated against other masters, as did his rivals. Instead of entering into a psychological duel with his opponents, he focused on his own attack. I compared his style to a lucid poem with not one extra line. I would take Capablanca as a model for my moves in the Byzantine labyrinth.

I enjoyed myself in South America until May. What did it mean that I received no messages, not even a 'Thank you', from Mistral? If Wendy Sade were around, she would no doubt say, 'She's remaining silent for the good of future developments.' My grandmother, on the other hand, would have said, 'That worthless Greek slut!'

RHO

The piece of paper I'd tucked into a book on chess history nine months ago, thinking it was merely one of my grandfather's idiosyncrasies, lay before me now, but as an idiosyncrasy of my father.

There was a single sentence in Arabic in one of the five triangles of a star drawn with a ruler. The other four triangles contained codes that were mixtures of letters and numbers. I solved two of them by shifting and shuffling the ciphers. I had to hold the Arabic sentence up to a mirror. But in three hours I was looking at five sentences. My father had probably hoped that a puzzle solver – preferably his son – would find the list. I arranged the decoded sentences in sequence:

Y.A.: The unpretentious man who practically begged me to marry his daughter, almost like he expected a savior in some mysterious intrigue.

A.A: Instead of an oriental aristocrat, I married an oriental witch.

My Son: On my father's account I suffered much. So that he won't suffer much on his own father's account, I entrust him to E.G.

Everything began with doubting the names.

I needed to take my indemnity.

— My grandfather, whom Nomo did not regard as

belonging to the Elect, lacked the respect also of his wife and daughter. But the Galata locals remembered Yahya Asil, who went bankrupt in all areas of his life, with a great deal of affection. I think that all he wanted, by marrying his daughter to a qualified man, was to obtain a promising heir to his exiled throne. His American tenant was a good candidate. Now, beyond the question whether Nomo had a hand in all this, there was another problem for me to deal with: if I could not achieve the status of the Elect myself, and learn what I needed to learn, I would fade into the twilight zone.

— The friendship between my father and Eugenio Geniale didn't surprise me. I wanted to get the Paul Hackett story from him, as well as a third-party interpretation of my father and mother's relationship.

— After discovering that I was Constantine XV, I figured out that my grandfather's and mother's names were Turkish rearrangements of 'Joannes' and 'Sophia'. If my father had solved the essence of these names without the help of clues, I should be able to get to the end of this road too.

— 'I needed to take the indemnity.' More than resolution, this sentence seemed to indicate the desire to fabricate an excuse. If my mother thought that my father had taken anything from the house on his expulsion from it, she would have reminded us of the fact repeatedly and with plenty of elaboration. So she probably knew nothing about this 'indemnity' of Paul Hackett's. If such was the case, it meant that my father wanted me to be aware of his point of view in the matter, if it ever came up.

I stood up from my desk and went to the balcony as the

late afternoon *ezan* started at the Bereketzade Ali Efendi Mosque, the first mosque to be built in the neighborhood after the Conquest. I looked across the Golden Horn to Stamboul, the heart of old Constantinople, and waited for an inspiration. I saw a curtain of fog wiggling and winking like an augur of glad tidings. Then a flock of loud cackling seagulls destroyed it. The nicknames of the members of my supporting team came to mind.

SIGMA

Not only did I get myself invited to dinner at Eugenio's, I imposed a menu on him. 'Do you want a belly-dancer too?' he said. 'No,' I replied. 'I prefer dancing with wolves.'

When I asked him to tell me about the relationship between my mother and father, 'Oh,' he said, 'I thought they'd gotten you to erase Paul from your book.'

I was glad to note that his tone grew more serious when he said, 'I knew your mother from her university days.' It meant he wouldn't be prejudiced. 'She was flirtatious and pretentious and used to hang out with the rich non-Muslim girls. Her nickname was "Princess". Unlike her father, she had business ambitions and was a go-getter. Yahya Bey probably spoiled his daughter because he saw this and liked it. I asked her once whether she wanted to be an MP from a right-wing party. "No," she said, "they can't guarantee a ministry for me."

'The Doğan Apartments were the preference of bohemian foreigners thirty years ago. When a British journalist I knew who was living there packed up and moved back to London, your father moved in. He was a sympathetic guy and knew enough Turkish to get by. The neighborhood put Paul down as a secret agent, but didn't mind because they figured he was fighting against the same enemy they were. He was intelligent and went on a lot of mysterious trips. He met your grandfather in a backgammon tournament. They took to smoking hookahs and playing backgammon at every opportunity. When a flat with a view in your grandfather's apartment building came up, Paul moved in and paid a symbolic rent. I was surprised to hear that he was flirting with your mother but didn't say anything, since he never asked my opinion. I knew the relationship wouldn't survive marriage. Your father tired of his job. He wanted to be a university professor of international relations. Yahya Asıl's son-in-law believed that would stave off financial trouble and allow him to remain in the city he loved.

'Princess Akile took off the carnival mask after the honeymoon and began oppressing her husband. In the sixth month of his marriage your father left his house and took refuge in mine. He'd decided to divorce her. Your grandfather acted as a go-between and they patched it up for a while, but the egg was broken. They lived like two strangers in the same house. Then you were born. Your mother tried to turn the job of caring for you over to the maid, but your father put his foot down. At the cost of his job, he became both father and mother to you. When your grandfather died, the relationship collapsed totally. Your father once said, "When her father was alive, Akile looked on me as the butler, but now she thinks I'm the maid."

'Your mother was a thin-skinned and jealous woman. I was considered your father's friend, but I had no idea that he was seeing a pretty Canadian secretary. Somebody sent a picture to the Princess of the two of them at a dinner party, and the expected result came to pass. He tried to see you several times, but your mother's devotees drove him away. Every year I sent him a photo of you that I took on the sly, plus a report on how you were getting along.

'To you I gave the message that I was always there if you ever needed my help, but a fragile orphanhood was never a part of your personality. You had fortitude. I always thought you were lucky to have inherited the best sides of your parents and grandparents.'

'What's the good side I got from my mother?'

'You're not full of ambition like her, thank God, but you're determined to reach whatever goal you set your mind to.'

So here was another question for the list I was going to present to Nomo, if I was ever admitted into their presence: why did you send my mother the picture of my father with his lover?

TAU

'Hello, big brother, where were you?'

'I was with Lady Jane, Mina, Yasemin, Priscilla II, Nevbahar and two dozen noble ladies whose names I can't remember, Hayal.'

'So you were at the race track.'

'If humans paid me enough attention, I wouldn't have to go to the horses.'

'I hope you won enough to buy me a Bulgari ring.'

'Iskender saved his skin, but just barely. I've been royally robbed.'

'That's odd, you've been royally robbed here too.'

'Little sister, can you explain that last sentence a bit?'

'Well, some dumb thief broke into your house and took a few silver picture frames, a silk rug, and your radio. Unfortunately he left behind that stupid bird named Tristan.'

'If anything happened to Tristan, I'd blame it on your evil eye, Miss Jealousy.'

'You better hurry home and do something about it, son of a worthless American.'

I stepped into the elevator, praying that this was not another insidious event in the form of a simple theft. Hayal popped out of the door, saying, 'I forgot my glasses,' as I opened it. I went into the living room, and thought I was going to have a heart attack. There, in the armchair next to

239

the balcony, sat Mistral. She stood up.

'Stay where you are, Mr White Knight. I'll give you a four-sentence explanation and a nine-line poem.

'When you ran off from Stockholm, I waited for you to get back to Istanbul because I had more to tell you than "Thank you". Hayal let me know you were back in town, so I came here with a poem. I hope you won't run away to Patagonia while I'm reading it:

> When someone says "Istanbul,"
> More mysterious than Byzantium,
> Prouder than an Ottoman,
> As friendly as Anatolia,
> Erudite but polite,
> Funny and shy,
> Handsome as a kingfisher,
> When somebody says "Istanbul,"
> I think of my beloved, Halâs.'

I stood stock still, frozen like a cat in the headlights. I thought of Wendy Sade, who was always right.

'Should I read the poem again, Mr Knight, or explain to you the lines you didn't get?'

'I'm busy counting to ten, Mistral. If in that time I don't hear another line turning this into a joke, I'm going to embrace you now and never let you go.'

*

My name is Halâs. In Arabic it means 'Salvation'. If you reverse it, 'Salâh' in the same language means peace, comfort, and devotion. This doubleness is like the symbol and soul of Byzantium, the double-headed eagle. Now if my grandmother doesn't find out that the Greeks call their country Hellas, I'll be thankful.

('soldier'), could be transferred to Greek as 'Askaris.'

'If it were Armenian,' he said, 'you would be quite right; but in Greek, definitely not.'

In my mind a light bulb lit up. I paced up and down in my room for several minutes and downed a double shot of malt whisky. I caught the first plane to London the next day. I needed to find my savior Askaris, but could only speculate about where he lived. During my training in London, Askaris mentioned Winchester a time or two. I would not have been surprised, actually, to find him living in this south-eastern district, once the capital of two kingdoms and now accommodating a population of 40,000 people. It was an hour from London by train. As a doctoral student I'd visited Winchester, which was home to Europe's tallest cathedral, and not been all that impressed. This time, as I strolled the streets crowded with native tourists, the shape and size of the buildings caught my eye. New ones constantly went up, but with due respect paid to history. As a result Winchester had acquired the feel of a storybook town. I felt like Gulliver waking up in Lilliput. Bored by the touristy atmosphere, I took refuge in the cathedral. Somehow I was not impressed by the information that Jane Austen was buried there. My head was swimming with silly research possibilities.

I thought I heard a voice say, 'Good day, young man!' I turned around with a frown. The 'Visitors Chaplain' – according to the tag on his chest – had perhaps singled me out as the most dejected visitor. I couldn't help thinking that he must be paying for some kind of mistake with this assignment. When I told him I came from Istanbul, he informed me happily that his brother-in-law had worked on the construction of the first Bosphorus bridge. At the end of our geographical conversation I asked the talkative priest how I might find an old acquaintance, possibly from Winchester, whose name I'd forgotten but whose picture I had with me. Gently squeezing my right arm, he said, 'The ageless waiter at the cathedral cafeteria, Alan Paxton, is your man,' and turned his attention to the obese couple who had just begun quarreling in front of us.

The heavy smell of meat emanating from the cafeteria enveloped the souvenir shop next to it. Lunch service had begun, and the early patrons all seemed to favor the same low-calorie items. The potatoes were evidently presented half-raw so as to match the color of the beef stew. The waiters were all over seventy and strutted around like wardens. Alan, as upright as an ostrich, was responsible for collecting empty glasses and trays. He surveyed the tables like a human periscope and immediately attacked the vacated ones. It was amusing to follow the action. Seizing the right moment, I thrust the picture of Askaris on my cellphone under Alan's nose. It was another Fellini moment. Alan gave a long whistle. After this overture he said, 'Nobody this ugly has lived in Winchester for the last seventy-four years,' turned on one foot, and waltzed away.

That was as much as to say that Askaris, with his perfect Oxbridge accent and sophisticated manners, was hiding in London. Back at the hotel, I called him on his personal cell phone and invited him to my favorite pizza place in Knightsbridge. I said that I'd come to London for the surprise birthday party of an old grad-school friend. I knew he would be a little apprehensive when I added, 'I have things to tell you.' He came into Il Pomodoro on the run. I knew he would relax when he heard that the subject I wanted to share with him was my relationship with Mistral. At that precise moment of relaxation I asked, 'So which Greek island would you suggest I take my beloved to on her birthday?'

'Rhodes,' he answered without a moment's thought. Then he added, stuttering, 'Santorini, Mykonos, Paros,' but it was no good.

Weeks earlier, when we were in Athens, Askaris had confided to me at the hotel bar that he'd spent an unhappy childhood on one of the Aegean islands. Immediately afterwards he apologized in panic. The event suggested something I could not put my finger on at the time. Apparently that heavenly venue was Rhodes. The time had come for me to visit the island to unearth the original name of Nikos Askaris. I didn't want to think about what the move might drag me into after that. My one hope was that I was dreaming all this up.

At nine the one-man orchestra at Il Pomodoro was about to begin his show. As I paid the bill I sought to put Askaris at ease. 'I think I should choose Paros among the options you offered. I just remembered that it was the favorite of George Seferis, the poet from Izmir.'

I sailed from Marmaris, in Turkey, to Rhodes on a tired sea bus. The Greek passengers looked like happily exhausted picnickers on their way home. When I was dragged away from Vladimir Holan's poetry by a snore, I shifted my attention to the family seated opposite me. The old woman wearing a headscarf and raincoat in the heat of June, fixing her eyes on the floor, made my neck sweat. I had trouble believing that she was headed to the island on the same holiday as her lümpen son, flirtatious daughter-in-law, and five-year-old grandson. Whenever the boat rocked through a series of waves, she would loudly say her prayers, which in turn caused the boy to break into laughter. His name was Candancan and he probably giggled more in these two hours than I had in my thirty-four years. His young mother, chewing gum 'like a clitoris riding a bicycle' in Iskender Abi's words, pointed to me and said to her unruly son, 'That man is a circumciser, you better behave!' The spiky-haired boy cautiously leaned toward me.

'Are you really a circumciser?'

'A circumciser and a king too!'

'Do you know the Lion King?'

'Whenever he sees me, he runs away.'

'Do you have a horse that gallops on the ocean?'

'I have a blue horse that gallops on the ocean, flies and turns somersaults in the air now and then. He's waiting for me where we're going. If you stay nice and quiet, I'll let you ride him when we get there.'

With Candancan glued to his seat, not to leave it again, I was quite amused to see the family peering at me with suspicion. When we arrived at the island he was in deep sleep on his grandmother's lap. I hastily left the boat before he woke up and was welcomed by Rhodes, with no magical blue horse. I was startled by my sudden assumption that I would fall in love with this island. There was a faint aroma of apricot in the air. I felt I was being pulled slowly into the scene by an octopus's tentacle. I chose the 'Splendid', in the Old City, as my hotel for its name. I compared the monumental locust tree in its courtyard to a dervish raising his hands to the sky. I wanted to sit under it and read Ritsos. But it would be impossible to make an action plan without taking my customary exploratory tour as soon as I got settled. It was a fine late afternoon. According to the receptionist, who assumed that he was speaking English with an urban British accent, I could enjoy the pleasures of the Old City because all the loud tourists were on the beach.

On the maps Rhodes looked like a giant leaf fallen on the sea. When that green mass met the blue Aegean, a bright yellow layer of earth came into being. If the castle on the hill was a shepherd and the warehouses on the waterfront the shepherd's dogs, then the groups of buildings squeezed in-between were flocks of sheep and lambs. The residents looked like aliens tired of waiting for a message that never arrived. They had Turco-Greek physiques and elegant postures. I walked randomly along the narrow streets free of souvenir shops. When the tourists started to come down to the Old City for their evening's entertainment, I continued moving through the avenues connected to each other by time tunnels. The urbanites leaving their offices zoomed down the streets in their cars. Every clock, inside or outside, told a different time. I would have believed it if somebody said that they'd forgotten to lift the blackout after World War II.

The taverns and cafés outside the tourist routes were filled with locals. In every bar I dropped into I saw primitive icons. The bizarrely literal translations into English on the shop marquees were almost tragicomic. This was the Turkish approach too, of course. The owner of the restaurant recommended to me was originally from Izmir and was named

Theo. He claimed that he could deduce my Turkishness from the way I sat in my chair. The Albanian waiter did not believe that I'd read a novel by their national author, Ismail Kadare. I tried to sound convincing as I said that I was combining business and pleasure when Theo posed the question, what was I doing all alone on the island? Mistral, for her part, thought I had an appointment in Rhodes with an Arab businessman.

I had breakfast early, then went the upper, Turkish, part of the island by way of the cool Sokratous Avenue. There were about 1500 Turks and thirty mosques still on the island. I strolled down the deserted cobblestone streets toward the coast. The low houses had gone unpainted since they were built and reminded me of dying Aegean mountain villages. I peeked through partially open curtains; the rooms were simply furnished. I eavesdropped on the gossip; it was the bookish Turkish of forty years ago. The best adjective for the attitude of the kids on the streets was 'melancholic'. I was overwhelmed by it all with a brief but intense feeling of ironic guilt.

Was I wandering through an open-air exhibition called 'The Charm of the Ruined and the Tired'? I concluded that the aim of the broken, rusty, cracked, torn, run-down, sunken, hollowed-out artifacts was to provoke an accounting in the mind of the traveler. Perhaps it was the low walls that time had harmed the most – I thought the mission of the ivy army covering them was to pull them skyward so they wouldn't fall down further.

I tried to remember who the Byzantine emperor-in-exile was when the Ibrahim Pasha Mosque opened for prayer in 1530. The architect had definitely taken into consideration the dimensions of the island's churches. An old man with a kindly face sat inside the grounds. He was probably waiting for the noon prayer in the place he hadn't moved from since the morning prayer. We said hello as I was on the way out: I was afraid even a three-sentence conversation would create a bond and then I would be in for his life story.

There were 'about a thousand' manuscripts at the Hafiz Ahmet Ağa Library – opened in 1793 – according to the library's best estimate. The collection of the Ağa and his son, Rhodes natives who rose to eminent positions under Selim III, was displayed in primitive conditions and left to the ravages of time. I remembered that two Koran manuscripts stolen from here had been sold at auction in London. The library, with its simple courtyard and outbuildings, was like the mansion of an exiled pasha. On a cushion in the shade sat a sweet-faced old woman who could have been a hundred years old. I would have bet that her family had been caretakers of these buildings for generations. At that moment a *ney* solo gradually filled the courtyard. It turned monotonous in ten minutes, or I would have stayed longer. As I continued along the labyrinthine streets, the case of the stolen Korans preyed on my mind. The back of my neck itched.

I felt a little relieved when I got a phone call from Theo, the restaurant owner. Over coffee the night before I'd asked him to find me an experienced English-speaking guide. I planned to put him on the trail of Askaris while I stayed in the background. I met Mikis for lunch at Theo's; he was a retired English teacher in his fifties and spoke like a machine-gun when answering a question. He was relaxed and charming. When I told him I was reading Odysseus Elytis, he asked, 'Are you really a Turk?'

In keeping with the image of a harried businessman who had to snatch his tourist sorties from his work schedule, I accompanied Mikis to the Walls of the Knights. I wasn't impressed by these fourteenth-century piles of stones. There was something about them that disturbed the harmony of the island. The Archaeology and Byzantine art museums – so-called – that we entered and exited were, in reality, little more than display rooms. The primitive quality of the icons and frescoes brought from Byzantine churches on the Aegean islands made me uncomfortable. The north coast of the island, where we drove in Mikis's little car, was infested by ungainly hotels for middle-class tourists.

By this time I was quite friendly with Mikis. That night, when the second bottle of wine was ready to be uncorked at Theo's restaurant, I had a flash of inspiration. I showed him Askaris's picture on my cell phone.

'Last month,' I said, 'as I took a friend around Cappadocia I ran into this fellow here. He told me he came from Rhodes. I don't remember his name now, but I was impressed by his knowledgeable and mysterious attitude. Would you happen to know him?'

If my assumption was correct that Askaris was a native of Rhodes, then Mikis ought to know him. They were about the same age and Rhodes was a small place of 50,000 people. In fact, when I asked Theo to find me an experienced guide my real goal was to increase my chances in this regard. Mikis took my phone for five seconds and handed it back.

'It's probably twenty years since I last saw him, but this is Yannis the Raven. He was four years ahead of me in elementary school. His mother was Greek and his father Turkish. To his alcoholic father and the other Turks he was Melik. He left the island during high school and came back only once, for his mother's funeral. Rumor had it that he was a professor, or a spy, or something like that. His father was a fisherman and died young in an accident at sea …'

'Well, this bit of information has raised my curiosity even more. If you could arrange a meeting between me and somebody in Yannis's family tomorrow, it would be worth the best tip of your life.'

Grapefruit juice, melon, white cheese, and two pieces of bread dipped in red pepper and olive oil constituted my breakfast under the locust tree the next morning. Mikis showed up with a grin on his face just as I was getting bored with the panting of the mischievous wind. It seemed, according to Mikis, that a man named Raci Cemal, who lived in Koskinou village fifteen minutes away, was a cousin of Yannis's father. We had an appointment to see the retired university teacher at five o'clock, after we came back from Lindos.

Lindos was a district on the eastern coast whose natural beauty was erased and historical richness robbed. It was, besides, blighted by innumerable sightseeing buses. Added to this was the interminable desert heat. We left hurriedly, without staying for lunch. We reached Koskinou after stopping for breaks in all the summer-camp villages along the way. The houses of Koskinou, which was apparently in eternal siesta, perched on a hill as green as fresh almonds and seemed to prostrate on command. I didn't see even a cat on the streets down which two people could hardly walk side by side. We came to a house with a garden at the end of a cul-de-sac. The elongated house in the midst of a grove of young olive trees looked like a caravan. Raci Cemal was probably in his seventies. His long white hair did not suit his rotund physique. He'd probably worn the same faded clothes for the last ten years. The house smelled of soap and was plain but tidy. He invited us into his study, where I was thrilled by the enormous library of scholarly and classical books. Raci Bey lived with his sister. She was a hunch-backed old woman – possibly owing to intra-family marriage – who tired me with her endless questions and offerings of food.

Raci Cemal had taken a PhD in sociology at the University of Minnesota and, until he retired, taught at rural universities. He confided that he never married because his dead mother had entrusted his sister to him; I hoped he would not refrain from giving information about his cousin Yannis. He'd started a novel five years earlier and planned to finish it in another five years. The title was *I Did Not Create a Character Able to Write a Novel Because He Won the Lottery; I'm Writing This Novel Because I Won the Lottery*. I told him the title alone was a poem. His sister, Rana Hanım, presented me with a white handkerchief she herself had embroidered with lace, and went out to visit her neighbor. She didn't fail to promise to call when she came to Istanbul. I immersed myself in Turkish conversation with our host, while Mikis pulled out a book of aphorisms in English. The more he giggled as he read, the more Raci Bey scowled. It was a standoff. Finally I managed to bring up the topic of Askaris – I'd met him in Cappadocia, he impressed me with his personality, I believed he lived on Rhodes, etc. I traveled to London often and therefore if I might get his address, that is if he had one, just in case, you never know after all, anyway I would be grateful.

When Raci replied that he hadn't seen his cousin since he'd come for his mother's funeral, I showed him the photo on my phone. He mumbled to himself and tugged his forelock. But it was against the rules of Turkish hospitality not to tell what he knew.

'My Uncle Arif,' he began, 'was a cavalier womanizer. He got the Greek spinster Tina pregnant and had to marry her. Tina was so ugly that there were jokes about her like, "She must have come out of the Byzantine palace." Two years after she had Melik, she and Arif split up. Melik stayed with his mother. Turco-Greek relations were more civilized on Rhodes than on the other islands, but still the Greeks saw him as a Turk and the Turks saw him as a Greek. I was his closest relative on his father's side. He wanted to run away from the island the first chance he got. He was hard working and ambitious and an introvert who read history books all the time. He lived with his mother and his blind aunt. They lived on money sent by his mother's brother, whom nobody ever saw. He went to live with this uncle when he started high school, and didn't come to his blind aunt's funeral. He did come back to the island for his mother's funeral, but that was twenty years ago. I was there. He was proud and withdrawn and cold to me. I wanted nothing to do with him beyond offering my condolences. He dropped English words into his sentences now and then, and his pronunciation made me believe he was living in England. I heard that he gave various answers to people who risked asking what he was doing nowadays. He'd developed a rude and shifty personality. I erased him from my books …'

'Raci, Yannis once told me his last name, but I don't recall it precisely. Was it Askaris?'

'You're very close. Laskaris.'

This was the name, unfortunately, that I'd come to Rhodes to hear. John IV Laskaris was the last emperor in the dynasty of Byzantine emperors exiled to Nicaea. He assumed the throne at the age of seven when his father, Theodore II Laskaris, died young of asthma. Michael, the founder of the Palaeologus dynasty, forcibly established himself as the young emperor's regent, then sent him off to a castle in Gebze, where he had the eleven-year-old boy's sight extinguished. I knew the story of the little emperor line by line. Michael's ruthlessness, in contrast to the tolerance John's grandfather had shown Michael, had always been an embarrassment to me.

What Michael did to the young emperor was not forgiven by the Byzantine people either. According to Russian sources, John Laskaris accepted his destiny, living like a saint and dying in exile. In *The Imperial Twilight*, which I accepted as the most inclusive book on the Palaeologi, the method of blinding the child emperor was described as the most 'humane' one: John IV's pupils were made to focus on the sun until darkness descended. However, the dissenting modern historian Michael Geanakoplos maintained that Laskaris in his adult years began to see again and fled to Sicily.

The business reminded me of the case of Cem Sultan. The kings of Europe, fearing the Ottomans, kept Cem as an involuntary 'house guest' as a precaution against his older brother, Sultan Beyazit. Similarly, the king of Sicily might have kept John IV under his thumb for a long time as a ploy against the Byzantine emperor, with whom he had frequent skirmishes. I expanded my hypothesis: John IV Laskaris was never able to regain his throne, perhaps, but he managed to marry and produce progeny, thus continuing the bloodline. And now the one wish of – probably – the last member of the family, who was also John's namesake, was to exterminate me and recapture the throne stolen from his many times great-grandfather. Nomo, who'd only just noticed this enterprise, was warning me without intervening. They too were helpless in the face of the 'divine justice' principle that was the cornerstone and dead-end of the Byzantine Empire. John Laskaris could help the Empire by eliminating me; therefore he should not be stopped. This kind of fatalism was a black hole involuntarily bequeathed to Byzantium by Justinian. Because Nomo would remain neutral, the last John Laskaris could not learn that I had unmasked him. It was an advantage I needed in order to neutralize him. I had to prepare for the worst-case scenario. But more than anything else, I wondered what long list of evils this ruthless avenger, who was more Byzantine than I was, had visited on my family.

CHI

Those residents under no obligation to stay in town in June had already departed for warmer places of the northern hemisphere. Even the summer wardrobes of those who stayed behind possessed the touch of a secret designer; I wondered about their beachwear. It was almost a joke not to hear laughter or loud talk on the streets of the most liberated town in the world. It was also strange to have no major structural flaws in the daily flow of life. Back in Stockholm I once more concluded that, if Stockholm was heaven, then my citizens who enjoyed Istanbul's traffic jams would consider heaven a boring place.

I stayed in Stockholm for three days this time. Mistral had a crowded daytime schedule and Nedim had left for Kulu with his family. Mistral's neighbor, Lennart Espmark, a retired librarian, took me to the off-tourist tracks of the town as if he were repaying an old debt. I was too tired to tell him that I owned the books of the Swedish poets Lennart Sjogren and Kjell Espmark. He had a time-share house in Marmaris, where he went with his wife during August, and he couldn't decide whether Turkish hospitality was a blessing or a curse laid on the Turks. He believed that the hillsides of the city, in which I could discern no disharmony of color or sound, held a special charm, and he wanted me to squeeze my impressions of the place into one sentence before we took leave of one another.

Mistral was happy with the way I enjoyed the town and her friends, but she noticed my moments of distraction when I was trying to figure out how my match with John Laskaris would conclude. 'Hey gunslinger,' she said, 'are you playing chess with yourself?' I thought I would be stepping into a trap of my own devising if I asked why she called me 'gunslinger'. She had to be satisfied with my excuse that the deadline for my research reports was stressing me out. I wanted to make myself believe that I was a character in a novel who gave up his throne to marry his beloved.

Lennart and his wife were not at home when I knocked on their door to say good-bye. In the IKEA sack I hung on the doorknob was a bottle of cognac and an envelope. In the envelope was my one-sentence impression: 'When Noah's Ark comes back, Stockholm, you won't be able to decide if you're a port or a passenger!'

*

I wasn't lying when I told Iskender that I wanted to scare somebody and that's why I wanted to borrow his 7.65 automatic pistol. I was going to threaten John Laskaris and make him take me to his boss. If he refused, I would confiscate his cellphones and wait for that boss to call him. Since I hadn't risen to the status of the Elect, my only contact with Nomo was through my sworn enemy – a twist worthy of a detective novel. On the evening of June 22 I called Laskaris, who was in Istanbul awaiting me, and told him to meet me in the quarters beneath the Tekfur Palace. In my briefcase I had a length of rope, a pair of scissors and strong tape. My knees were knocking despite the two double cognacs I tossed back. My trembling stopped as I shook Laskaris's hand for the last time, but a headache sprang up in its place. I sensed symptoms of irritation in this creature, who, with his bulging eyes and beak of a nose, deserved his moniker, 'The Raven'. He looked like an employee trying to resign before he could be fired. I sat in the armchair at the head of the table, took out my gun, and said, 'Come and sit next to me and start talking. Tell me everything about the crooked plot you've cooked up, your majesty, my dear John Laskaris.'

Leaving an empty chair between us, he sat down with an impudent smile on his face. I was about to open my mouth again when I felt the cold steel touch of a revolver at the back of my neck. Laskaris laughed. He'd probably been waiting for this moment for fifty years. He laughed until tears ran down his face. Finally he wound down somewhat and stopped to rest, still gasping.

'Aren't you going to turn around and say hello to your prospective executioner, my dear helpless great-great-great grandson of the ungrateful traitor Michael?'

'Before you turn around, put what's in your hand on the table,' said a deep voice behind me, and my blood froze.

That voice belonged to Iskender. I turned in wonder to see his real face. The person I called 'Big Brother' for twenty years and treated as my confidant had not a trace of shame on his face. Instead, he was biting his lip to keep from laughing.

'May God send you to hell, you thing without a shred of honor,' I said, and spat in his face. I turned to Laskaris.

'Before you start your own journey to hell, false emperor,' he said, 'you're going to hear more than you wanted to hear.

'After he escaped to Sicily my great-great-great grandfather John IV, the last emperor of the Laskaris dynasty, waited in vain to be restored to the Byzantine throne. The necessary conditions did not occur, however, and he died while still in exile, married to a noble Sicilian woman and the father of a son.

'Official Byzantine historians, who concocted the story that Constantine XI died fighting on the walls, also set down, on orders, that John IV died in exile in Gebze. This way, the possibility of a Laskaris ever obtaining the throne again was totally erased.

'My modern-day grandfather, my maternal Uncle John, and I all worked for Nomo in disguise. We were looking for tangible proof of our rights. I studied history at Cambridge with my uncle's approval. He had the respect of Nomo, and after university I went to work for him. My Uncle John died of heart failure when he was on the verge of retirement.

'I've been with Nomo for forty years. For six years my mission was to handle communications between your grandfather and the organization. Byzantium possessed the finest historical documents of its time. While looking for the proof I needed, I also worked to prevent a competent Palaeologus from coming to power. This part of my mission wasn't much trouble – your grandfather was an honest man, but not good for much. A dreamer, a hedonist, a parasite. He survived all those "bankruptcies" of the businesses he sank only thanks to Nomo's salvage efforts. In his sixties, he was persuaded to give up business and move to Galata. Several properties were bought for him so that he could lead a comfortable life in Istanbul.

'I have no doubt that the nature of your grandfather's death has been concealed from you. It was on a winter midnight. He was leaving his usual bar when he was hit by a stolen jeep fleeing police pursuit. After the accident there were some surprise developments in Nomo. One member, whose hope in the Palaeologus family had diminished, brought up the possibility that the son-in-law Hackett might do for the throne. After some hesitation, the other members reacted favorably. After all, Hackett was a well-educated American, a historian who had absorbed both West and East. Besides, he was a secret agent. It was a relief to me when I was assigned to compile a report on his private life.

'I needed to arrange for you to become emperor in place of your father. That would gain me a lot of time during which I could find the evidence I was looking for. I wrote a false report that your mother was on the point of divorcing your father after getting wind of his mistress. It didn't take long for the slander to become true. In the Anglo-American colony of Istanbul there was a sharp Canadian girl who had just broken up with her Turkish fiancé. She worked odd jobs and was having trouble paying off a bank loan she'd taken out to fly back to her country. I had my man offer her a sum that would pay off her debt and cover a first-class ticket to Canada, in exchange for seducing Paul Hackett. Your mother was furious when she saw the pictures of them having candlelight dinners and walking hand in hand in Emirgan Park. Four months after your grandfather's death, your parents divorced.

'To show that you were fated to wear the purple, I spiced up my report with a bit of the occult numerology the Byzantines loved. My idiot boss, Angelos, took your birth date, which happened to be the day after the fall of Constantinople, as a divine omen. The development I didn't expect was your father's falling truly in love with that hired woman. Together they went to Canada. With Nomo's permission I had them followed. Your father was not an alcoholic but he always loved his wine, and two glasses would loosen his tongue. Whenever he got the chance he would joke about his married life. He would chortle to himself after relating, for instance, how his wife's and father-in-law's names were converted from Byzantine names, and how on returning he made them pay "indemnity" in the Byzantine manner. It took three years for the Thessalonican immigrant I put on his trail to discover that he was stealing rare books from his father-in-law's house. The man from Thessalonica introduced me once to Paul as an antiquarian book dealer interested in Byzantine books. Five minutes after we shook hands Paul Hackett said, "I think I know you from somewhere," and a little later, "Oh, I remember where – Istanbul." I left the bar instantly. The next time he met our man from Thessalonica, he told him, "I'm pretty sure now that I saw your weird friend once with my father-in-law." This was your father's death sentence. He experienced the same fate as your grandfather – hit by a mysterious jeep as he emerged from a bar.

'According to the Thessalonica man, all of your grandfather's rare books were sold, except one. A Toronto book dealer bought them up for the Research Institute of Byzantine History at various auctions. I don't know when Paul's wife sold the last one, but I found it in London at a coy bibliophile's shop in 2007. It was in manuscript form and its author was

Manuel II, the father of Constantine XI. This work, in which the most philosophical Byzantine emperor recorded his personal remembrances and impressions, contained the written evidence I was searching for. It stated in detail the places and dates of John IV Laskaris's Sicilian residence. I bought it and hid it from the Institute's library to keep the information out of the hands of meddling historians. For me, the best time for the reality of the situation to emerge would be when the Byzantine throne was vacant. Manuel II's written testimony would be enough for me to stake my claim. That I personally carried the genes of John IV could easily be established by the family tree that my grandmother had commissioned, plus the related church registers.

'It was Nomo's idea that Iskender would be your mentor and protector. It was I who selected him. His Greek grandmother was my mother's next-door neighbor. His father was a Turk from Rhodes who moved to Muğla with Iskender after his wife died. He is devoted to me, but he also knows that I'm the legitimate successor to the Byzantine throne.

'As I said, I procured the manuscript by Manuel II in 2007. In my report to Angelos I suggested that the throne be offered to you in 2008, as that was the 555th anniversary of the Conquest and you were ready to take the test. I decided to take precautions against you in Trabzon. You surprised me with the purple square that you said you found in your hotel room. If it was really Nomo who had it put there to test you, I would put you in a difficult position by not relaying to them your reaction. If, on the other hand, it was not their doing but yours, I would avoid falling into your trap by saying nothing. When I saw that suspicious look in your eye, what do you think I did to renew your trust in me? It was Iskender who shot at you in Cappadocia and I who saved your life by pushing you to the ground! But there wasn't much change in your attitude, so I asked Iskender to follow you more closely. When I heard that you were going to Rhodes, I knew you were about to unmask me. Then, when you asked Iskender for his gun, it was of course inevitable that we would come to this point.

'If you hadn't gone to Rhodes on your own, I would have invited you there before our Haghia Sophia excursion and this scene would have played out probably just about like it is now. If I could have called up the spirit of John IV, God knows, he would have been only too happy to have you killed with two bullets to the eyes. But I have to obey a different scenario. So I've rented a small boat in your name. You will be taken to it unconscious and a Slavic prostitute will be waiting for you there, also unconscious. The report I submitted to Angelos indicates that you're a sex addict who is quite fond of making love to prostitutes in rented boats on the Bosphorus at night. Whisky will be poured down your throats. You and your whore will meet the bottom of the Bosphorus when your boat hits the rocks at one of the most accident-prone points of the Straits. The newspapers will cite the accident report saying that you lost control of the boat as the result of extreme intoxication.

'A month later Manuel II's manuscript will be donated to the Institute's library. In time, Nomo will invite me to assume the Byzantine throne. I will of course be surprised at this unexpected turn and will do my best to be worthy of their trust …'

It was a tragic performance, almost, the way he acted out this tirade. As I listened to him, however, my fear gradually faded. I thought I might simply get up and leave, like walking out on a bad one-man play. Laskaris barked a command to Iskender in Greek. When he loomed closer with a rag in his hand, I couldn't help myself.

'Haven't you ever seen a police movie, you idiot?' I yelled. 'Don't you know this psychopath is going to get rid of you the first chance he gets after you kill me?'

Laskaris's man leaned over and spoke into my ear.

'There are things in this universe you know nothing of, son of the dishonorable American,' he said. The softness in his voice surprised me. I thought my heart would stop when he abruptly picked up the gun on the table and emptied it into Laskaris, who was sitting five steps away. I sighed for the lyrical sound of bullets bursting from a gun with a silencer. Iskender embraced me and kissed me on the head.

'I swore to protect you, Halâs, even at the cost of my life. You're my friend and my brother. Whoever tries to harm even one hair of your head will have to deal with me.'

At this juncture three men entered the big room. Kalligas seemed to have a body bag in his hand; Pappas carried a bottle of water. A tall white-haired man in his sixties was in the lead. He said, in English, 'Your Majesty, my name is Basil Angelos. To express myself fully, I'll continue in English, if you permit.' He had an American accent and carried himself like a diplomat. As we took our seats around the table, Pappas hastily handed me the water. Iskender, muttering, helped Kalligas put the corpse into the bag.

'Like the traitor Laskaris said, I was his boss and directly

connected to Nomo. His con game fell apart when he failed to pass along your message to me from Trabzon. We checked his background, then contacted Alexander – sorry, Iskender – who was his employee. We told him to inform us before acting on Laskaris's orders. Laskaris had failed to repay an advance he'd taken to buy a rare book long ago. While he was with you we went through his London house and found the book by His Majesty Manuel II. Our scholars found Laskaris's claim not worthy of consideration. But since we knew he would never leave this country alive, we sent the book to the Institute's library. Laskaris's debt was paid.

'We waited for you to confront Laskaris face to face. What you got out of him was much more than we already knew. With your permission we'll remove the body, Your Majesty. As you know, your testing period is up in two weeks. It will be my honor to escort you to the holy Haghia Sophia. I'm certain you'll complete the final stage and rise to aristocratic status. Then, after the investiture ceremony, the next item on the agenda will be implementing the last item of the emperor's will. Now I would like to give you my private phone number ...'

On returning to ground level, I shook, feeling as if I was emerging from a nightmare. A summer breeze caressed my face and I stumbled. I accepted the first taxi I saw as my personal savior, and bought a bottle of tranquilizers at the first pharmacy. As I gratefully climbed into bed, one little fact nagged at me. If Laskaris kept the news of my finding the purple square in my hotel room to himself, how did Angelos learn about it? From Kalligas? Pappas? Was a chip implanted in me? Perhaps they were not ordinary security guards either.

At least I knew well that, instead of bringing together the mosaic pieces of the past, I had to get ready for the tricks of the future. And if I was now a true Byzantine like Manuel II and his princely sons, I was safe beneath the wings of Nomo. Wasn't I?

PSI

'… In old panoramic photographs of Istanbul the church of churches looks as innocent as a wooden toy. Her kneeling pose makes her look like she's holding a priceless object in her lap that she's protecting from danger. The brick-colored plaster covering the exterior looks like it would peel off in the first rain, but it's 1,500 years old. It took seven and a half years to collect the material for its construction, and five years for the construction itself. Haghia Sophia is the Shakespeare of churches. Her dome is 180 feet above ground level, with a diameter of 100 feet. It has survived all manner of natural and man-made disasters, including earthquakes. Haghia Sophia is close to God with her symmetrical arches and sky-wide domes; and close to humans with her ornamented pillars and colorful detail. I've never seen any other church that could aspire to this level of architectural grandeur and beauty of interior design.

'… In 1934 the sacred space became a museum, as if it knew what to expect of the future. Each of its mosaic mazes possesses a rich and unique combination of religion and art. In them I saw everything: a fairy-tale palace, a time tunnel, a lighthouse, an aquarium, a caravanserai, a virtual hot springs, a suburb of heaven, a purgatory, an art studio.

'… The drunken hooligans of the Fourth Crusade did not overlook Haghia Sophia as they plundered Constantinople, with the permission of the Venetian Doge. It is the historians' crime that they did not record the Crusaders' orgies with prostitutes in the church, but invented stories about how flames rose from its dome when the city surrendered to the Ottomans.

'… If visitors from another planet came to earth in some future millennium, it would be Haghia Sophia that would present them with the common message of humanity …'

These lines belonged to my father. When I first saw them, with an 'X' over each paragraph, I immediately read these paeans of praise and found them a wee bit exaggerated. But I read them again before my Haghia Sophia expedition, and determined the first stop in my quest to sort out the last item of the will.

In another one of his notes my father complained about the mysterious gaps and mistakes in Byzantine history. For instance – as an example of incomplete information – he pointed out that the mathematician Anthemius and the geometrician Isidore are known as the architects of Haghia Sophia; but in fact the Emperor Justinian put them in charge of every detail of construction. And then there were the two mistakes that I knew of personally: one, the Emperor Constantine XI did not die on the walls but was hijacked; and, two, the last emperor of the Laskaris dynasty, John IV, died in Sicily, not Gebze. The few historians or clergymen courageous enough to record these truths were mocked if not persecuted.

*

The lengthy queues at the ticket office of Haghia Sophia were discouraging. With over 2 million visitors a year, the long-retired church was now the country's favorite museum. The doors had only been open for ten minutes and already the long line of old and half-naked tourists standing in the summer heat was hurting my eyes. But while I was still convincing myself that I was an emperor in the camouflage stage, the line melted away and I was in. The courtyard was a maelstrom of chaos. While harried guides tried desperately to organize the straggling Mediterranean tour groups, the perfectly orderly Japanese groups looked on in amazement. I spotted Pappas and Kalligas hovering nervously around the main gate. I was getting tired of them. Just before entering the church I called Pappas over and said, 'You'll soon be rid of me, pal.' I couldn't keep from pinching his two cheeks and saying, 'I don't know why, but I always felt close to you.' Angelos called my cellphone just as I passed through the Emperor's Door to tell me that he was at the café next door in the event that I needed help. I started to sweat. Then I realized that I didn't really care so much anymore about my many times great-grandfather's will. I didn't want to take this job that I couldn't quit, true, but it would also be unfair to say that the only benefit I had of it so far was meeting Mistral. For me, understanding Byzantine civilization was of the highest importance.

As I slowly walked deeper into the interior toward the dome, the temperature inside seemed to increase. With each step the colossal pillars seemed to elongate and the dome rise higher into the sky. I felt an intense joy of life together with a deep respect for death. The gilded ceiling contained engravings, designs and carvings from assorted layers of civilization. It was an eye-catching and heart-warming symbiosis. I was in a space beyond church, museum or palace. Coolness filled me from inside out; my eyelids drooped.

Was the Christ depicted in the mosaic on the wall about to conduct a hymn of lamentation? If so, a magnificent chorus would respond in perfect harmony, and all the emperors would bow their heads. I woke to the fluttering of a pigeon over my head. Yes, there were pigeons flying freely inside the church. I had come to in the Omphalion, the circle where the emperors received their crowns. As the tip of my shoe touched the border, I once again felt regret for the major handicap of the Byzantines: the lack of a firm principle for the succession of emperors. At this point a fat tourist in his seventies, apparently oblivious to the magnificence of Haghia Sophia, materialized next to me. He seemed to be from rural America. His witty comment, 'Is this where we line up to be the emperor?' left him gleefully chortling at his own joke and me disgusted with it. It would have been meaningless to respond to him with a line from his countryman Ezra Pound: 'Dreams are the only reality.'

We ascended to the upper gallery by way of a curving ramp made of smooth and slippery cobblestones. A well-dressed French woman in my group said, 'This reminds me for some reason of "The Phantom of the Opera".'

I approached the masterpiece of mosaics: the Deesis. The lower half of the great panel was gone. Christ, life-like and in color, was posed between his mother Mary and John the Baptist. This must have been the Mona Lisa of Christ depiction. Despite the large warning sign below it, and the female security guard's nonstop admonitions – 'Do not use flash' – the tourist platoons pressed their camera buttons without let-up or mercy for the fragile mosaic. Clearly this was a crowd that would ignore environmental pollution until it lapped at their doorstep.

The divine Christ appeared to be indicating something just across the way, with both his upraised right hand and his eyes. There, a carved slab recessed in the floor between two pillars stopped me. Here was the tomb of the Doge of Venice and butcher of Constantinople, Enrico Dandolo (1107-1205). (The ironies of history are scandalous.) It was on the orders of Dandolo, an enemy of Byzantium, that the army of Crusaders had plundered the capital of the world. The peerless palace complex; the Mese, which was the Milan of the times; the coastal residences of the Golden Horn that Venice imitated, were all devastated. Rich and poor were slaughtered together. Small girls and nuns were raped. It was the most monstrous massacre history ever witnessed! While the two-faced western world closed its eyes to the tragedy, Venice recorded it as the noble Conquest of Constantinople.

So it would be natural for any Byzantine emperor to top his revenge list with Venice. I was sure I would find the 'decree' somewhere on the arch-enemy Dandolo's tombstone. It was a marble slab about three by five feet, inscribed with HENRICUS DANDOLO. I leaned over and was about to spit on it, here where tourists seldom came, but restrained myself at the last moment. I focused on three small dark marble rectangles wedged beneath the slab. They seemed to have something scratched into them with a stylus of some sort. I touched the left one with my index finger and rubbed it, hopefully, from right to left. I felt something. All three produced a similar impression. In a state of excitement I left the museum, went home, took an inspirational shower, swallowed a tranquilizer and went to bed. I returned an hour before closing time, carrying a briefcase inside which was a

OMEGA

Mistral and her father accepted my invitation to visit at the end of August. My beloved never left my side; Costas Baba spent three days in Galata and then went to Prinkipo Island for a week. He bestowed grateful prayers – in Turkish – on me for finding so many of his old friends who were still alive. I envied their joke-filled, relaxed father-daughter relationship. On the same day that we sent Costas back to Athens, Mistral and I flew to Stockholm. Before we all parted, he said to his daughter, 'If you don't marry a Turkish man, I'm going to find an old Turkish woman and settle down on Prinkipo.'

I was going to have a life-or-death meeting with Nomo in London and I wanted to talk to Basil Angelos first. I went two days early to see the gentlemanly Angelos. I felt like I was solving a puzzle before entering the torture chamber. I dropped in at a Golders Green chess club. The regulars were old Jews who'd migrated from Istanbul, and together we cured our homesickness. Uncle Salvador from Balat not only challenged me to a match but destroyed my plan to let him win as soon as he sensed my strategy. I went back and forth between far-off Underground stations with enigmatic names. I scrutinized the faces in my compartment, frame by frame. In the Latino boy I saw an illicit love story, in the face of the Ethiopian girl a sonnet on hope. I loved children from a distance. I inhaled the incense of times past at shops dealing in rare books, maps and antiques. I fell into a trance at zoos and aquariums. (Was the spark that would light my fire against Nomo waiting for me in a nightmare?)

I stayed at the Le Meridien, where I was a regular, and met Angelos in the dim bar. Before leaving Istanbul, I'd undergone the traditional formalities and officially ascended into the ranks of the Elect. Angelos had taken my resolution of the last item in Constantine's will in a sealed envelope to Nomo, who ratified it against the original document. Three other men, I knew, had risen to the level of the aristocratic Elect over the last 500 years, but they were all eliminated at the final step of decoding the will.

I also completed the legal procedures necessary to become Chairman of the Board of Directors of the corporation called Monodia. I was about to take the reins of Nomo. Wasn't 'monody' what the solo songs of Greek tragedy were called? The Byzantine Andronicus Kallistos, who took refuge in Italy after the fall of Constantinople and died in London, composed a requiem titled 'Monodia'. In it he mourned the loss of 'Constantine, who was wiser than Cyrus, more just than Rhadamanthus, and braver than Hercules' more than he did the capital itself. I could not think of a better name for a company whose major job was to finance revenge.

A thick envelope and a dossier fell out of the package Angelos brought. I picked up a bottle of vodka from Tesco and went up to my room to work on them. The thick envelope contained a handwritten letter that summarized – in Turkish – the history of Nomo. It told me about the Monodia Board of

Directors, which consisted of four members: a representative each from the Palaeologus, Cantacuzenus and Comnenus families; and the emperor. The emperor, who was of course the head, could run the organization however he wished, except in the matter of dissolution. To dissolve it he needed the assent of at least one other member. The Palaeologus representative was expected to be a loyal supporter of the emperor. In fact, in the emperor's absence he was acting chairman of the Board.

Monodia was governed by British law, and had instituted many precautions against takeovers aimed at the emperor. For instance, three of the Board members were required to give the emperor signed but undated resignation letters. As chairman, he could put these into play at any time to forestall developments of an undesirable nature.

The dossier contained the balance sheets, as of June 30, 2009, of seven investment firms. Monodia owned six of them. There were graphs and tables in abundance to illustrate their net worth. They were based in New York, Hong Kong, Frankfurt, Tokyo, Milan and Edinburgh, and they had taken their names from combinations of the letters of the Byzantine alphabet. Their profits derived from rental income, real estate, and the interest on bank accounts and government bonds. Each one had a bottom line of less than a billion pounds, to avoid attracting the attention of the global economy. As consolidated in Monodia's ledgers, their total worth was 5.5 billion pounds, with the original properties worth 4.2 billion and the semi-annual profit coming in at 183 million pounds.

In the short time I spent scanning the reports I began to tense up. I noticed that I was wrinkling my forehead just like my mother. I walked around the room and came back to my desk with a fresh drink. More than simply relaxation, it was an actual pleasure to be solving a problem. For the first time I was going to act like the son of Akile Asil and squeeze the Board into a corner. I'd found the spark I was looking for. I read the financial reports with new enthusiasm and took notes underlining the Board's passive policies.

I called Angelos after breakfast and told him I wanted the meeting next day to be moved up to half past eight from ten o'clock. I carefully modulated the tension in my voice. I went out and bought a suit and tie for the meeting at the Hackett, simply because it was my father's namesake. On my return I ran into Selçuk Altun and his wife getting off the elevator in the lobby. It was certainly a surprise. I raised my Hackett shopping bags in humorous homage, and wondered about the possibility of seeing him as a Nomo member.

*

Canary Wharf was at the spot where the twilight-colored Thames River begins turning from the east towards the city. In the 1980s, investment companies began moving into the skyscrapers that were stabbing it in the heart. Lancaster Tower at Churchill Place looked like an aquarium washed and turned upside down to dry. One-fifth of the building's thirty-four floors belonged to Monodia. The boardroom was of course on the top floor. I entered the elevator with Angelos and imagined myself descending past all those floors two hours later as a man who'd tendered his resignation.

I couldn't feel right about a floor where twenty-four

people were working. It was as depressing as a government office whose modernization is perpetually postponed for lack of money. I was directed to the office of the Chairman of the Board. Furnished with antiques, it actually served as the royal chambers of the emperor-in-exile. I was momentarily excited to think that it was my privilege to be its first occupant. Not to take the chair tricked out in mother-of-pearl would have been to spoil the game. I tried not to smile. Angelos ritualistically placed two files before me. In one were the undated resignation letters of the Nomo members of the Monodia Board, and in the other their short CVs.

The Palaeologus representative was Theofanis Torosidis, born in 1963. He'd read history at Oxford, was fluent in four languages, including Turkish, and had been a member for eleven years.

The Cantacuzenus representative, Stelios Moras, was born in 1949 and was a graduate of Georgetown University in political science. He commanded three languages perfectly but his Turkish was mediocre. He had been a member for eighteen years.

The Comnenus representative was Dimitrio Ninis. Born in 1940, he was educated in economics at Yale. He too was fluent in three languages but weak in Turkish. He'd been on the Board for twenty-six years.

The A-team was eager to meet me. 'Bring them to me,' I told Angelos. The first to enter was Theofanis Torosidis, whom I knew as Theo Pappas. He offered an apologetic smile. I pinched his cheeks and said in Turkish, 'So, Pappas, is it you again?' I continued in English, 'That tragicomic clown act of yours worked. You must be an excellent director and historian.' I no longer needed to wonder who had arranged the purple squares in Trabzon and saved me from Laskaris's trap. The Oxford historian had been my tutor, observer and protector for a year. He was the acting head and brain of Nomo.

Moras had the looks of a well-adapted domestic bridegroom, and Ninis the air of a tired professor. They did not act like natives of the Aegean. Still, they were not disagreeable, and I welcomed them heartily.

In the boardroom, after we'd taken care of a certain well-known item, the official meeting could begin. I sent Angelos out and invited Nomo to the square table. I pulled out their resignations, tore them up theatrically, and said, 'Let's discuss the matter of the emperor's will. If we have any misunderstandings on this point, my presence at the next meeting is out of the question. I tore up those resignations so that you'll feel free to express your opinions. If I continue as Chairman of the Board of Monodia, I won't request any resignation letters from anybody. If somebody needs to quit, he can do what is required of him on his own.' I paused and looked at Nomo. They seemed hypnotized.

'I'm grateful to you, not for the rank bestowed on me by five people, but for helping me develop an awareness of the greatest civilization in history. I owe a debt of thanks to all of you and to your ancestors who devoted their lives to preserving our precious legacy.

'Gentlemen, when Constantine XI said, "Burn the Doge's palace," he did not give us 500 years to do it in. He assumed that one of his grandsons would carry out the mission while Venice was still a state. But his descendants were unable to fulfill their duty. Meanwhile the successors of Venice lost their soul by surrendering first to France in 1797 and later to Austria. In 1866 Venice joined Italy not as a state but as a city. Instead of a Doge, it got a governor. Eventually its palace that looked like a Byzantine bathhouse became a second-rate museum. Therefore it was Venice herself who implemented the last item of Constantine XI's will. After 1866 any further action, in my opinion, would be the equivalent of taking a corpse out of a grave and shooting it.

'I have to open a special paragraph for Venice here. I know it better than I know Istanbul and I enjoy it no less. There are two Venices. The first one, which was once the wealthiest city-state on earth, is now serving as an amusement park for rich and shallow tourists. The other Venice is a glorious page of the Byzantine heritage. The immense Byzantine impact on the architecture of churches and official buildings erected in the Middle Ages is noted in every tourist's guidebook. But what isn't known is the way in which her palaces that run like a string of pearls on either side of the Grand Canal clones the Byzantine Golden Horn. The whole world would have known this if the Latin army had not devastated the Golden Horn. At least the stolen masterpieces of art are being displayed in Venetian museums as Byzantine items, and who knows how many priceless Byzantine manuscripts are under lock and key in the Marciano Library. For this reason alone I think Nomo should feel responsible for Venice.

'In short, Constantine XI's last wish has been fulfilled by the euthanasia of the dukedom. Yet, one of his distant grandsons, by decoding his will in 2009, has at last rescued the soul of the emperor from agony. Please know that I have no intention of dissolving Monodia. On the contrary, I want your contributions to a new mission and vision for Monodia.'

Torosidis asked to speak. His accent was like a Shakespearean actor's. He started to rise but I said to him in Turkish, 'Please stay seated as you speak. And, Pappas Efendi, come to the point.' His team bowed their heads and tried not to laugh. Torosidis was responding well to my teasing.

'You've honored us by considering our views, Your Excellency,' he said. 'We completely agree with your remarks. Constantine XI will rest in peace from now on since his legacy has finally been passed on to a wise and honest descendant of his.'

As the others nodded in agreement I said to Torosidis, 'Whose idea was it to name me Constantine?'

'It came from my father-in-law, Vasilis Spiropoulos, Excellency. Your grandfather knew him as a landholder from Izmir whom he once met in a Monte Carlo casino. He was actually the Palaeologus representative before me. With your permission, Mr Ninis, who worked with my father-in-law, can tell the story.'

I saw that Dimitrios Ninis was waiting for my permission to speak and I made the necessary nod. (Better not to abjure the customary rituals.) The oldest Nomo launched into his remarks as if they were a sermon.

'Mr Spiropoulos used to visit your sainted grandfather regularly, Your Majesty. After your grandfather died, he continued to visit twice a year to keep an eye on you. He had high hopes for you. He told us how impressed he was by your ability to turn the period after your parents' divorce into an opportunity for maturing instead of breaking down.

He believed that you would be more astute than Manuel II, whom you resembled in your scholarly interests.'

I remembered the mysterious Mr Spiropoulos, who always went around with an ornamental walking stick although he never limped. The compliments he paid my mother in his inadequate Turkish made me uneasy. It was a comfort to learn about Nomo's concern. But, perhaps at the devil's behest, I posed a crucial question.

'Okay, what were you going to do if I ordered the Doge's palace to be burned down?'

He looked me in the eye and said, 'We took an oath to carry out commands consonant with the legacy of Constantine XI, Your Majesty. If it is your wish, I can have that building razed to the ground in seventy-two hours.'

I tried to register my displeasure with the enthusiastic tone of his voice in my facial expression.

As I moved on to my second topic, I felt I should acknowledge the good will I'd experienced with the first discussion.

'Let me make a few brief observations and then, if we come to an agreement, I have a suggestion to make. Perhaps we can begin a new era in Nomo's history.

'Monodia's resources have been quite conservatively managed. In the profit-loss statements I found no income stream other than interest and rentals. Now, if mutual bonds from telecommunications, energy and the health-care sectors were bought and sold along with investment funds; and if gold and financial instruments such as treasury bonds were acquired, the accumulated profit would be multiplied by a factor of five at least. Sure, there's always a risk factor in this business, but look: during the recent global recession some of our real estate, which was considered a risk-free investment, lost twenty percent of its value and we took a big loss in our rental income.

'Friends, my goal is to double Monodia's bottom line in seven years – that would be eleven billion pounds! To do that we need to increase corporate profits by one hundred percent each year. An institution with a cash value like ours can reach that goal in the medium term. Of course we'll apply all our profits to the service of the Byzantine cause. This is my new mission for Monodia. We could begin by channeling our resources to the restoration of historical treasures. Nor should people and institutions who deserve to be penalized be forgotten. This sentence does not imply terrorist activity, by the way.

'We've got time to make a proper list, but we shouldn't sit still in the meantime. Let me mention my embarrassment, for example, over the so-called memorial to Constantine XI in Athens, stuck behind a huge statue of a bishop like a toy Sancho Panza.'

I continued with a certain amount of Nomo-bashing, but gently. Finally I stood and said, 'If there is no objection, the meeting is adjourned.'

Photos of the properties Monodia owned in partnership with various entities covered the conference-room walls like a spider web. I observed those tributes to ugliness with a sour expression. I used my notes in the Board of Directors meeting to make the directors and managers sweat. In the end it was decided to set up a division for buying and selling mutual bonds, investment funds and mining shares. On top of everything else, Monodia's interior décor was to be modernized, subject to my approval.

The time came for my salary to be fixed. Torosidis, who as an administrator and deputy chairman came to work every day, took home thirty thousand pounds. Ninis and Moras got fifteen thousand each. In addition they all received shares of the annual net profit. I cut my salary from ninety thousand pounds to half of that. 'And I wouldn't even take that much,' I said, 'if I weren't spending a good deal of it on scholarships for poor children.' I closed the meeting with a decision to have the third-quarter meeting, scheduled for November 22, at the Four Seasons Hotel, which stood on the foundations of the Great Palace of Byzantium.

I invited Nomo to dinner at The Providores. I planned not to ask personal questions on this night of socializing, but I couldn't resist the urge to ask Torosidis, 'Pappas, what part of Istanbul do you come from?' My right arm, it turned out, was the only son of a Fener priest. To ask how he ended up at Oxford after the Fener Greek High School would have been superfluous.

*

By the time I boarded the plane to Stockholm, it felt as if I'd aged five years, but I had gained greatly in self-confidence. Mistral thought Monodia was a mid-level investment firm in which one of my grandfather's friends was a partner. When I informed her that I was the Chairman of the Board, she said, 'Ah, now I see the reason for your squared-up shoulders.'

'If you know a beauty ready to live in Byzantium, I'll propose to her,' I said.

'I know a spinster ready to go anywhere on earth with you,' she replied. Then she phoned Costas of Edremit and said, 'Papa! Halâs just proposed to me. What's become of your idea that a Turk wouldn't want an infertile woman?'

I'd found the love of my life, but evidently I wasn't to discover the joys of fatherhood. It was a dilemma worthy of a Byzantine aristocrat. Maybe destiny didn't want to enrich history with another Byzantine Sultan after me.

We planned to marry at the end of the fall semester. Mistral would continue her academic career at an Istanbul university, and I would find some kind of keeping-up-appearances job. I called my mother and Hayal, who were not surprised at the news. Akile said, 'You'll have to give the good news to your grandmother yourself, because she'll kill me if I tell her.' And Hayal said, 'Big brother, tell Mistral to wear flat shoes to the wedding – she's not shorter than you.'

In Istanbul I was immediately welcomed into my grandmother's presence. When I broke the news, she started rapidly thumbing her prayer beads. Her mind was troubled by a more prominent nuisance than the infertility of the bridal candidate.

'Halâs, my son, take that blonde girl to the imam before you marry her. Let her pick a holy name like Emine or Ayşe and convert to Islam.'

'Grandma,' I said. 'I proposed to Mistral and didn't ask her to do anything beyond moving to Istanbul. Maybe she'll be impressed by you and volunteer to convert, who knows?'

'Son of a worthless American, do you think you're pulling the wool over a child's eyes?' she said, and threw her prayer beads at me. I caught them in mid-air and we started laughing. I hugged her on the way out and kissed her on the cheek. It smelled of rose water.

I woke at dawn in orgasmic delight. In my dream Nomo and I had mounted the four horses stolen by the Venetians from Constantinople, and were riding back to Istanbul on air. I was in the front and wearing a purple caftan. Our laughter mingled with the joyful neighing of the Quadriga. The brass plate left behind under the empty niche in the Church of San Marco said, 'Home, Sweet Home.'

I went into the living room to watch the movement of dawn into daylight. The ancient Galata wind and the seagulls all hushed; the *ezan* was about to issue from the city's 3000 mosques. I went into the study and took my fanciest Venetian notebook from the desk drawer. I wrote 'B. Homework' on the first page and burst into laughter. On the back of the page I drew a chessboard. Over it I wrote, in the favorite poly-alphabetic code of the fifteenth-century Italian city-states, 'Saving the Quadriga'. Had I discovered the pleasure of composing puzzles instead of solving them? I went back to bed. When I was a child, if I couldn't sleep I used to recite three little nonsense prayers my grandmother gave me to shut my eyes. This time it was lines from Karacaoğlan that sprang to my lips:

Square in the heart of her fair breast
Lies the sacred fount of Zemzem
If I drink from it they'll kill me
And if I don't, I'll die.

(March 2009 – July 2010)